MW01200496

Tanglewood Plantation III:

Adventure in New Orleans

by

JOCELYN MILLER

Cover Graphic
by
Jamie Tate

ISBN: 978-0-9886214-1-1

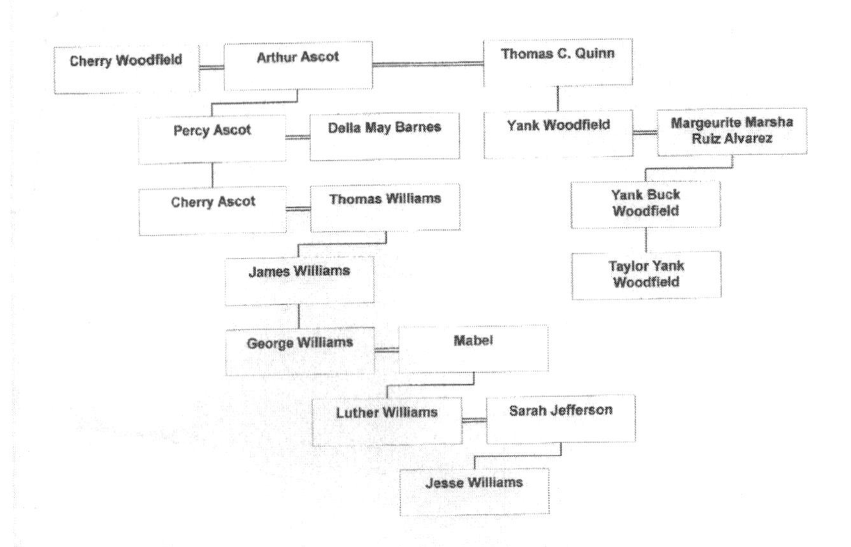
Descendant Chart for
Cherry Woodfield
Cherry Woodfield
Arthur Ascot
Thomas C. Quinn
Percy Ascot
Della May Barnes
Yank Woodfield
Margeurite Marsha Ruiz Alvarez
Cherry Ascot
Thomas Williams
Yank Buck Woodfield
James Williams
Taylor Yank Woodfield
George Williams
Mabel
Luther Williams
Sarah Jefferson
Jesse Williams

ACKNOWLEDGEMENTS

My sincere appreciation to my editors, Carolyn Carson and Sally Bright.

Thanks to my husband, Bernie, for his endless supply of creative ideas and support.

In New Orleans, LA, thanks to Mr. House at the Cabildo for the wonderful tour and history.

Thanks to the Voodoo Museum for a bird's eye view into the mysterious world of Voodoo.

Thanks to New Orleans and the French Quarter for such a tantalizing history.

Thanks to Jamie Tate for another beautiful cover.

Special thanks to Kelly Clark and Nancy Russell of the Dry Tortugas National Park for the abundance of pertinent information regarding Fort Jefferson. Their efforts enabled me to highlight life at the isolated island prison during the days of the American Civil War.

In the beginning…

Tanglewood Plantation

Summer Woodfield doesn't have an inkling of what adventures await her when she inherits the family estate, a dilapidated antebellum rice plantation in Georgia. Not only is she confronted by ghostly apparitions upon her arrival, but is whisked back in time to the American Civil War. Confused and terrified, she experiences the war not as the mistress of the manor, but as a slave on her own plantation!

Join Summer in Tanglewood Plantation, Book 1, as she experiences the war from the darker side of history, rekindles a 150 year old love affair, and unravels the mysteries of her heritage.

Tanglewood Plantation II

Adventure in the Everglades

Another time travel adventure begins for Summer Woodfield when the ghost of the hapless slave, Cherry, returns to haunt her. Cherry is in peril and Summer is not one to turn her back to a ghost in need. Clues of Cherry's last known existence lead Summer to the Florida Everglades where she accidently stumbles across the portal to 1864 and the chance to save her old friend.

Together again, Summer and Cherry fight for their lives amidst renegade war deserters, blockade runners, the Seminole tribes and the big brute of a man who has kidnapped Cherry from Magnolia Plantation. What Summer doesn't expect is the attraction she feels for the dashing Captain Ruiz, a blockade runner who rescues her and Cherry from the sea when their skiff overturns in a storm.

Tanglewood Plantation III
Adventure in New Orleans

Summer has promised her soon-to-be husband, Guy Mason, that her time travel days are over and she's determined to keep her word. However, promises fly out the window when Captain Ruiz returns in ghostly form to create chaos in her modern life. What's a girl to do when her dashing paramour of 1864 shows up in the twenty-first century asking for help?

Once more, Summer finds herself in the midst of the Civil War and in more danger than ever; Captain Ruiz is in prison and she must set him free before he is tried and executed! With the help of an imprisoned French prostitute, Lila de Peau, Captain Ruiz, Summer and Lila escape on a seafaring adventure that returns to Buck Key and eventually New Orleans, the Captain's home town, which is now under occupation by the Federal troops.

Caught up in the hustle-bustle excitement of the occupied French Quarter, Summer unwittingly falls into the mysterious world of Voodoo. This proves a blessing in disguise when she is drawn into a dangerous plot set against her beloved captain by a ruthless Confederate traitor who has conspired with the Yankees to recapture Ruiz.

Join Summer as she battles her way through another time travel adventure, and where she finds surprising connections and conclusions to the mysteries surrounding her visits to the past.

Where we left off in Tanglewood Plantation II...

Often, she found herself in Evaline's old bedroom, the one with the doorway to the attic. She had waited months for an indication from Cherry that she was now at peace. Cherry had not visited her again, here at the balcony doors, frantic with fear and with Quinn on her heels—not since before her adventure in the Everglades. Perhaps this was a good sign, but she needed *more*, she needed to know for sure.

Just one little sign, Cherry, so I know all is well....

It was on one of those days when, again, she found herself standing in Evaline's room staring at the door and chiding herself for doing so, when she heard a rustle in the attic. Her heart leapt! *Cherry!*

She raced to the door, anxious to see Cherry at the top of the stairs; Cherry, smiling, no longer sad, no longer frightened. With her hand on the latch, she swung the door wide open, stuck her head into the stairwell and shifted her eyes upward to the top of the stairs. Just as quickly, she slammed the door shut and stood back, eyes wide.

"My God! It can't be!"

With trepidation, her hands now shaking violently, her heart beating in rapid *thump, thump thumps*, she opened the door again and gingerly stuck her head around the corner; there was no denying it.

"*Verano!* Where have you been? I have been waiting for you!"

There are a hundred places where I fear
To go,—so with his memory they brim.
And entering with relief some quiet place
Where never fell his foot or shone his face
I say, "There is no memory of him here!"
And so stand stricken, so remembering him....

Edna St. Vincent Millay

Chapter 1

"He spoke to me, Jesse. Captain Ruiz, the one I told you about. What am I going to do? Guy made me promise to stay put, '*no more time travel*', he said—and adamantly!

"That makes sense, don't you think?"

"Of course! But I have no control when it happens. I'm whisked away no matter what I happen to be doing at the time. Oh, my God, *Ruiz!* What am I going to do? What if he pulls me into his time zone?"

"Maybe you can ignore him? And why are you hearing from this guy, anyway? What does he have to do with us—with the old Tanglewood Plantation? What about Percy? Arthur Ascot? Why don't they visit you? We're all the same blood at least, but who's this captain that he should call out to you? "

"You know I can't answer that; I have no control over who appears to me. All I know is that I opened the attic door and there was Ruiz, plain as day, handsome as ev…." Her voice trailed off.

"Uh huh? Handsome as ever? You'd better get yourself under control, girl. This here is the real world; this is real time. Your Captain Ruiz is *dead,* and Mr. Guy loves you very much. You love him, too—don't you?"

"Of course I do! We're getting married in two weeks, and I'm preg…."

"What?" Jesse literally leaped out of the porch rocker. "Whad' you say?"

"Darn! I wasn't going to tell you until after the wedding."

"You're having a baby—here? At Magnolia?"

"Yep. The cat's out of the bag now."

"Summer girl, I'm so excited!"

"Well, we are too, but it's kind of embarrassing. We're not even married yet."

"This isn't 1865, friend. These days, you and I could get married and have a baby."

Summer raised her eyebrows. "Oh ya? Is there something I don't know about you?"

"Don't be silly. And don't be embarrassed. I won't say a word, but I'm so excited I could burst!"

"Me too." she sighed.

"You don't sound too happy."

"I *am* happy—very happy—and Guy is over the top with joy, but now, Ruiz….What am I going to do about Ruiz?"

"What if you really, really concentrate and block him from your mind?"

"You've never seen him." Summer wiped a tear from her cheek. "He's not easy to block."

"Good God girl, you're crying!"

"You know, when I saw him a strange feeling came over me, like something warm and wonderful rushed through my veins. My heart nearly beat itself out of my chest. There's just something that draws me to him, and I'm so scared." she sniffled. "I'm pregnant, I'm getting married, and I love Guy— in *this* world—*this world….*"

"What's to be scared of, then?"

I'm scared because I love Captain Ruiz in the *other* world, the world in which we met. I don't understand it at all. I don't know what the connection is, either."

* * *

"I simply have to avoid the attic," she mumbled, cleaning up the last of the dinner mess in the kitchen. "I just won't open the door."

"What?" Guy asked, setting his coffee cup on the table. "Open what door?"

"What?" she asked in return.

"I didn't hear what you said."

"Oh, I…I can't remember," she lied while reprimanding herself for mumbling out loud.

"What's going on with you? You've been doing this more and more lately—talking to yourself."

"I'm sorry. Guess it's the pregnancy. Scary thought. Are we ready for this?"

He stood and circled her in his muscular arms. "Of course we are, silly. We love each other, don't we?"

She rested her head on his chest. "I didn't say I didn't love you. I guess it's just the thought of motherhood, the hormones. You know, pregnant women are known to…." She felt a sudden hot breath on the back of her neck, and turned her head slightly to see the cause. Then, she heard it—she heard *him*— Ruiz!

"I love you, my Verano. I have been waiting for you."

Her eyes shot to Guy's. *Did he hear that?*

He raised his eyebrows. "Now what? You look like you've seen a ghost!"

Reluctantly, her head tilted backward as something brushed against the tender spot at the crook of her neck. *This is insane!*

Guy released her, a stern look on his face. "*Have* you seen a ghost, Summer?"

"No…no," she said, but now invisible hands caressed her breasts as well as the tantalizing business on her neck. She stumbled backward, grabbing a kitchen chair and sat, hoping to dislodge Ruiz's hold.

"Are you okay?" Guy asked.

"I need you, Verano. Help me." Ruiz said, and in an instant he was gone; the heat of his breath, the feel of his hands—*gone.* She shuddered.

"I—I'm fine, Guy. I think I'll just rest a moment. Could you make me a cup of tea?"

This was a serious conundrum. Why was she gifted—if it *were* a gift—in this mischievous business of ghosts and time travel? Why her? She and Guy were soon to be married, *happily* married.

Soon after returning from her exhausting adventure in the Everglades, she discovered she was pregnant with twins; it was a fact she had rather not disclose to anyone except Guy. She couldn't go traipsing off on another time-travel adventure and put the twins at risk. She promised Guy that if another old ancestor came to visit, she would *'stay home.'* He was adamant about it, and she was ready to comply. Besides, Captain Ruiz wasn't even on her family tree, so why should he be haunting her?

The last time-travel adventure was harrowing enough, though she did bring Cherry home to rest. It was well worth it. Even the affair with Captain Ruiz was well worth it. She remembered him perhaps *too* fondly, but he was dead, killed in the horrific sinking of the ships over 150 years ago[1]. Besides, he lived and died well before her time. She should forget him but… but here was the nagging question; *why does he need me?*

Try as she might, she could not get him out of her mind, and the feelings of his presence were not helping.

* * *

One brisk fall day while finishing up details in the nursery—the same nursery of her Woodfield ancestors—she heard a commotion in Evaline's old room.

"Oh no," she said, setting down a new stack of baby jammies. "Tell me it isn't Ruiz!" He was making her pregnancy far more difficult to endure. Every time she felt his presence, he said the same thing; he was *'waiting'* for her; he *'needed'* her. And she, so pulled to him in the first place, tried hard to resist. She loved Guy with all her heart, but somehow, she loved Ruiz, too. She would always love the dashing captain, and resisting his call to help was quite difficult.

She opened Evaline's door. "Ruiz, what are you—". There he stood, as handsome as ever, his dark hair flying free about his ears, the white shirt open, exposing a hint of dark chest hair. The black boots rose nearly to his kneecaps, and with legs spread apart, arms crossed over his chest, he presented quite an enchanting picture.

"Verano, where have you been? I have been waiting for you."

"Captain!" Why was she surprised? She knew it had to be him, but he rarely materialized and remained, for the most part, invisible. It

[1] This event occurred in Book II

was the feel of his breath on her neck, his hands on her breasts that made her aware of his presence. But now, her heart thumped wildly at the sight of him.

"Captain...."

"I need you Verano, come to me." He held his arms out and she was so very tempted to comply, to be encircled by the wildness of his love, but then she remembered her promise to Guy: *I will not succumb.*

"Look at me, Captain. Can you hear me? Look at me; I'm pregnant. I can't go with you. I'm getting married, Ruiz."

His dark eyes penetrated hers. "I have been waiting for you, Verano."

Can't he hear me?

"I need you, Verano. I need your help. Come to me, my love."

He remained in place, in the entrance to the attic, his arms outstretched.

"Captain," she said, stepping closer. "Captain, look at me." She placed her hands on her expanding belly. "I'm pregnant, Captain...I can't...."

In a microsecond, he was inches away, his hands pulling her to him. "I need you, Verano. You must come to me."

"But...." She didn't finish. His warm lips were upon hers. She *felt* them, she received them, she *wanted* them....

Chapter 2

"Where am I?" Summer instinctively placed her hands over her pregnant belly, only to discover that she had no belly! *My babies...where are they?* A terror ran through her. *Is this a dream?* If so, it was the nightmare no mother wants to experience— the disappearance of her children.

Calm down, she told herself. *Don't get crazy. I've been through this before.*

Wherever she was, the sun was peaking on the horizon across the water...*water!* It was beautiful and clear, a Caribbean blue that shimmered in the early morning light. A slight breeze ruffled her hair as she scanned the horizon ahead. *No land there.* She turned for a panoramic view and was shocked to find herself on the brink of falling into a moat that ran between her and an immense brick wall.

"Where the heck am I?" she repeated. Her question was partially resolved when two armed soldiers in blue uniforms approached, rifles ready to fire.

"Who are you?" one of the soldiers asked. "How'd you get here?"

"I…I…." She shrugged in defeat. "I have no idea how I got here." It was the truth.

When the soldiers looked her up and down, she, too, looked to see what she was wearing, remembering how odd her 21st century clothing appeared to the folks in the nineteenth century. She was certain it was that—the nineteenth century—that she had awoken to, as the soldiers were of Yankee persuasion, and certainly a uniform that she would recognize. The last she remembered, she wore a pair of sandals, maternity jeans and tee shirt. When she looked down at her clothing, she discovered that it was the same: sandals, jeans and tee shirt, but the jeans zippered snuggly at the naval and the tee shirt hugged a flat belly.

"Come with us." The taller soldier signaled the direction with his rifle. "Move ahead."

"You can put those rifles down, you know. Obviously I'm not going anywhere." *I don't think I am, anyway.*

"Walk," the other said, ignoring her comment. They were, to her mind, enjoying the fact that they had captured an intruder here on this bump of land; wherever and whatever it was, she couldn't place. The brick wall seemed to consume the entire island, from her viewpoint.

Having some experience in the past ventures of time travel, she sincerely hoped that Captain Ruiz was involved in this one. She assumed, now that she thought back on it, that the tantalizing kiss was the portal to this mysterious place.

"Can you tell me the date?" she asked, feeling the point of a rifle in her back. "The year, then?" she asked, when they had not replied to her first question.

"Can you at least tell me where I am?" *Exasperating!* The soldier continued to silently push her forward with the rifle until they crossed a small bridge entering the compound inside the brick walls of the strange construction. There, she was aghast at what seemed an indefinite row of arches that circled around a large field spattered with soldiers, cattle, buildings, and a various assortment of disheveled characters who stared upon her entrance. All eyes continued to stare as she passed the ruffians and soldiers. She tried to ignore the catcalls and insinuations, as the soldiers were certainly not protecting her against the perpetrators. *It's the clothes,* she told herself. *I must look like a harlot.*

"What is this place?" she demanded, beginning to feel quite uncomfortable.

"Keep moving," the soldier ordered, and she did, as the barrel of the rifle nudged her over the great yard to a very large building directly across from the entrance.

When they stopped beside a wooden door, the taller soldier ordered her to lean against the wall. "And don't move," he ordered. This gave Summer the opportunity to face her captors. The shorter soldier pointed the barrel of the rifle at her belly, and she was instantly relieved that the twins were most likely put in storage elsewhere.

"Do you not see that I'm unarmed?" She stared the young man in the eye, which she could barely see due to the cap pulled squarely down over his brow line.

The tall soldier knocked on the wooden door. "May we enter, sir?" he asked. Upon reply, the door was opened, and she was guided in by rifle barrel to stand before an officer sitting behind a large desk. He did not disguise his surprise at the appearance of the scantily clad woman. "How the devil did she get here?"

"Don't know, Captain. We found her just out the sally port,[2] and she says she don't know either."

The captain's chair scraped across the wooden planks of flooring as he stood. A strong whiff of body odor assaulted her nostrils as he came forward to scrutinize her through eyes so squinted in his appraisal that they disappeared behind the chubby folds of his face. His mustache and beard were neatly trimmed, but his uniform jacket was unbuttoned and faded, the armpits soaked in sweat and his shirt in need of pressing.

"So, young lady, how did you get here?"

"I don't know."

"Sir!" interjected the first soldier. "Address the captain as *'sir'*."

He enforced this command by nudging her with the rifle barrel.

"Sir," she added. *No sense making more trouble than necessary.* "Where am I…*Sir*?"

"You may call me Captain Giles." He said, giving her the once-over. He indicated her to sit in one of two chairs facing his desk.

"You're excused, soldiers."

---

[2] Sally port: a guarded entryway generally associated with forts and prisons.

"But sir…."

"You're excused! One of you stand outside. I don't care which, and the other, get back to your watch. They saluted, turned and left, closing the door behind them.

"There's no need for armed guards, is there, miss…miss…?"

"Woodfield," she replied. "Summer Woodfield, and no, you can see I'm not armed."

The captain sauntered back to his desk, plopped into the chair, and again scraped its legs across the wood planking as he pulled himself forward until his protruding belly met the edge of the desk.

"What happened to your clothes, Miss Woodfield? If you came here to offer your services to the sol…."

"Certainly not!" she interrupted.

"Were you dropped off by boat?"

"I don't know, sir. And what is this place?"

"Tortugas. Dry Tortugas. This is Fort Jefferson[3], a prison camp."

"Out here?"

"A good place for a prison camp, wouldn't you say? The water is so clear that we can sometimes see the sharks swim by; a good deterrent to escape attempts. "

She shuddered, remembering her own shark encounters[4] when she and Buck retrieved the gold coins from Ruiz's sunken ship.

"Fort Jefferson is a prison, Miss Woodfield. We house military and civilian prisoners here and, believe me, they are here for serious crimes."

"I see."

Where are you from, Miss Woodfield?"

"Bluebell, Georgia."

"Hmmm." He twisted one end of his dark mustache. "You're on the side of the Confederacy I assume, coming from Georgia. However, you don't seem to have the peculiar Southern accent."

"I was born in Chicago. I suppose that makes me a Yankee, like you, *Sir*."

"Why are you living in Georgia, then?"

"I inherited an estate."

---

[3] Fort Jefferson, in the Dry Tortugas, was built from 1835 – 1875 to protect the nation's gateway to the Gulf of Mexico. During the American Civil war it was used as prison.

[4] This event occurred in Book II

"In Bluebell, Georgia."

"Correct."

"So, tell me if I'm correct in my summation: you were born in Chicago, Illinois; you inherited an estate in Bluebell, Georgia, which is where you presently live. You are scantily clad, inappropriately dressed, need I say, and you appeared mysteriously at the sally port of Fort Jefferson on the Dry Tortugas, which are islands at the mouth of the Gulf of Mexico—to further answer your question— and you have no idea how you got here."

"That's correct, *sir*."

"Hmmm." Captain Giles cleared his throat while he ruffled papers on the desk. All was silent as Summer awaited a reply, but the captain seemed lost in thought as he stared blankly at the papers in hand.

He's wondering what to do with me, I'm sure. She wanted to leave the small office and look for Ruiz. Could he possibly be alive? Her heart raced in anticipation. Why else had she landed on this obscure island if not because of Ruiz?

Captain Giles drummed his fingers on the desk while Summer wriggled in her chair. The room was stuffy, stifling to say the least. Thoughts of the unborn twins popped into her head, and she felt her stress level rise. *I should be old hand at this time travel by now,* but she wasn't pregnant the other times. True, she did give birth to her great-great-grandfather, James, as Evaline[5], but he wasn't her own child— it was Evaline's child— and, at that time, she was Evaline.

"Can I go, sir?" she asked, tired of the silence and of her own nerves twisting her gut. It was far better to be busy than to sit in silence thinking and wondering what happened to her other life and her babies— and Ruiz.

"Go? Where?" He leaned backward in his chair until it rested against the brick wall. "In case you hadn't noticed, there is no place to go until the supply boat comes. I'm not quite finished with you yet. I don't know how you got here, or why you are here. Perhaps you're a spy for the Confederacy, Miss Woodfield?

"What? A spy? No sir, I am not a spy. I wish I could explain my appearance, but I can't. I don't know how I got here—at this prison—. unless…Ruiz…," she murmured under her breath.

His chair thumped upright as he leaned forward across the desk. "Ruiz? Did you say 'Ruiz?'

---

[5] This event occurred in Book I

"Uh, yes. Is Captain Ruiz here?"

"He is," he replied, eyeing her suspiciously. "You are familiar with Captain Ruiz?"

He's alive! "Yes, I do know—*knew*— Captain Ruiz." *How could he have survived?*

"You are aware that Captain Ruiz is a scoundrel, a thief, a murderer, and a blockade runner? He is scheduled for trial on the mainland."

"I'm surprised he's here, since I watched him die."

"He's far from dead, young lady. We're holding him here until his trial. Hopefully, they'll lock him away for good."

Summer slumped in her chair, totally mystified as to the new and disastrous situation onto which she materialized. *No wonder he needs my help!* But, how could she? How could she, alone, fight the Federal Army on an isolated island in the Gulf of Mexico to save Ruiz? How?

"I see you are distressed by this news. Am I to assume you and Captain Ruiz are…" he drummed his fingers on the desktop… lovers?" The arches of his eyebrows rose as if pulled by strings. This move revealed the color of his eyes, a sly slate gray, and she didn't like the way those slate eyes were rolling over her body.

"Stop your wild imaginings, captain. Am I under arrest for knowing Captain Ruiz?"

He quickly averted his eyes, cleared his throat, and busily straightened the stack of papers on his desk. "No, but you are under observation as a possible spy. I will send a letter to Washington requesting any information they may have on you. That is, *if* Summer Woodfield is your true name."

"It is, and I can assure you that I'm as obscure to Washington as…as this island was to me before I unhappily landed here."

"We shall see, Miss Woodfield. Guard!" The tall soldier who had earlier escorted her by rifle-point appeared in a matter of seconds.

"Show Miss Woodfield to my quarters, and have Mrs. Giles give her appropriate clothing."

"Yes, Sir!"

"Your wife is on this island?" she asked.

"Yes, and a few other officers' wives as well. While you're here we can put you to good use. Perhaps the laundry or the kitchen would keep you busy until we find your true identity, *and* your reason for being here."

"Come on," the soldier said, waving his rifle.

"She is unarmed, Sergeant. No need for weapons."

She flashed a smirk at the discouraged soldier and rose off the chair.

"And what is the date today?"

"Why, it's September 18th."

"And the year?"

Captain Giles shook his head. "Don't tax me, Miss Woodfield; I know you are aware of the year."

She waited, the tall soldier obviously growing impatient as she stared at Captain Giles.

"September 18, *1864*, Miss Woodfield. Now go!"

Chapter 3

The officers' quarters was a large imposing three story structure on the north end of the complex directly across the field from the sally port.

"What on earth…?" There was no mistaking the shock on Mrs. Giles' face when she opened the door to find Summer standing shamefully dressed in her threshold.

"Beg yer pardon, Ma'am. This woman was found at the sally port and the captain has requested that you find her some decent clothing to wear."

"Well….uh…I guess you had better step inside, young lady. Quickly!" Mrs. Giles shooed the guard away and scanned the hallway. "Oh my, what will they all think?" she said, closing the door and turning to view the half-clad woman before her. "You can't walk around like that here, young woman. There are men here who…who…."

"I realize that, Mrs. Giles. I had enough looks and comments just crossing the yard."

"I'm sure you did; you should be ashamed."

"Not to be rude, but I'm very tired of explaining myself. I don't know how I got here. I realize that my clothes are improper, but you wouldn't understand even if I explained the situation. Could you *please* find me something appropriate to wear?"

Mrs. Giles digested this comment while standing back to peruse Summer's frame, which was undoubtedly several sizes smaller than her own.

"Oh, I just don't know." Mrs. Giles shook her head. "You're a tad smaller than I am, but let's look in the trunk."

A tad? Summer followed the woman, whom she imagined had a broad behind beneath the deceiving hooped skirt. They left the small living area and entered an even smaller sparsely furnished bedroom where she opened a brown-stained trunk set against a wall. "Let's see now…."

One by one, Mrs. Giles removed articles of clothing: a blouse of white cotton, a large skirt in plaid, another skirt, a petticoat of muslin and lace, another blouse. When the pile of clothing reached knee-height on the floor, the woman stopped her search to catch her breath and to hold up a grossly colored calico blouse in purples, yellows and orange. "Oh, this may fit. I was a bit smaller then."

Summer gingerly took the blouse from Mrs. Giles' hands and held it up to her body. Mrs. Giles clapped her hands. "Oh yes! It will fit! Now we must find you a skirt, a petticoat, an apron, pantaloons. And your feet! Oh, my. What on earth are you wearing on your feet, dear?"

"Sandals. They're fine."

"A proper lady does not traipse around Ft. Jefferson sporting *sandals*. You need stockings and proper shoes."

The temperature in the small room seemed to have risen several notches by this time. Mrs. Giles' armpits showed spreading sweat stains with her exertion combined with the heat of the day. "Oh, I do think I must sit a moment," she said, and propped herself on the end of the sagging bed after retrieving a folded fan from a dresser.

"It's very hot in here," Summer agreed, bending to retrieve more items of clothing. She held a skirt to her waist, but the skirt's waistband would have circled her own three times.

"We may have to do a little sewing, dear."

"We may have to take a foot off this waistband," Summer replied, but seeing the hurt in Mrs. Giles' eyes, she felt a pang of remorse. *No sense taking my predicament out on the poor woman.* "Just a little joke. I do appreciate your kindness. Yes, we can alter this skirt. It looks like the others are about the same size."

"There's a petticoat in the pile on the floor, but look in the trunk. Perhaps there are some pantaloons, too." Mrs. Giles fanned her face rapidly while Summer's own beads of sweat dripped from her face into the dark cavern of the trunk, nearly empty now.

"I think I'll skip the corset." She dangled the dreaded undergarment at arm's length in front of Mrs. Giles' sweating face before dropping it back into the trunk. It was, to her relief, much too big.

"Yes, I suppose you don't need one, and especially in this heat."

"Now, all I need is a needle and thread."

* * *

After an afternoon of sewing alterations—a job at which Summer had little talent—she donned the proper garb and paraded her attire, the ugly calico blouse tucked into a full and floor-length brown cotton skirt. Mrs. Giles was delighted. Because of the excessive heat, Summer had only buttoned the blouse half-way up her chest; but Mrs. Giles, upon seeing this oversight, stood off the bed and took the liberty of buttoning the blouse clear to the neckline.

"Yes, yes, you look quite proper now!" the woman exclaimed, standing back. "Oh, dear, your hair! Where is your hair?"

Summer put a hand to the short blond crop. *The hair...* "Uh, well...I sold it. Yes, I sold it. I needed money."

"Tsk, tsk." Mrs. Giles shook her head. "You are just a catastrophe, my dear."

"This is a bit much to wear in this heat, don't you think?" Summer asked, changing the subject. She grasped the skirt, which laid over the muslin petticoat, and held it out on either side, allowing a slight breeze to circulate beneath the layers of clothing.

"Indeed." Mrs. Giles agreed.

"Do you have a hoop I could wear? At least it's light and airy and would keep your nice skirt from dragging on the ground."

"I'm wearing my one and only hoop, dear."

"Honestly, Mrs. Giles, I don't think I can endure this outfit; I'm cooking under here." She desperately wanted to rip the long-sleeved high- necked blouse off her body. When she was in Evaline's body, the clothes were not so stifling due to the fact that the slaves were not required to wear the entire ensemble of pantaloons, petticoat, corsets, blouse, crinoline and apron. They were lucky enough to have a pair of shoes and a winter coat.

"I suppose you traipse about your hometown in the brazen attire you arrived in?"

"Where *is* that brazen attire, by the way," Summer asked, seriously thinking of chucking the layers of clothing and resorting to her own comfort.

"It's where you will never lay eyes on it again, I can assure you."

Summer's shoulders slumped at this news. Defeated! She had no choice but to roll with the punches. As usual, everything was out of her control; she was a voyeur in a different century and had to abide by its strange rules. And, as usual, the rules were not kind to women.

"I never caught your name, dear, or where you are from."

"Summer Woodfield. I was born in Chicago but live in Georgia."

"A Confederate?"

"Just a stranger, Mrs. Giles. Simply a stranger in a strange land,"

Chapter 4

"Home, sweet home," she mumbled, doing a once over of the designated shared room. Captain Giles couldn't have chosen a hotter or more obscure spot than the top floor, northwest corner, of the officers' quarters building. "Damn sun." She pulled a flimsy curtain across the one window, knowing that it wouldn't make much difference. The sun was setting and would be blazing into the small room until its last wink of the day before sinking into the horizon. The window overlooked an endless expanse of turquoise waters which, if not for a row of cumulous clouds, would have blended with the blue of the tropical sky.

Captain Giles had returned to his pudgy bride and small apartment at dinnertime, informing Summer that she would be rooming with a Miss Lila de Peau of New Orleans. Miss de Peau had procured the job of food server as well as housekeeper and laundress, in exchange for avoidance of a prison term for theft from Yankee soldiers who paid to have a romp with her in the back alleys of the New Orleans French

Quarter. This Captain Giles shared privately with Summer while Mrs. Giles disappeared to arrange dinner.

They had supped on fish, which the captain informed her had been fresh caught that day, rice (which Summer supposed was from the very plantations the Yankees had pillaged and destroyed), and bread, which was speckled with mysterious dark dots. It was not the most lavish meal Summer had experienced during the Civil War days, but it certainly sufficed, and amply so when Mrs. Giles paraded into the dining room with what she called "pineapple cake". The cake was so delicious that Summer was hard pressed to refrain from asking for another slice. No wonder the Giles' packed extra pounds; Mrs. Giles was a wonderful baker!

The starving days at Magnolia Plantation[6] momentarily flooded her memories as she sat relishing the meal. In her mind's eyes, she wondered how her ancestral family was doing since her disappearance; but she shooed the thought from her head because she was helpless to do anything that could improve the situation, which surely would be quite pitiful at this time.

Now, as Summer perused the room she shared with a yet unknown roommate, she could see that the woman had taken over both small and sagging beds, one piled with personal belongings, one slept in and hastily made. She systematically opened and closed the four drawers to the one dresser in the room, and shrugged. *Not full, but doesn't matter. I have no clothes anyway.*

She unbuttoned the horrid blouse and removed the insufferable clothing down to the shimmy and bloomers. The air was stifling, unmoving. To open the window would only invite more humidity and mosquitos. She removed the pile of items from one bed and placed them on what was, obviously, Miss de Peau's sleeping bed and lay down.

* * *

"*Mon Dieu*![7] Who eez theez?"

Summer strained to focus on the figure overhead; a frizzy head of hair, one hand on hip and the other holding a lantern to shine on the face of her intruder. Had she fallen asleep? She was confused and glanced toward the window; night had fallen.

---

[6] This occurred in Book I

[7] "*Mon Dieu!*" Dear me! Or, my God!

When the vision of the stranger sharpened, she saw that it was a young woman of small stature, small features and eyes wide, glaring unkindly. She was nearly childlike. *This is a hooker?*

"Qui êtes-vous? Sorteez de mon lit![8] Shoo! Shoo!" The young woman waved her free hand, indicating for Summer to get up.

"I don't speak French," Summer said, lifting herself to a sitting position. "Do you speak English?" she asked, trying to sweep the cobwebs out of her head and focus on the situation.

"English, yes, of course. Who are you? What eez it you do in my room?"

"Captain Giles put me here."

"Oh, of course. Yez, Capitaine Giles gives no concern for my comfort. He puts a strange woman in my bed and does not tell me! Mon dieu!"

"I'm to stay here until he figures out what to do with me."

"Oh!" She took the lantern the few steps to the other bed. "Vous faites un désordre! You disturb my things and make a mess. Look at theez!"

"You have room in the drawers; I looked."

"And you are snoopy, snoopy, too."

"Don't worry, I have no clothes. I have nothing."

The woman set the lantern on the dresser. "And just why eez theez?"

"It's a long story, Miss de Peau, and I don't think you'd understand."

"And why do I not understand? Do you think I am stupeed? Did Capitaine Giles tell you I am stupeed?" She plopped a fist on each narrow hip.

"No, of course not. It's a very complicated story, and sometimes I don't understand it one bit." *So true!*

"Humph!" Miss de Peau was not happy. "Well, I guess you are to take theez bed Meeez…what eez your name?"

"Summer. Summer Woodfield."

"Zummer Woodfield," she repeated. "You call me Lila, and I weel call you Zummer."

"Fine. Will do. Uh… Lila, are you familiar with Captain Ruiz? He's a prisoner here."

---

[8] *"Qui êtes-vous? Sorteez de mon lit!"* Who are you? Get out of my bed!

"Oh! Capitaine Ruiz! Of course, of course! Everyone know of Capitaine Ruiz, and I want to know of Capitaine Ruiz better, if you know what I mean, Zummer." Lila put a hand to her breast in a theatrical move. "He eez— shall we say—un belle homme—a beautiful man."

Summer raised her eyebrows. "And, does Captain Ruiz want to know *you* better, Miss de Peau*?"*

Lila feigned shock at the crisp retort and then smiled. "Oh, I get eet. You want to know zee capitaine better yourself! How do you know zee capitaine, anyways?"

"We sailed together from the Bahamas. He was injured and I thought he was dead."

"Oh, I assure you, Zummer, he eez not dead. He eez, how you say…*virile*…oh, mon Dieu! He make my heart boom! Boom! Boom! And my bottom so *chaud*, so hot!" She said, gyrating her hips.

Summer felt her face fire up at the insinuation of the waifish Miss de Peau— prisoner and prostitute— that she was ready and willing to bed the captain, *her* Captain Ruiz!"

"For your information, Captain Ruiz and I are *lovers*, Miss de Peau." Summer blurted. *Jealous! I'm jealous! The man is a ghost, and I can't control myself!*

Lila stood back at this remark. "Well, I am zo sorry to tell you that your lover, Capitaine Ruiz eez to be on trial and perhaps executed. Mon Dieu, I am so sad about theez occasion."

"So I've heard." Summer stood, suddenly feeling quite the giant compared to the petit French woman. Her height made her feel oafish and unfeminine, and not that she was tall, but the woman was so short and dainty in comparison. "You must take me to him, Lila. Where is he kept?"

Lila looked her up and down. "I do not theenk zo. How do I know you are a lover of zee capitaine? How do I know ze capitaine will want to zee you? He never say a theeng about Zummer."

"Did he ever mention *'Verano?*[9]*"*

Lila folded her arms over her chest and eyed Summer suspiciously. "Yez. I theenk I hear him say *"Verano"* one or two times when he first come to theez place. What does theez mean?"

"It's what he calls me, Verano. It's the Spanish word for summer."

---

[9] *Verano* is the Spanish word for the summer season. Captain Ruiz calls Summer by this name.

"When he come, he is no…how you say…*awake.* He eez no awake. I feel zo sad for him; he has big bandage on *le tete*—heez head."

The accident…but how did he get here? She couldn't grill Lila further, she needed to see Ruiz in person. "Will you take me?"

"We zee tomorrow. I work ze whole day from ze sun to ze dark. I sleep now."

With that, Lila removed her skirt and blouse, resettled the belongings that Summer had placed on her bed, onto the floor, blew out the lantern and climbed beneath an army issued blanket, leaving Summer in the dark.

A knock on the door startled both women.

"Mon Dieu! What eez it? I go to sleep now. Go away."

"Open the door, Lila."

"Oh," was Lila's disgusted reply in the dark.

Summer sat up on the lumpy mattress listening to Lila throw aside her covers and step barefoot to the door.

"What eez it?" she asked, opening the door a crack.

From her position, Summer was surprised to see Captain Giles's face reflected in candlelight. Lila stepped outside, leaving the door slightly ajar.

"Yez, yez, of course. I know theez. I will." She then reentered the bedroom and closed the door behind her, her small feet slapping against the wooden floor as she made her way back to bed.

"What was that about?" Summer asked in the dark.

"Eet is what to do with you tomorrow."

"And what is that?"

"*Bon nuit*[10], Miz…ah Zummer, bon nuit. Tomorrow we talk again., *C'en est assez!.*[11]

* * *

"Fais vite! Fais vite![12]" Lila de Peau ordered, rushing down the dark stairway while Summer, barely awake and cursing her present predicament and lack of morning necessities— eye drops, coffee, a flush toilet, real toilet paper; all the basic needs of any civilized human

---

[10] *Bon nuit.* "Good night."

[11] *C'en est assez!* Enough! (of it!)

[12] *Fais vite!* Hurry up!

being— scurried to keep up with the petite French woman as she noisily transcended the stairs, the echo of her boots rat-a-tating on each tread

"Do not make me late, Zummer!" Lila warned, as they exited the massive officers' quarters from the back, turning right to walk along an arched walkway in the predawn of another sweltering day.

"Hey Frenchie!" a voice called from somewhere in the center yard. "Got a mornin' wake-up for ya!"

"Put eet in your beeg mouth!" Lila replied, never missing a step.

"Hey you— new gal!" another voice called. "If you get lonely, ask for Frank!"

"Shut ze face!" Lila yelled. "Eef she lonely she go to a real man, like ze áaine Ruiz!"

"He can't get nothin' up if he's dead!" came the reply, which hurled Summer back into the reality of the situation; Ruiz, was in serious trouble! She shivered with thoughts of what she was about to face. What shape was Ruiz in? How could she get him out of here? How could she save his life? Perhaps this journey would prove too much for her abilities. *Abilities? My only ability in this century is survival....*

Dawn dimly illuminated the hollow darkness of the brick arches ahead. A sudden flicker of flame caught Summer's eye. "Oh!" she exclaimed, feeling her heart jump as the face of a man briefly illuminated as he lit a cigarette.

"Hey, Frenchie," he said, as they passed. "I'll have a dozen fried and three chops!"

"Oh you weesh, you bad boy!" Lila replied, her worn boots echoing the tat-tat-tat as she hurried along the brick walk.

"I'll have the same!" a voice called from a dark recess.

"Me, too!" cried another.

"Where *are* these men speaking from?" Summer asked, double stepping to keep up with Lila's pace.

"They are there, there, there," she answered, impatiently and sporadically poking her arms into the air. "Theez way," she said, turning left into a short passageway which exited out into a spit of land. Two brick dwellings sat before them on terrain patchy, with grasses and sand, and ending at a gently lapping tide upon the shore.

"Les cuisines", she said, stopping abruptly.

"Let's what?"

"*Les cuisines!* Zee kitchens!"

"Is this where I work?" Summer asked.

"Oui. Follow, follow, follow and do not be like zee snail."

The sand created an uncomfortable layer between Summer's feet and sandals (which she had managed to hide from Mrs. Giles) as she followed Lila to the second building

"Ze boulangerie eez in theez one."

"Boo—what?"

"La bou-lan-gerie. *Ze* bakery! Mon Dieu, must I explain every leetle theeng?"

"Well I…honestly, Lila, you will have to be patient with me. I've never been here before, and I don't speak French." She did not need Miss de Peau's cocky attitude so early in the morning, *and* without her coffee first to fortify herself against the day ahead. To stress the point, she removed her sandals, banged them hard against the door frame, glaring at her feisty roommate while brushing what she could of the sand off her feet before replacing the sandals.

"Mon Dieu," Lila whispered beneath her breath before opening a wooden door which led into a sweltering one-room structure. When the blast of warm kitchen air from the ovens reached Summer, she felt faint. That, combined with the outside heat, created a nearly unbearable atmosphere.

"Attention mais amis[13]*!* Theez eez Miz Zummer. She will work weeth us now." Lila shouted.

Summer took stock of the faces that appeared as Lila introduced the workers in the bakery. Fanny, a heavy-set white woman, slapped a large ball of dough onto the wooden worktable and grinned toothlessly. Cesar, a strapping young black man who sported a gold earring in one ear, grinned ear to ear as he stuffed a mound of dough into a long metal bread pan. Fat Jack, a mocha colored obese man of indistinct nationality, sat at a small desk a few steps away from the cooking area.

"Miz Zummer is our Capitaine Ruiz's lover." Lila thumped her hands over her heart and fluttered her eyelashes, causing a raucous uproar from the kitchen staff.

"Excuse me!" Summer interjected. "You have no right…," but it was futile to finish, as the crew was now snickering amongst themselves.

"She eez all yours!" Lila said, throwing a kiss to the crew. She left, closing the door behind her, leaving Summer to face the heat and kitchen crew alone.

"Where ya come from, girl?" Fanny asked, punching the wad of dough, flipping it over and punching it again.

---

[13] "*mais amis!*" my friends

"Georgia," she answered, having not moved from the spot of entry.

"Wha'd ya do to git to this hellhole?"

"Why I…I…I just arrived yesterday."

"Ya must'a done somethin' to git yourself here," Fat Jack said from his station at the desk.

Summer straightened her shoulders. She would have to come up with a story—eventually. "None of your business."

A brief moment of silence followed as Fanny and Summer locked eyes.

"Grab yourself a apron and git on over heah," Fanny ordered, nodding toward three limp fabric pieces hanging on pegs against a wall next to Fat Jack.

She gingerly made herself to Jack's desk, as it couldn't be avoided in order to choose an apron, and stood looking at a row of three fabrics. Jack's piercing eyes made her uncomfortable.

"Hello," she said, looking him square in the face." She felt if she didn't stand her ground, there would be trouble ahead.

"Mornin'," he mumbled and returned to writing with a stubby pencil in hand at what appeared to be a list.

"Ain't no social hour!" Fanny yelled. "Grab one and git on ovah heah. The men gonna be wantin' bread soon as roll call's done."

In her haste, Summer grabbed the closest—and dirtiest—apron, which was not an apron at all, but a large square of cloth, and tied the top corners around her waist.

"Grab that ball theah and start kneading!" Fanny ordered, nodding to a ball of dough resting next to her.

Kneading? Oh, great. This was a food art Summer had never experienced—the making of bread! She took the big ball and set it in front of her, watching as Fanny kneaded and then lifted her ball of dough, slapping it back onto the wooden table.

"Like dis," Cesar said, taking her ball of dough and going through the moves in order. "Knead dat ball, punch dat ball, pull it up and slap it down. Den, do it agin."

"What kinda dumb girl ain't never made bread?" Fanny asked, spit showering out through the black spaces in her mouth onto Summer's face and onto her wad of dough. "You some kinda fancy girl come from one of them plantations?"

"You could say that," Summer replied, determined to not let the big woman further fracture her already fractured morning. "Thank you,

Cesar," she said. "I think I got it now." Still, though, out of the corner of her eye she watched Fanny knead, punch, and slap the dough ball, and followed suit.

"Oh, my God!" Summer yelled, jumping back. "A cockroach!" The brown insect scurried quickly across the upper edge of the table. Fanny lifted her ball of dough and slapped it down as hard as she could on top of the roach, stopping it in its tracks. "Theah." She grinned wickedly, showing Summer the roach imbedded into the dough, one antenna still wiggling. Then, as if there had not been an interruption, Fanny continued kneading.

"Are you joking? You're leaving that cockroach in the bread?" Summer stood away from the table, the bottom of her apron clutched in her hands at her chin.

"It's food, ain't it? Don't have time to pick every critter out of the dough, and don't you start doin' it neither or the bread will never get baked with the time it'd take to pick every cotton-pickin' bugger out'a it."

Summer looked at her own ball of dough, focusing in on the small discolorations dotted throughout. With horror she realized that what she had thought was grain, was actually an assortment of small insects that had found their way into the flour supply, or had lost their lives crossing the expanse of the table, and would soon be traveling down the throats of the men of Fort Jefferson—like they must have traveled down her own throat last night at dinner!

* * *

Lila reappeared at full daybreak to start collecting food for the mess hall. The telltale signs of a busy, steamy morning presented itself in soaked blouses, shirts, limp hair and the level of ill temper of everyone in the kitchen, including Lila.

"Allons! Allons[14]! I need ze bread, *se presser!*[15] Zee men are lined up for zee food!"

Even before Lila's hurried entrance, Summer was feeling faint from the heat and afraid she would collapse to the floor like a ball of dough if she didn't get some relief. The bread making was endless! Pan

---

[14] "*Allons! Allons!*" Let's go!

[15] "*se presser!*" Hurry up!

after pan baked in the hot ovens. What first had smelled quite heavenly—the baking of bread—was now nauseatingly familiar. *Too much of a good thing,* she supposed. She wiped her forehead with a damp and filthy corner of the apron and tried to focus on Lila through eyes wet with salty perspiration.

"Oh, eez zee little American tired and hot?" Lila said, creating a puckered pout with her lips.

"Shut up," Summer whispered. The room began to spin; she lost her balance and fell backward, caught by the rough-hewn wall. Cesar was quick to grab her.

"Git out o' dat chair," he ordered Fat Jack, who obeyed immediately, lifting his wide body off the seat he had coveted since Summer first appeared in the bakery at dawn.

Once in the chair, Summer gladly took the cup of water that was handed her and, in rapid succession, gulped it down until the cup was empty. She then fanned herself with the bottom of the soiled apron.

"Thanks," she said to the group which now stood around her like an arch of statues. "I'm okay; just got too hot."

"You come with me," Lila said, helping her up. "We feed zee men, then we have food ourselves."

"The bread ain't cut yet," Fanny barked.

"I weel cut it there," Lila replied. "Give me zee knife."

Exiting the kitchen was no relief, as the sun beat relentlessly onto the parade grounds and beamed throughout the arched walkway. Summer carried four of the long bread pans while Lila managed six. Cesar balanced a double stack of pans on a large tray.

The mess hall was long and rectangular, filled with countless wooden tables and benches. At one end, in a fine row of tables stretched across a narrow end of the hall, the food was set out; a strange smelling porridge in a huge iron pot and the bread that the kitchen crew had so tediously baked.

She and Lila stood side by side behind the tables where Lila sliced the loaves and Summer set a thin slice on each man's tin plate as he passed. Cesar ladled the foul porridge from a large kettle. The insects were not at all limited to the bakery, as black dots of all sizes were visible in the mess of porridge. All the while, armed guards stood by the women. Summer wasn't quite sure if it was to protect them from the men, or because of the knife in close proximity to the prisoners; perhaps it was both.

"There are so many men here, Lila. Do they just run free?" She searched the endless stream of men for the familiar face of Captain Ruiz.

"There eez no place for them to go."

"I haven't seen Captain Ruiz."

"He eez not free, Zummer. They do not let him out."

"Why is that, if he can't escape?"

Lila shrugged. "Theez I do not know."

Summer eyed the ragged stream of prisoners and they eyed her, some winking, smiling, or just complaining over the thin slice of bread they had received.

"Move eet, Move eet!" Lila demanded when a complaint met her ears. "Theez eez what you get. You take your complaints to ze capitaine, not to me! Mon Dieu! You men are lucky to have theez!"

Finally, with the breakfast served and cleaned up, Summer, Lila and Cesar, having returned to the kitchen, took several pieces of bread from the one large loaf that was always on reserve for the crew. Lila and Cesar each took a cup of porridge, but Summer declined.

"Porridge too good for the plantation gal?" Fanny sneared.

"I don't eat bugs."

"You will gal, you will."

* ⚜ *

As if to follow through on her words, Summer picked the bugs out of her bread as they sat on the dock that stretched a few feet into the water behind kitchen and bakery.

"Don't put your feet in dat water," Cesar warned.

"Don't worry. I learned my shark lesson," she said, bringing a now hole-ridden slice of bread to her lips. The bread was good, despite its additional and disgusting seasoning of insects.

"Eez that so?" Lila asked. "And where did you learn your shark lesson?"

"Not far from here, most likely." She scanned the horizon, but saw no other islands. Just mentioning sharks brought back the despair she felt after Ruiz was—or so she thought—killed.

"What do you know about Captain Ruiz?" she asked her new-found friends. "Last I saw of him, I thought he was dead for sure."

"I helped t'bring him ashore when dat supply ship bring him." Cesar said. "He was in bad shape, dat man. Couldn't but walk a step or two on his own. Had a bad head wound."

"I wonder how they found him?"

"Et was a patrol boat find him in ze water somewhere out there." She gestured to the expanse of topaz blue, an endless sea from their vantage point.

"First he go to hospital and then here. He wait for ze trial."

"I really need to see him, Lila. Will you take me? *Please?*"

Chapter 5

Summer's heart beat so loudly she was surprised it didn't echo down the arched corridor. *Ruiz! She was going to see Ruiz!* Lila rat-tat-tatted ahead of her at her usual quickened pace, but neither spoke. Summer's head was full of memories and her stomach full of butterflies. She was ashamed of her excitement but couldn't help the fact that she was here, in a different century under different circumstances, and Guy hadn't even been born yet. She tried to shoo Guy out of her mind, and as she followed Lila through the night darkened arches, it was surprisingly easy to put him aside.

They continued down the corridor until Lila stopped. "Theez ez it." She knocked on the heavy door, which thudded dully beneath her small fist, but being short, she couldn't call through the barred square of a window. "Call him," she said to Summer, indicating the window.

"Ruiz," she whispered. "Ruiz, it's me, Verano."

A groan wafted through the bars.

"Ruiz, it's me. Wake up!"

"Que Paso[16]? Who goes? What do you want?"

Oh how her heart fluttered at the sound of his voice! "Ruiz, it's me, Verano! I'm here!"

Within seconds his hand—his precious hand—tried to reach through the bars, but it was too big. She grabbed hold of his fingers, and on tip-toe kissed them. "Oh, my captain, you're alive!"

"Is it really you, Verano? Stand in the moonlight so I can see."

She glanced across the parade grounds. Indeed, there was nearly a full moon rising over one wall of the fort. She shifted so that her face caught what bit of light it could without disappearing from view.

"Verano, my love! Oh I have prayed that I would see my Verano again. My love, I was so desperate thinking that you had drowned!"

"And I so desperate thinking that you were dead!"

"Oh, Mon Dieu!" Lila exclaimed. "Zee love birds are making me sick!"

"Lila *estás aqui?*" Ruiz asked. "Lila is here?"

"She brought me to you, Ruiz."

"Gracias, Lila," he said through the bars. Vayase! Now go! "

"Theez eez my thanks for bringing your lady love, mon cher? 'Go Lila, go! Go like you are notheeng! Go like you are a cockroach in zee bread! " Despite her complaints, Lila turned and left, the rat-tat-tat of her boots disappearing down the long corridor.

Summer could not get enough of the feel of Ruiz's fingers through the bars. Her heart was full of love for the man, and she was desperate to help him free himself from this place.

"How did you get here, Verano?"

"Oh, it's such a long story. I was looking for you, my love, and here you are, alive!"

"When we sink, I see you in the water, and then no more[17]. Then…then I am in hospital. Where is your maid, Cherry…and Buck?"

"Oh, Captain, such a sad story. Cherry is dead, but her child lives! Buck has the child— a boy— a beautiful boy."

"Buck, he is a fine man. I am so sorry for your friend, Verano. I know how you love her. I did not get you safely to New Orleans and your home like I promise. Forgive me, Verano."

"There is nothing to forgive, captain. We are together; that's all that matters now."

"But we are not together, as you can see."

---

16 "*Que Paso?*" What's happening?

17 Event from Book II

"We must get you out of here. Why don't they let you out in the daytime like the others?"

"I am waiting for trial. The Yankees, they do not like me; they want me dead."

"Can they…can they execute you?"

"This I do not know. I must have the trial first. But you are here now, and we will think of a way."

"We have to think of a way to get you out *before* the trial."

"Supply boats come from New Orleans. Perhaps I know someone on them. It is my home and I know many people, but I cannot see the faces from this place."

"Who do you know who would be working on a supply boat?"

"Hmm…there is Pasqual, and Henri. Oh, let me think…José…I don't know, Verano. I remember those names only. My head, it is not quite the same, but my heart, Verano, my heart is full now that you are here."

Pasqual, Henri, José; Pasqual, Henri, José. Summer repeated the names over and over in her head as she made her way back to her room.

* * *

"So you and your lover are now so happy, *oui?*"

"Yes, and I thank you, Lila, for bringing me to him."

The room was dark as she entered. She had hoped that Lila was asleep but then, how could she be? Summer was sure the woman was hoping for details. *Well, she has another think coming.*

"And? Did you make zee lovey-lovey through zee bars?"

Summer ignored her, disrobed and climbed into bed, the moon now shining through the window. "Did you ever love someone, Lila? I think if you did, you wouldn't be so unkind."

"I have not zee time for love, my spoiled American. I was beezee with staying alive."

"So I've heard."

"And what did you hear?"

"I heard that you were '*beezee*' over in New Orleans, and *that* is why you are here."

"Oh, mon Cherié, I make much money in zee Quarter from zee Yankeez. I don't know why they put me here when I make zee men zo happy over there."

"Are you remorseful, Lila? Do you feel ashamed?"

"Ashamed? *Pourquoi?* Why should I feel ashamed? I must live. I have no man to take care of me—no family. If I do not take care of Lila, then I have notheeng."

"Good night, Lila." Summer sighed and turned to face the wall. So, Lila slept with men for money. Was she, herself any better? She had a husband at home in her own century, a man she loved very much, and two babies on the way *somewhere*. But, here she was drooling over Captain Ruiz, butterflies in her stomach, her heart pounding like a jackhammer at the thought of meeting up with him, and now she was planning his escape. Of course, they would end up in bed together should they succeed in the escape. She would shamelessly give herself to him and then feel remorseful afterward with thoughts of Guy—but it wouldn't stop her. Maybe she didn't do it for money like Lila, but yes, she was just as guilty.

* * *

Three days later a supply boat arrived from New Orleans. Summer followed Lila through the sally poor to the pier in order to pick up flour, and whatever else had been designated for the bakery. She paid close attention to the faces on the boat, and listened carefully for any names mentioned during the unloading.

"Excuse me," she asked a young fellow of Spanish descent. "What is your name?"

"Mi nombre es Miquel, Señorita."

"Oh." *Darn.* "Miquel, do you know of any men named Pasqual, José, or….uh, Henri? They may work on this boat."

"Oh, *si, Se*ñorita. I know many José's, but not on this boat today. I know Pasqual, and he is here."

"Could you show me?"

"Pasqual! Veines aquí! La Señorita quiere habla con usted.[18]"

Pasqual arrived, sweating and swatting at mosquitos, as was everyone else on the pier, including Summer. He removed his straw hat. "Hola, Señorita."

---

[18] "*Veines aquí! La Señorita quiere habla con usted!*" Come here! The woman wants to speak with you!

"Hello, Pasqual." She said, and glanced around to make sure no one was standing too close. "Pasqual, do you know Captain Ruiz?" She whispered and put her fingers to her lips. "Shhh…."

"Si, Seńorita. El Capitain Ruiz. Eres un hombre simpatico—a fine man, the Capitaine."

A sigh of relief. "Do you know that the captain is imprisoned here?" Again she looked around and noticed Lila watching her.

"No!" he said, surprised.

"Yes, he is here and goes to trial soon." She glanced again at Lila, who was still watching.

"He needs your help. He will be executed if they find him guilty."

Pasqual seemed a bit bewildered and looked to Miguel, still standing with them, who translated Summer's words. Pasqual's eyes grew larger.

"And just what eez this little tete-a-tete I zee happening here?" Lila interrupted.

Summer rolled her eyes at the intrusion. "May I have a moment without you butting in?"

"No, certainly not." Lila crossed her arms.

"You are *snoopy-snoopy*, Lila, to borrow your own words."

Lila shrugged. "Eh."

Summer anxiously tapped a sandaled foot on the ground when Pasqual and Miguel were called back to work. "Damn, Lila. I need to speak with those men," she whispered. "I swear, if you breathe one word of this, I will ring your skinny neck."

"What? What eez it I have done?"

"*Snoopy, snoopy*, that's what." She pulled Lila off to the side, away from any other big ears. "Swear, Lila. Swear on your skinny neck that you will not breathe a word…."

"Okay, okay, Zummer, I swear," she said, putting a hand over her heart.

"We must get the captain out of here before his trial. We can't let him be found guilty and executed."

"Oh, Mon Dieu! What you ask! I do not want to see zee capitaine executed, but I do not want to spend zee rest of my life here for helping him escape!"

"That's why we must be successful. We need the help of those men, Lila. We need a plan. We need to get the Captain out on the next supply boat—or any boat—as long as he's away from here."

* * *

"The men are fishermen," Ruiz said later that night. Again, the moon shone silvery upon Summer as she stood on the outside of Ruiz's prison cell. "They have their own boats. If Pasqual, Henri, José or Miguel are on the next supply ship, tell them I will pay handsomely to bring a boat for us. They will trust me, they know my family. This must happen soon, in the dark. Tell them to bring two boats so they can return home. We will sail to New Orleans, to my home."

"Wait…what kind of boats are these? How far is New Orleans?"

"My Verano, do not worry! You do not remember the little boat you tip over when I first find you?[19] I can sail anything; I am a Capitán of the seas!"

It was arranged. Two weeks later the next supply boat arrived and luckily, José came along with Miguel, who was happily looking forward to sharing in the promised reward. Summer was instructed by the captain to tell the men to bring a boat to them on the first night of no moon and to wear dark clothing. Summer would meet them at the small dock behind the bakery, and it was imperative that they come silently, weather permitting, as guards on the A and F Bastions, which overlooked the back of the fort, would be on duty. Miguel was confident that he could break the lock of the prison door, but the sound would resound against the walls of the prison and perhaps alert the guards. This would not be easy; the plan put everyone in danger.

---

[19] This event occurred in Book II

Chapter 6

"Hey, Frankie, et eez me, Lila! I cannot sleep zo I come to have company."

"Frenchie? What'r you doin' up here?"

"Like I say, I cannot sleep. Zee American eez snoring, and I am lonely."

"Did anyone see you come up here?"

"No! I am zo careful! "

"What's going on over there? You okay Frank?" A dark figure approached from Bastion A, walking along the apron of the fort, the grassy stretch of land between A and F bastions.

"S'okay, Charlie. Look whose come to visit, Frenchie!"

"Hey, what brings you here?" Charlie asked.

"She's lonely," Frank snickered.

"Well we can take care of that, can't we Frank?"

"Oh now wait, you naughty boys. Eef you have no money, then Lila talk only."

"Well, shit," Charlie said, setting his rifle against the F Bastion brick wall. He reached into his pockets, while Frank did the same.

"Yankee note only!" Lila warned.

"Of course. Reb money ain't worth shit anyway," Frank said, reaching into his pockets. "I got tokens[20] and some notes[21]."

"Not zee tokens."

"Then it looks like thirty cent," he said, squinting at the notes in the darkness.

"Hmph. Lila worth more than thirty cent."

"Where you gonna spend it, Lila? Thirty cent is better'n no cent. Wha'd you have, Charlie?"

"Thirteen cent," he said, glumly, looking at the crumpled notes from his pocket.

"Hmph! you get no fancy-fancy."

"Well hell, Lila, don't need no fancy-fancy. A quick poke would set me just fine."

"Me, too." Charlie piped in."

"Oh you bad boys. Lila lonely zo...okay. Who eez first?"

* * *

As Lila entertained the guards overhead, Miguel worked furiously —and as silently as humanly possible—to release the lock on the heavy door that imprisoned Captain Ruiz. Summer stood by nervously watching the grounds for guards, but they were nowhere to be seen. This seemed odd to her, though she was not thoroughly familiar with the routine of the parade grounds at this hour. After twenty-five stressful minutes passed, Ruiz was free! Summer, Ruiz, Miguel and José hurried to the boat ramp where the men had tied two dories. Miguel and

---

[20] From 1862 to 1864, Civil War tokens were produced by private sectors to compensate for the shortage of coin currency. These coins became a popular and accepted Yankee currency with guaranteed redemption for merchandise and services. In 1864, congress made token production by the private sector illegal and value of the token was dimished.

[21] In 1864 the government issued fractional paper notes as low as three cents.

José took one, with promises of a grand reward awaiting them at the captain's home in New Orleans. Summer and Ruiz hurriedly boarded their own, untied the docking line and were prepared to shove off when Lila came running onto the small dock.

"I go with you!" she whispered.

Oh crap. Summer did not remember including Lila in the actual escape, just the diversion while the prison door lock was broken.

"Yes, yes, hurry!" Ruiz returned; and once she was onboard, they shoved off into the dark night, the waters calm and lapping gently against the boat. Breathing was barely audible as he rowed quietly away from the prison to the larger sailboat that was anchored a distance off shore. Aside from the flickering of lanterns, all was quiet and still at the fort. They had escaped!

"Just where is New Orleans from here?" Summer asked, once settled on the sailboat.

"Far away, my love," was the reply.

"Eez this what I get? No '*thank-you Lila'* for keeping zee guards beezee?" Indeed, Lila had been oddly quiet until now.

"Oh, mi poco puta.[22] Of course I thank you with all my heart!" Ruiz exclaimed.

"And me, too, Lila," Summer said begrudgingly to the French woman. She was not at all expecting a threesome on this journey, and especially with such an annoying creature.

"And did you make lots of money?" Ruiz asked.

"Eh! Zee soldiers are poor, but I do have Yankee money for us. Let me see: Frankie, thirty cent. Charlie, thirteen cent. William, forty cent—he have more money than the others. Joseph…."

"Wait a minute," Summer interrupted. "Did you have *sex* with these men?"

"Oh such a stupeed woman! Of course! It eez my beeznez, no? How you think you have time for zee capitaine to get free? I get all six soldiers on zee bastions. Zee word catches fast, no? I have one, two, and then four more!"

"Muy bien, Lila! For you, a great reward!"

"Oui, capitaine. Lila get a big reward for entertaining zee soldiers."

[22] "My little whore,"

"Verano, while we talk of reward...." Ruiz looked up at the starry sky. "We go to the shipwreck and look for my treasure. We must have money."

Summer was glad the night was pitch black or Ruiz may have seen her face flush. *His treasure? It's gone!* Should she broach this subject in front of Lila?

"We must find it, Verano. Perhaps the water was not deep where the ship go down."

"What do you speak of?" asked Lila. What treasure eez theez? We will find treasure?"

Summer exhaled. *Oh boy, cat's out of the bag now. Here goes.* "Captain, the treasure is no longer there. Buck and I dove to retrieve it. We thought you were dead...."

As summer relayed the entire story to Ruiz, it was punctuated by Lila's exclamations over the diving with sharks, the rescue by the Seminole tribe, and the birth of Yank on the Island. It all brought back such vivid memories to Summer that she found herself sobbing at the end of the tale, at the death and burial of Cherry and the three gold coins Buck threw into her grave. Of course she could not tell of her own rescue by Guy and the park police, and the murder of Captain Jack, or the retrieving of Cherry's bones for burial at Magnolia Plantation[23].

In the dark, she felt Ruiz's exasperation, perhaps even his anger at the loss of the treasure.

"We will find Buck," he said, standing at the ship's wheel. "We find the island where the *Diablo Volante* sink. From there, you find us the island where Buck and the child are.

"It's a tall order, captain."

"*Que?*" he asked.

"I will try," she said, feeling the tears come again. Perhaps she had angered him, disappointed him. Her heart sank, taking her elation of the escape with it.

Ruiz navigated through the night by the stars. Summer couldn't sleep, and watched him exhaust himself with the arduous chore. At one point she offered to take the wheel, but he wouldn't hear of it. Lila had curled herself up in a corner of the boat's deck and had fallen asleep.

"Don't be angry with me, Ruiz. Buck and I thought you were dead. Buck needed the coins to live. After all, he had Cherry's baby to raise."

---

[23] These events occurred in Book II

"I am not angry, Verano, just tired. This war, it touches everyone in a bad way. I worry about the hacienda, the family."

"What about your family, Ruiz? You've never told me." Her stomach rumbled at the thought that Ruiz may have a wife. Surely he was old enough to, and then some, but he never mentioned one before.

"Mi madre—my mother is of concern, and…and my child."

"*Child*? You have a *child*? Do you have a…a…a wife?" As her voice rose, her heart fell deeper into the pit. *He's married?* It never occurred to her while they were romping in the captain's quarters[24], that he could have a wife!

"One time I had a wife. She is *muerte*—she is dead. She die when Marguerite is born."

"How old is Marguerite?

"She is one year. I have not seen her since she was born, since we bury Isabella."

"Oh Ruiz, I'm so sorry; I didn't know. Why didn't you tell me?"

"I was happy with you, Verano. You take away the sadness, my little American."

"You're sad, now, Ruiz. I can feel it, even if I can't see your face. Can I take away your sadness now?"

"Come over here, Verano."

He wrapped her in his arms, she standing between him and the ships wheel. They stood together for a while, she leaning into him, feeling his breath on her cheek, and loving him all the more for eclipsing the dashing captain for a brief moment, to show the tender, saddened man beneath.

"How do you know where to find the gold on the ship?" he asked, as if suddenly remembering he had hidden it from sight.

"Uh…I must confess, Ruiz. I was in your room one night, just curious, you know. I heard you coming and I hid. That's when I saw you put the box with the coins in the panel behind your bed."

"You and Buck are very brave, diving for the treasure."

"We were, and I do hope Buck and Yank are alright, but I don't know how we can find them."

"We will find them. Miguel was good to bring this boat. He also bring us water and some food. We must watch for the Yankee ships and be *muy cuidado*—very careful."

---

[24] This event occurred Book II

Summer wondered how long the Gulf waters would remain so calm. She knew personally how quickly the swells and waves gathered and roared with an approaching storm. Until then, she hoped they could make it undetected, wherever it was that they would make land.

* * *

"There it is! The mast!" Summer could hardly believe her eyes when three days later she spotted the mast of the Diablo Volante still sprouting from the waters off the shipwreck island. Their luck had sustained them throughout their journey as they had not spotted one Yankee ship in the Gulf. She shuddered in deja vu as they sailed toward the monument, and couldn't help scanning for dorsal fins.

As they sailed past the mast, Ruiz stared mournfully at the sentinel that marked the very spot where he had lost his prized possessions, the gold coin, and the Diablo Volante. Summer took her eyes from him to glance at the beach where Cherry had once sat and watched as she and Buck dove for the treasure.

"Theez eez where you stay?" Lila asked.

Time slowed to a crawl, and Summer did not hear Lila's question. Instead, she stared at the shoreline, the island that had saved them. If she tried hard enough, she could still see Cherry sitting on the shore, waving with relief when she and Buck surfaced from their dangerous dives. As the beach passed in slow-motion, a sadness boiled deep inside and rushed through her veins. Absentmindedly, she waved to the island, to Cherry anda time that was, and would be no more.

"Who you see?" Lila asked, searching the shoreline.

"Oh, no one," Summer replied.

"You are a strange one," Lila said, shrugging her small shoulders. "Eh, capitaine? Is she not?"

Ruiz stared longingly at the mast of the Diablo Volante as it faded into the distance.

"Sorry captain, but here you are; you have survived and are alive and free!"

"*Si, son liberté.*[25]" he said, halfheartedly.

"Oh my poor capitaine. Von bateau, no?[26] I am so very sorry." Lila pursed her lips into a little pout for the captain's benefit. "Perhaps I

---

[25] "*Si, son liberté* "Yes, I'm free."

[26] "Von bateau, no?" Your boat, no?

can make you happy a leetle?" Lila peered at Summer and smiled wickedly.

Summer ignored the remark and looked away, off into the horizon. Clouds were gathering in the west. "Look over there, Ruiz. Is it a storm?"

Ruiz tore his eyes from the mast, viewed the western horizon and headed for shore. "We stop tonight."

"Please, not here, Ruiz! Not on this island!"

"Look there, Verano. *Mira aya!"* He said, nodding toward the darkening sky. "We cannot be in this small boat in such weather."

"Further up the shoreline then," she pleaded. "There are sad memories here, Ruiz. *Please!*"

Ruiz complied silently, maneuvering the sail. Soon after they passed the shipwreck island, another island appeared in the distance.

"We must stop there, Verano; the sky is dark and the winds come."

Mangrove Islands were a challenge. Unless there was a beach, or somewhere to dock the boat with solid land to walk upon, they could be in grave danger. Ruiz sailed the boat around the tip of the island and there, tucked between the foliage, was a spot of solid ground. He lowered the sail and dropped anchor. With the sailboat secure, they climbed into the dory and made shore where Ruiz tied the dory to a sturdy tree. They then continued on foot further inland with Ruiz carrying a torn canvas sail that he had found on the boat. It was necessary to remove themselves from the brunt of the winds that were now gathering, preceding the darkening sky.

* * *

"I'm amazed, captain!" Summer exclaimed, observing in awe the shelter he had created with the torn canvas sail.

He smiled at her and winked, which sent her spirits up a notch; things were not the same between them. The first elation and excitement of their initial meeting at the fort had faded with the reality of their situation, and perhaps with Ruiz's worry of his family and the lost treasure.

Summer scolded herself. She did not know the reason she had been thrown back in time if it was not to save Captain Ruiz. It appeared that she was not to be his lover, though she desperately wanted it to be so. She was here; he was here, and yet that magic spark that she had so enjoyed in anticipation, had flattened like a calm sea in response to his seeming indifference. Did he not love her as she loved him?

This predicament only further confused the purpose of this particular time travel event; she had a man she loved, and she had babies on the way in the 21st century. Cherry was dead and finally home—buried at Magnolia—or so she thought. Was she expected to resolve every unresolved issue of the ancestors? And, speaking of ancestors, the significance of baby Yank was understood, as he was Cherry's child. But just what did Captain Alejandro Ruiz have to do with any of it? He was nothing but torment and heartache!

Chapter 7

Summer could not remember exactly where Buck's Key was located, but she was fairly certain that the day she, Cherry and Buck traveled with the Seminole, that they stayed pretty much on the outside of the islands until it was necessary for Cherry to give birth.

With the last of the food supply consumed, and the storm having passed the night before, the trio of escapees set off again in the small sailboat that had been supplied by José and Miguel.

"We are on a new day and new journey, my little sailors!" Captain Ruiz exclaimed as he shoved the dory back into the Gulf waters. When they reached the sailboat, anchored in the deeper waters, he jumped aboard and indeed, his low spirits seemed to have blown away with the winds of the storm; before them stood Captain Alejandro Ruiz of the *Diablo Volante.* With sails up, off they went into whatever lay ahead.

"We find Buck today, yes?" he asked, maneuvering the sail to catch the wind.

"I believe so," Summer replied, not 100% sure that it would happen, but she did not want to deflate his enthusiasm and good humor.

"We find zee treasure today, *oui?*" Lila asked.

"First, we find Buck and Yank and see how they are doing," Summer snapped. The treasure hunt was beginning to annoy her.

"*Buck, Buck, Buck*. We find theez *Buck* and then zee treasure." Lila turned her back to Summer. "Mon Dieu! Elle est une femme très difficil![27]"

Ruiz laughed. "Two women in one small boat; it is not so good a circumstance!"

* * *

"It's there! I'm sure of it!" Summer pointed in a northeasterly direction to an island with a small sandy beach landing. Surely this was the very one where Cherry had delivered Yank into the world! A Seminole dugout was beached on its shore, indicating the presence of humans. Captain Ruiz turned their boat toward an approach.

"Seminole," He said aloud.

"They've been helpful in the past," Summer recalled.

With their sailboat anchored offshore and the dory secured next to the dug-out, they proceeded inland looking for the natives, and for Buck and Yank. Ruiz walked ahead with Summer following behind, and behind her, Lila, whose whining over her fear of the Seminole was reaching full blown panic.

"You know theez Seminole, Zummer? Are they kind? Are they wickeed? Do they kill us? Please, talk to me, Zummer, I am so nervous!"

"Shh. Calm down! The Seminole are not going to kill us. They're friendly and helpful—for the most part."

"And weech part eez not friendly?"

The women's long skirts snagged on vegetation, as they followed Ruiz along a narrow path to an opening in the sub-tropical forest. Ahead stood a small dwelling set on a tabby foundation[28]. Off to the right was a chickee hut[29]. To the left of the hut was a tall tree, and

---

[27] *"Mon Dieu! Elle est une femme très difficil!"* "My God, she is a very difficult woman!"

[28] A tabby foundation is cement made from lime, sand, and shell.

[29] A chickee hut is a raised, open air, thatched roof dwelling in which the Seminole people lived.

low on the tree, over the place Summer remembered as Cherry's grave, the face of a woman had been carved into its the trunk. Summer froze.

"What eez it? Move! Allons, allons!" Lila ordered, as she was stuck on the trail behind Summer swatting at the mosquitos that attacked as soon as a body was still.

"This is it, Ruiz. This is where Cherry is buried. This is Buck's Key ! Buck! Buck!" she called.

The homestead was quiet and still, aside from the birds calling from the woods, and even they hushed as their peace was shattered by the intruders.

"Where eez zee treasure? Where eez theez Buck?"

"He's here, somewhere." Summer walked beside the chickee hut where there appeared to be a stove built counter high on a tabby base. The center was a wide crevice charred and full of ash. It was surrounded by a rough counter top created with planks of wood "Look, Ruiz, it's a stove, or…is it a barbecue?"

"Un barbacoa!" Ruiz said. "Buck is most ingenious and I am most hungry!"

"Well, lawd be praised!"

The trio turned to find Buck, standing tall and fit, a string of four large fish tied with rope to his waist and in his arms a toddler, white as milk against Buck's ebony skin.

"Lawd, lawd, is what I see, what I see?" He was a handsome picture in his Seminole pants covered in part with a brightly woven skirt that reached to his knees. His chest was bare, hairless and shiny with a day's moisture.

The toddler stared at the trio with eyes of blue sapphire. "Da," he said, pointing. Buck set him on the ground.

"Lawd, I thought you was dead, cap'n!"

"So did I, my old friend!"

The men embraced and patted each other on the back.

"I looked but I could not find you in dat water, cap'n. Dat mast broke and hit you square in da head. You was dead, cap'n, for sho.

"Ah, *si,* I would have been, but Yankees find me drifting on a plank of wood. My mind, it is not the same, but Buck, I remember you, my friend, and I am happy to meet you again."

"And lawdy, Miz Summah. I search and search for you! Where did you go?"

"It's a long story, Buck, but we sure are glad to be here."

"And what am I?" Lila asked. "Am I a notheeng? Do you not introduce Lila?"

"And this," Summer said, indicating the small, sweaty and disheveled French woman, "is Miss Lila de Peau of New Orleans. Miss de Peau, this is Buck, and this adorable little guy hanging onto his leg is Yank Woodfield. Oh Buck, just look at him! He's walking!"

"He is, Miz Summah. He walkin' good. Don' talk yet, but I swear, I would be dead if my Yank wasn't here."

Summer bent to get a good look at the little guy. *Not a speck of Cherry.* Not one little inkling that this was Cherry's child, a child born to a full blooded Negro[30]. She shook her head. It was a shame that there was nothing of a reminder of the woman in the child. "Hello, Yank. You don't remember me, but I was here the day you were born."

Yank hid his head behind Buck's muscular leg. "He ain't used to people, not white folks anyway. The Seminole come sometimes."

"I thought they were afraid of him."

"Not now. Dey was afraid o' Cherry, I think. Now dey say Yank's somethin' special, like a God; a white god born from a black woman. It's been good with the Seminole comin'. We trade."

Ruiz's ears pricked. "And what do you trade?"

"Dey bring me swamp deer sometime. Ain't got none here on da island. Sometime dey bring clothes for Yank and me. Sometime a pig, a gator."

"What do you give them?"

"Gold."

"Zee gold!" Lila exclaimed. He has zee gold!"

"You give them my gold?"

"We thought you was dead, cap'n. Me n' Miz Summah, we done dive for dat gold so's we have money to live—money for Cherry's boy."

"I know, I know, Buck. But…I need my gold, my friend. I need money."

"Well, here you is. Guess what's fair is fair; what's yours is yours."

Summer exploded. "Captain Alejandro Ruiz! You can't take it all away from Buck and Yank."

"Why not?" Lila asked, obviously very put out. "Et eez for zee capitaine, no?"

---

[30] This event occurred in Book II

"Shut up, Lila!" Summer had had enough. "It is not your gold to even question!"

"Well…I get my reward, do I not, capitaine?"

Ruiz ignored her, and walked off around the chickee hut, his hands locked behind his back. "Let me think. Let me think," he said. Summer followed.

"Ruiz, you can't take it all away from them. I won't let you."

"*You* won't let me? It is my money, Verano!"

"You *stole* the money."

"It was owed me. Remember? It was money owed me from the cigars."

"I guess you could look at it that way, but you still can't take it all, Ruiz. It's not fair. Buck and I worked hard to bring that treasure up from the ship; we risked life and limb. I don't want any of it. I just want Cherry's boy to be taken care of, and that means Buck, too. He's caring for the child. He loved Cherry, and he loves her child."

Ruiz sat on the side of the chickee hut. "Oh, yes, you make sense, Verano, but what am I to do? What are *we* to do? You come with me, yes? We go to New Orleans, to my home. We need money."

"We'll think about it, okay? We'll sleep here a few days, and work it out with Buck."

* * *

"What does zee baby want?" Lila asked while Yank tugged on her skirt.

"Da. Da.," he repeated, raising his arms.

"He wants you to pick him up." Buck said.

"Da!" Yank insisted.

"Oh, mon Dieu! Okay, okay, I get you." Lila lifted Yank into her arms, where he immediately proceeded to wrap his small fingers in her curly hair.

"Ouch! That does hurt, leetle one!"

Yank laughed. So did Buck.

"He likes you," Buck said.

"He like to pull my hair, eez what he like."

Yank then pulled on the neck of her blouse.

"Oh, he start young, theez one. No! No!" she scolded.

"He knows a pretty woman when he sees one." Buck said, to which Lila, who gave her most magical and coquettish smile in return.

Summer rolled her eyes. *That woman….* "I hope she doesn't plan on having sex with Buck for the gold coins. I wouldn't put it past her," she whispered to Ruiz. They sat close together on stump chairs eating the fish that Buck had caught and cooked, along with bananas he had picked in the sub-tropical forest.

"And what is so wrong with *amour,* my little American. I would like some *amour* with you— tonight." Ruiz nuzzled her neck and she was back to square one, filled with desire for the man.

"Would you, Ruiz? You are so distant."

"I have much on my mind." He straightened himself on his stump chair. "I have many worries."

"Let's forget them tonight, my captain." She put a hand on this thigh and felt her own tremble.

"Yes," he whispered, and moved her hand upward to feel his hardness.

Later, Summer and Ruiz took the coconut shells the group had used as dinner plates, to the water's edge to wash. They then walked up the beach, and it was there, on leaves of palm, where their desires were satisfied.

Chapter 8

On the trio's third day on the island, a group of Seminole men arrived in dugout canoes. They were dressed in the traditional costume that Summer remembered: the colorfully woven shirts and skirts worn over brightly colored leggings. On their heads they wore exotic turbans adorned with plumes and feathers in pinks and whites. The new visitors caused the women to pause and take note of their own dowdy clothing. Summer still wore the skirt and ugly calico blouse that Mrs. Giles had given her, and both women's clothing were filthy and smelled of sweat.

"Why they look at us like theez?" Lila asked, obviously uncomfortable with the stares she received from the six men who stood by their canoes with surprised looks on their faces.

"They weren't expectin' to find a bunch o' white folks with me." Buck replied.

"They don't like white women—or men, for that matter," Summer said, nodding to Ruiz. "They don't appreciate what our kind has done to them."

"Dat's da truth," Buck muttered. "Ain't nothin' but fightin' wid de army.

When the dark glaring eyes lifted from the white intruders—only after Buck's assurance that the strangers meant no harm—the Seminole busied themselves with unloading the various cargoes from the two canoes; dried meats: woven cloth, vegetables, pumpkins, a squealing pig, clucking chickens in a wooden cage, an alligator tail that smelled to high heaven, and other sundry. When the supplies were deposited to their proper destinations, the Seminole conversed with Buck in a language they appeared to have created between themselves; *Pigeon Seminole*, Summer surmised.

"Dey will spend da night and we'll make a feast in thanks for da gifts," Buck translated for his guests.

Little Yank was not a bit put off by the Seminole. They played with him in a masculine, sporty way that delighted the little fellow. He laughed with glee as they took turns wrestling with the toddler, and chasing him around the chickee hut. Eventually, playtime ceased, and Buck went off with the colorful crew of Seminole to fish while Ruiz was told to remain with the women.

Ruiz was quite disgruntled that he could not join the men, but Buck had told him that the Seminole did not trust him and would not fish with him. He was disturbed; but considering the unfriendly looks he got from the visitors, he realized it was best to stay out of their way. Later, while the other men fished, Ruiz scoured the shoreline for clams and oysters to complement the evening feast.

Summer and Lila, along with little Yank—who followed Lila like a lovesick puppy—gathered wood for the evening fire. When the firewood was ready to ignite, the coconut dishes were lined up neatly on the make-shift counter/cooktop combo that Buck had built. A few vegetables and squash brought by the Seminole lay ready to cook over the yet-to-be-lit flame. Summer and Lila sat on one end of the chickee hut watching Yank play in the dirt. Lila had surprised Summer with an innate talent for creating a festive atmosphere with flowers and plants set about the chickee hut in artistic display.

"Zummer, I am zo happy we are going to New Orleans—ooh la! I cannot wait for zee excitement of Le Vieux Carré and to see my friends. But now, we make theez chickee-chickee pretty for zee…zee…what we call them?"

"Seminole," Summer said. "They are Seminole Indians."

"For zee Zeminole, no?" Lila spread her arms to encompass her floral mastery in decoration of the hut. "It eez ze best we can do for our company—*les sauvages*. They do not deserve my decorations, but I am zo happy thinking of Le Vieux Carré that I cannot control myself!"

Les sauvages. Reflecting back on the horrific behavior of Quinn[31] and his treatment of the Seminole who helped their small group when she, Cherry and Buck were lost in the mangrove tunnels, Summer found it difficult to think of them as 'savages'.

"They're people like us, Lila. Not savages, just different. Look how much they've helped Buck and little Yank."

"Humph. Theez is true," she relented. "Oh, Zummer, that man, Buck, he eez a handsome one, no? *Un beau homme!*" She leaned into Summer. "I want him, you know?"

"Lila, please! Do *not* play with Buck's feelings. He is not one of your clients, and don't make him one."

"Oh, but theez I do for free!"

Summer was certain that Lila loved to agitate her and did it on purpose. Normally, she tried to ignore the taunts, but she loved Buck; they had been through so much together and both had loved Cherry. The perilous journey they shared linked them together in the past, and in the present. Lila's wish of partaking in sex with Buck riled her something awful, even though she was sure Buck would welcome the act, having been so long on the island without a woman for company.

"He has no woman for long time, no?" Lila asked, as if reading her mind.

"And you just had *a few men* about a week or so ago. How can you have sex with so many men and not be ashamed?"

"I tell you, it eez my beeznez; et eez how I make live. Mon Dieu, you do not understand? But you have lovey-lovey with ze capitain, no? You theenk I don't know theez? You feel shame?"

Summer blushed. Lila was right; she was also guilty, though Lila could never guess why. Why did she insist on berating Lila when she was acting quite shamefully herself?

* * *

[31] Quinn, a character from Book II

The men returned from fishing when the sun sat low on the western sky; a big red ball with offshoots of orange and pink streaks, its affect causing all to stop to stare at the mastery of nature. The fishing had been successful as all seven men returned with many pompano, which had been cleaned and prepared for cooking before entering the homestead.

The fire was lit; fish and vegetables were wrapped in banana leaves and roasting. Buck was quite adept in the kitchen, having learned much from his Seminole visitors. While he spoke the English language, which many of the Seminole were anxious to learn, they, in turn, taught Buck how to survive in the islands.

Before long, the expanded group sat in a circle beneath the palmed chickee hut roof, their coconut bowls full of the aromatic feast. Summer could not help wriggling in her seat on the floor, as the Seminole constantly kept their eyes on the white visitors.

"Buck, ask your Indian friends if they will take us to a port where we can buy a bigger boat," Ruiz asked. "Our sailboat is small, but our next journey is long and perhaps a little comfort would be a good thing for the women." Buck translated the request to one of the guests in particular—the one wearing the largest headpiece of pink and white plumes. The man looked hard at Ruiz, who did not look away, and then answered the question, never removing his eyes from the captain.

"He says he can take you to da trading post, but only if I come wid y'all cause I know da English."

"A trading post? How far?" Summer asked.

"It's past a place dey call Chokoloskee. Two days."

"You been there?" Ruiz asked.

"Once. You gets to know yo' way around dem islands."

"Will you come, Buck?" Summer asked.

"I come, me n' Yank. I ain't been der in a while."

"I will need the gold, Buck."

"Yes, sah."

Summer eyed Ruiz with unmistakable malice, a look he didn't miss.

"Oh course," the captain continued, "we will share the gold. I will not take it all."

Summer saw a look of relief in Buck's eyes. He was an honest man and would have given Ruiz all of the gold, had he insisted. Perhaps Ruiz wanted to remain on good terms with her, or perhaps he liked Buck enough to share the gold and not leave him destitute with a small child.

Whatever the reason, Summer was relieved, and loved the captain even more.

Chapter 9

"Chokoloskee ahead," Buck said as they approached another isolated patch of land, one of many on their two day journey to reach the trading post. It was a three dugout canoe caravan that had made its way from Buck's key to this landmark. Buck and Ruiz each on opposite ends of the craft, paddled religiously behind their Seminole guides, keeping pace with the natives who were born into this land of water and swamp. The women sat between the two in the middle of the canoe, daring not to stand for fear of their movement tipping the canoe over and dumping them into the water. Lila held fast onto little Yank, who appeared delighted to be wrapped in her arms.

What made Chokoloskee different from the other islands they had passed was the fact that this one had a boat landing. Small as it was, it still allowed for docking, while many of the other islands were covered in the impenetrable mangrove. Also, a shack stood at the edge of the tree line, set back from the water's edge. Mangrove roots promised to overrun the small dirt docking area, eventually, if not kept under control.

"Who lives there?" Summer asked.

"A white man. Dey call him Shady Joe."

As if on cue, Shady Joe appeared from the crude door of the shack to peer at the passersby. From Summer's point of view, he looked quite thin and grizzled, his unkempt hair blending into a long and scruffy brown beard. He nodded to the canoe fleet as it passed, but Buck did not return the nod. Shady Joe watched the caravan until it was out of view.

"Whew, that guy was creepy," Summer remarked.

"You don't wanna tangle wid dat man no-how. War deserter—like me, I guess—but he don't cotton to black folk…or da Seminole."

"Not me, mon Chér!" Lila said. "That man will not have me, not for $100!"

Buck looked back over his shoulder. "Wha'd you mean, gal?"

A small gasp from Lila's lips did not escape Summer's ears.

"Oh, *mon ami,* I make zee mistake," Lila whispered into Summer's ear. "Do not tell Monsieur Buck how I live."

"Hmph! Propriety at last, *mon ami?*" she whispered in return.

Lila elbowed Summer lightly in the ribs. "Shh, sil vous plais!"

"Can't hear ya, gal." Buck said, craning his neck trying to get a peek at the French woman.

"Don't fret, mon chér, eet was a silly joke."

Within an hour, the caravan paddled upstream into a river. Soon they tied their canoes to a rudimentary dock, stood on land and viewed the trading post[32], which harbored more people than the escaping group had seen since their hasty departure from Fort Jefferson. It was not a large crowd by any means, but what a group it was! A mixture of black, Seminole and white meandered around rudimentary wooden tables. Lean-to's, tents and blankets spread about the grounds, were manned by various vendors. Furs, dried meats, vegetables, squash, weapons, shell jewelry and even more various and sundry items were displayed for trade and sale.

No white women were at all visible in the crowd of gatherers, but several Seminole women were present along with many children from infants at breast to teenager. Many of the youngest children looked to be a mixture of black and Seminole[33].

"Vernano, miren esto! Look at this! We will not find a boat here," Ruiz exclaimed spreading his arms wide. "We have nothing here but Indians and…and criminals!" He gestured to a few disheveled men hovering near a tent fronted with jugs. Summer assumed it was liquor

---

[32] In 1864, what is now the Rod and Gun Club in Everglades City, Florida alongside the Barron River, began as a fur trading post for the first white settlers.

[33] Escaped African/American slaves and black Civil War deserters were welcomed into the Seminole tribes, and fought side by side with the Indians during the Seminole wars.

they were drinking, for when they threw a coin or two on the ground next to an old Indian woman sitting on a blanket, they received, in return, jugs from which they drank heartily before returning them to the old woman.

"Ay, ¡maldita sea[34]! We need to get to New Orleans, and there is not even a decent town!"

"Let's give it chance," she said, taking Ruiz's arm, leading him away from Lila. Buck lifted Yank to his shoulders and followed Lila around the grassy trading post as she perused the items for sale and trade.

They look like a family, Summer thought, watching the trio from the corner of her eye. An odd family; one large and muscular black man, one white petite French woman, and the other, little Yank, white as blinding snow and topped with a mess of hair so light it was almost white.

"Captain," she began, breaking her visual hold on the others. "We will have to ask around; that's all we can do. Perhaps we could go by land?"

"Verano, have you forgotten? There is a war, and I am an escaped prisoner. They want to hang me, and you do not want me dead, *si?* I cannot travel by land; it must be by sea."

She loved the way he spoke—his accent, the gleam in his eye, and the gesticulations of his arms doing the talking for him. Sometimes he crossed his arms over his chest, his feet spread apart, and looking very much like her beloved captain when they had first met.

Focusing again on the present, she thought a moment, searching the vendors' faces, and hoping one would look like a person with a boat for rent or purchase. *Don't be stupid, this is not the 21st century!* "We will have to ask, starting with them," she said, pulling him toward the three disheveled characters, and not considering for a moment of her own and the captain's disheveled appearance and body odor.

"Excuse me," she said, and would have continued, but Captain Ruiz pushed her behind him, blocking her from view. She had forgotten that women were not to be so forward in this century, and especially approaching strange men.

The men, smelling of sweat and alcohol, looked to the feminine voice, only to see Captain Alejandro Ruiz of the *Diablo Volante* standing before them, self-assured and arms crossed over chest.

"Whad'ya want?" one man asked.

"A boat." Ruiz answered.

---

[34] "*maldita sea!*" Damn!

That's right, just cut to the chase, Ruiz. Smmer rolled her eyes at the captain's straight forwardness.

"Do I look like I gotta boat on me?" another replied.

"I need a boat—a good seafaring boat."

"Who you got behind ya?" the first fellow asked, bending to catch a glimpse of Summer .

She stepped from behind Ruiz and cleared her throat. "We would like to purchase a good sea-faring boat. Do you know where we could find one?"

The men broke out in laughter. "Sure lady," the third fellow said. "Don'cha know there's a boat store right up the road there?" He thumbed a direction behind him. Again, the men laughed at the joke.

"Callarse el pico[35]!" the captain said with much authority in his voice punctuated by his reddening face. "We have a question. Do you have an answer?" he demanded.

The men straightened a bit at this new demeanor in the stranger.

"Maybe," one said, an eyebrow arching upward. "Depends on what you wanna pay."

"First, I see boat. Then we discuss price."

"Maybe you want to trade the woman?"

Ruiz glared at the man.

"I guess not," the man said. "Follow me."

Summer held tight to the captain's shirt as the men took large strides; she did not want to fall behind. She glanced back at the trade area to see Buck looking oddly at them as they walked toward the river, and she nodded to him, hoping he would get the message to follow. *May as well have backup.* If her travels taught her anything, it was to be extra cautious. She didn't trust the three strangers; they smelled like trouble.

Back at the docking area, Ruiz followed the men, who turned upriver and away from the Gulf waters. They walked several yards to where a few boats were secured, all the while Summer's nerves tightening. *Not good.* She looked behind, hoping to see Buck on their trail, but he was not in view; not a soul was in sight.

None of the boats were large enough for what Summer figured Ruiz had in mind, except for one. It looked older than the hills, but it was long, wide, and had two canvas sails. "How much?" Ruiz asked, pointing to the larger boat.

"Depends."

---

[35] *"Callarse el pico!"* Shut your mouth!

"How much?" Ruiz asked again, agitation in his voice.

"The woman and a hundred in Yankee dollars."

"No woman," Ruiz said.

"Two hundred Yankee dollars then," the man said. He appeared to be the leader of the threesome. The other two men stood back a ways, eyeing Summer.

"It is not a good bargain," Ruiz said. "The boat is old. I do not know if it is seaworthy."

"It got us here. Where you headed?"

The two ragged creatures continued to stare rudely at Summer, taking in her filthy skirt and settling their eyes on her ugly blouse, or what it covered. She absentmindedly reached to button the blouse to her neck, as her habit was to leave it unbuttoned to the cleavage; the weather could be brutally hot this time of year.

"It is not your business, where we go." Ruiz replied. "I give you fifty—in gold."

To Summer, it looked like all three strangers lost their eyeballs at the mention of "gold".

"Gold, eh?" the leader said, regaining his composure.

"Gold, Finn!" one of the fellows standing behind piped in.

"Shut-up," Finn said. "100 in gold."

You are crazy, my friend," Ruiz said. "Fifty coins is what I pay, and no more."

"Shit, Finn, take it!"

Finn turned and slugged his companion in the jaw, sending him stumbling backward until he tripped and fell into a growth of ragged shrubbery.

Ruiz stood still. When Finn turned to him again, Ruiz showed no emotion. "Fifty gold." he reiterated.

Seventy five in gold and the woman."

"I am *not* for sale," Summer said, completely annoyed at the thought that she could be sold—and for a mere seventy-five coins in gold and a boat!

The captain pushed her behind him again. "You sell or no?" he asked.

Finn's companion had managed to climb out of the shrubbery rubbing his jaw. "Wha'd ya do that for?"

"Shut up," Finn ordered, and suddenly nodded to his companions. Summer missed this particular move, as her view from behind the captain was limited.

Without a moment to think otherwise, Finn's companions had followed his signal and wrestled Ruiz to the ground. Finn had Summer by the scruff of her collar.

"Where's the gold, sister?" he growled in her ear. "Give us the gold or your Spanish bastard is a dead man."

"I…I don't' know where it is!" she exclaimed, very worried about Ruiz who was struggling to overpower his captors. It took the two filthy beasts to sit on him to keep him under control.

"Come on, sweetheart," he said, and half dragged her toward the other docked boats and canoes. "I know one of these is yours. Where'd he hide the gold?"

"Do you think he's stupid enough to leave gold on the canoe?" It was difficult to speak, as Finn had the back of her collar gripped in his fist, forcing the fabric to cut into the front of her throat

Finn threw her to the ground. "Where the hell is it then?"

"I don't know, you lowlife. Take the fifty in gold and be happy, that is if he'll even give it to you at this point."

"He will if he wants to see his little darling whore again." Finn reached down and pulled her up by the collar. As he brought her to a standing position, he grasped her breast. She fought off his hand, but it was futile. He laughed, dragging her back to where Ruiz was imprisoned beneath Finn's accomplices.

"Listen, you bastard. See this woman of yours?" He thrust Summer forward, still maintaining control of the horrid blouse collar. "You can watch us have lots of fun with her till you tell me where the go…."

Finn's voice cut short. From her vantage point, she spotted the eyes of Finn's thugs growing large and wide. In a fraction of a second, she was sent flying onto Ruiz. The two ruffians ran off alongside the riverbank, leaving Ruiz to collect his wits.

"Are you okay?" she asked, her hands on Ruiz's chest, but only for a moment. Ruiz pushed her aside and sprang to his feet. Summer turned to see Buck with a stronghold on Finn, the thick muscular black arm clenched around the man's throat. Finn's eyes bulged under the powerful grip, his face bright red.

"And for you, my friend," Ruiz said, punching Finn squarely in the gut with all the power he could muster.

Finn fell to the ground, rolling and coughing, his arms hugging his wounded belly. "Son of a bitch," he growled from his injured throat. "I'll get you, I'll find you wherever you go!"

Ruiz reached into a leather pouch tied to his belt and pulled out a few gold coins, throwing them at Finn. "Get Lila and the baby!" he ordered. Summer began to run toward the trading post, but Lila and Yank appeared from behind the brush, she carrying a large satchel.

"Get in the boat!" Ruiz barked. He sent Buck back to the canoe to get whatever belongings they had left. When he returned, he took Yank from Lila's arms.

"I ain't goin' wid you, cap'n." He set his eyes on Lila. "When you gits tired o' New Orleans, you come on back to Buck's Key, little gal."

"Come weeth us, *mon chér!* Bring zee baby!"

"Vienes[36], Buck, my friend. Do not stay in this place! You come to New Orleans."

"Come on, Buck," Summer said. "What kind of life can you and Yank have on that little island?"

"I'se a free man on my homestead. First thing that ever belonged to me."

"You're a free man anywhere, Buck."

"Miz Summah, it'll take a long time a'fore anyone looks at a black man and thinks he's free. We stay here. Besides, the rest of the gold is back on da key. I keep it safe for you, cap'n!"

"Farewell, my friend. We will meet again!" Buck helped Ruiz ready the larger sailboat and pushed them away from the dock. With the sails set, Ruiz steered the boat down the river toward the open gulf waters.

With one last look at her old friend and little Yank, Summer wiped away her tears. Buck was right. One day he could return to the mainland, but for now, perhaps it was best they stayed on the island, away from the prejudice and madness of the war.

* * *

Soon, the women were well schooled in the jargon of sailing a larger ship. When Ruiz yelled an order, they obeyed—or at least understood the lingo; tacking, heeling, point-of-sail. In the absence of Buck, they became the crew, and Ruiz, of course, the captain.

---

[36] *"Vienes"* Come

Chapter 10

"Zee Mizzizzippi!" Lila was elated. The nine-day journey had been to her both beautiful and frightening. To Summer, though, it was smooth sailing compared to the harrowing adventure she had shared with Buck and Cherry on the Atlantic when their skiff overturned, dumping them into the sea. They were saved by Captain Alejandro Ruiz then; but now, here he was with them, and who would save them had they capsized? Hopefully not the Federal fleet, which they had mercifully managed to avoid thus far.

Sailing up the Mississippi into New Orleans was a different matter altogether. Surely their escape had been publicized, and all ports were on the lookout for the captain. Ruiz's beard growth, black with hints of gray, gave him the look of a questionable renegade. He couldn't help it, he was of stocky and muscular build; his masculinity revealed not only in the scruffy facial hair, but the flowing black crown of hair that shone in the sun and fluttered in the wind. His stance emanated self-assuredness, and his voice was one of authority. He was a very noticeable figure, sailing up the river.

Just the same, it did not steel him, or the women, for the sight of the Federal fleet which saturated the Mississippi and the port of New Orleans. The closer they came to the city, the more ships came into view, and the more he tried to appear nonchalant as he sailed the vessel past the larger ones. Because of the large enemy fleet, Ruiz did not dock but sailed past the harbor.

"Why you not stop, capitaine?"

"We must head to Valecherie," he said.

"But, *capitaine,* theez is where I get off zee ship!"

"Not now, Lila. I cannot stop here. Look at the war ships. Look at the soldiers! I promise, I return you to Le Vieux Carré.

"C'est des conneries!"[37] *Mon capitaine,* please! I want to go home!"

"I know, my little friend, but you do not want me arrested, do you? We have traveled far, and I *will not go back to prison.*" He growled the last words as he scrunched his eyebrows and glared at her.

As the port of New Orleans faded from view, Lila sat at the bow, pouting and staring ahead at the riverbanks, lush and green, and at a river full of war and cargo ships.

"You know he's right, don't you, Lila?" Summer felt a sudden compassion for the woman, for surely she was just as much out of place as she; two women traveling into a future unknown.

"Yes," Lila whispered. "I just want to go home to zee my friends, to make zee money. I weesh Monsieur Buck would come weeth us, but then…" she sighed. "Then he would know what I do to make zee money and perhaps he do not like that." Lila began to cry.

In turn, Summer felt a tear roll down her own cheek; it was a terrible war; a war that displaced people; it tortured the countryside and littered the land with death and destruction.

"Captain Ruiz said he will take you home again, and he will."

"I could make lots of money in LeVieux Carré weeth zee Yankeez. I could make zee money and perhaps go back to see Monsieur Buck and zee leetle bébé again."

"I'll bet you do that, one day." Summer wondered if this were true. She had no visions of the kind that had haunted her in the Everglades on the treacherous journey with Buck and Cherry. Lila was

---

[37] *"C'est des conneries!"* "This is bullshit!"

not mentioned in any of the papers at the historical society. *Time will tell.* If anything, time was the ultimate truth.

* * *

At last, Vacherie! They sailed past the port, one made for larger ships to dock and upload the thousands of pounds of pecans that made Vacherie a major stop on the Mississippi cargo route.

Soon, Ruiz pointed out a dock tucked into an alcove alongside the river. "It is the "*Bella Vista Plantation,*" my family home.

"Why are we passing it?" Summer asked.

"First, we must look for the *Federales.*" Ruiz sailed closer to shore and spotting no soldiers or guards, he tacked and headed to the small dock. Once there, he secured the boat, lowered the sail, and they stepped onto dry land.

The plantation was far from the docking area, as was consistent with Tanglewood Plantation and many plantations alongside the rivers of the South. Ruiz insisted they stay off the overgrown path in fear of the Yankees; he was a wanted man and took no chances.

The woods were thick with brambles and vines that sprouted sharp and angry thorns, making their travel difficult as well as hazardous. By the time the clearing showed through the mangled vegetation, the trio appeared as if they had traversed a war zone with nature, complete with facial scratches, cuts, bleeding hands and ripped clothing.

"Mon Dieu! I could be in Le Vieux Carré having coffee and beignets!" Lila whispered, followed by curses. "But no, I am *here*, bleeding in zee forest!"

"Shh!" Ruiz ordered as he peeked through the brush and down the long expanse of grassy land to the large plantation house

"Just as I thought, soldiers!"

Yankee soldiers meandered close to the grand portico; some gathered in small groups, some standing alone, and all armed with long rifles. The manor house stood in splendor, its architecture hinting at the Spanish ancestry of Ruiz's family. On either side of the great grassy lawn were the pecan trees, tall and full of green leafy branches that spread their great arms into the next tree, and the next, and the next. Spanish moss draped gracefully from limbs of the live oaks that stood regally on either side of the impressive structure. On further scrutiny, viewing into the forest of pecan trees, black bodies came into view; black bodies bent in the act of plucking the dropped pecans from the ground and placing them in large satchels that hung from their shoulders.

"I thought slavery was dead," Summer said.

"It is dead in many places, but not here. Here, they get food, a home, and are not treated as animals."

"But, I thought Lincoln freed the slaves."

"My little American, did you not hear? They get food, a home, a good life. If they run, where will they run to? It will be more trouble for them. The proclamation does not include all the parishes[38]. Our people chose to stay."

Without another word, Ruiz led them back through the cutting brambles and strangling vines to the boat. Again they boarded, shoved off and sailed further upriver away from the plantation. Soon, he pulled into another dock that stretched fifteen feet out into the Mississippi. A small clearing was visible on land. "We stay here tonight."

"Where are we?"

"We are still on my land, but the soldiers will not come to this place. The woods are thick and…" he held up a bleeding arm. "…and unpleasant."

Lila removed the remaining food items from the satchel she had brought from the trading post; corncobs, pumpkins, which were beginning to mold, and salted alligator meat. "Et eez zee end of zee food."

At this remark, the captain began to disrobe. "I fish," he said, and stark naked, jumped into the river.

"Oh!" Lila exclaimed. "Zo cold!"

What on earth? But then Summer realized there was no need to be embarrassed over Ruiz's nakedness in front of Lila. There was nothing Lila knew better than every square inch of a man's anatomy.

"He eez very handsome, no? *Weeth* clothes and weethout. Make you want zee lovey lovey, no?" Lila asked as they stood dockside watching Ruiz's air bubbles surface.

"Oh, shut up!" But Summer couldn't deny the fact that the sight of Ruiz's naked, muscular body, and the sheer boldness of his nakedness in front of the women, did, most definitely, raise the temperature.

"How can he feesh like theez? *Oú se trouver*[39]*?*"

---

[38] Slavery continued in some parishes of New Orleans after President Lincoln's Emancipation Proclamation in 1863. *"…occupied New Orleans and a handful of parishes were specifically exempted from the law."* http://www.nola.com/175years

[39] *Oú se trouver?*" "What will he find?"

"He's trying to catch a catfish. I saw fishing done this way once before. Let's hope he comes up with a big, fat one. Sure would beat eating alligator for a change."

* * *

She woke with a start. *Guy.* Guy woke her. It took a moment to realize she had been dreaming. Guy wanted her; he stood naked and tall, yet she was entangled with Ruiz, *literally.* In the midst of passionate love making with her dashing captain, she had opened her eyes to see Guy standing at the foot of their bed with tears in his eyes.

"Why?" he asked.

Summer stood up off the deck floor. Mosquitos buzzed in a feeding frenzy about her head, biting and feasting on her blood. Ruiz snored softly beside her, covered head to foot in clothing, a must for protecting oneself from the unrelenting insects. She waved away the pests and scratched her face. Looking to the bow she saw Lila's small form, dark and shadowlike; she was asleep. Everyone slept, except Summer.

The guilt of her attachment to Ruiz struck like lightening. Again, that night, she and Ruiz had made love, and most willingly. When Lila dozed off, they clung to each other behind the sterncastle out of view. They muffled the sounds of their love act, and when it was over they dozed, wrapped in each other's arms. Then, the dream. Guilt overcame her; it dimmed her happiness. She knew that what she did now with Ruiz was unforgivable in her time…but was it unforgivable if she were in a different century—a different time zone—and with a ghost? It was a haunting question.

Chapter 11

"You stay here and I will see if I can get into the house."

It was pre-dawn. The minutest hint of sunrise showed as a faint glow rising low behind the trees. Ruiz left the women and disappeared into the of the woods and brush.

With nerves at high pitch, Summer and Lila stood staring into the darkness. "What if they shoot him? They had guns, Lila. Oh my God, this is unbearable!" Summer covered her ears, expecting on all accounts to hear shots that would take her lover from her.

"Eet will take him a while to get there, mon ami. I theenk we are far from zee big house."

* * *

Time moved at a snail's pace. The sun rose high overhead, and still no sign of Ruiz. *At least no gunshots.* Summer reminded herself to count the blessings in this venture—so far. Life changed on a dime; *expect the unexpected.*

When the sun hung high overhead, both women's nerves were electrified.

"Where is he? What's happening? I can't stand this!" Summer paced back and forth in the small clearing.

"We go look, yes?" Lila asked, stepping out of the sailboat onto the dock. Together they fought their way through the brambles and vines that were hell-bent on cutting them to shreds. Fearful of getting lost, they kept the river to their right as they struggled through the foliage. Eventually, after much sweating, cursing and bleeding skin, they came to the dock with the path to the plantation. Instead of taking the main path, they followed the freshly broken one in which they had cut through the woods and brambles the day before. With scratched faces and hands stinging of new wounds, they peered through the growth to the stately manor house. No soldiers.

"I don't see anyone, do you?" Summer whispered.

"Theez make me nervous. Yesterday there were many soldiers. Where are they now?"

Summer looked to the left and right of the majestic home, and to the dense pecan orchards—which appeared to be the only way they could approach closer— but the workers were busy in the orchards at their days' work. Should they approach? Could they be trusted?

"We must get closer. We weel talk to zee *d'esclaves*[40]".

Choosing the left orchard, they made their way, staying close to the clearing.

"Who dat? Who go der?" A large, aproned woman wearing a red turban was the first to catch sight of the bedraggled women. "Ain't y'all a messed up pair o'gals I ever did see!"

"Hello." Summer greeted the woman and the other workers who stopped to stare at the strangers.

"We...." *We what? Do we dare tell them we are with the captain?*

"Wha'd yo say, gal? Wha'd y'all doin' heah?'"

Summer looked to Lila for help.

"Where are zee soldiers?"

"Dey gone, thank the Lord!" A man stepped up beside the red-turbaned woman. "Der only 'bout two lef'. Dat Yankee cap'n say he

[40] slaves

want to keep 'em two heah waitin' for da Cap'n Ruiz a'comin' back. But we don' know where da cap'n is. He done gone ta prison, but jes like da cap'n— he a slippery fella—and he git outta der alrighty."

"Hesh up, Roscoe!" the red-turbaned woman said. "Yo jes don' know when ta shut dat fat mouf o' yo's."

Summer stifled a laugh.

"*Mon amis*," Lila piped in. Zee other Yankeeez are gone, for true?"

"Yes'm, dey is. Dey don' ride outta heah dis morning a'fore da sun come up. I seen 'em go."

"And wha'd you women's doin' heah?" Roscoe asked.

"Can you keep a secret?"

"Yes'm!" all the workers said in unison. The women were now surrounded by several curious pecan pickers who were apparently all ears at this point.

Summer leaned in to the red-turbaned woman and Roscoe. She put a finger to her lips. "You must be quiet about this…Captain Ruiz is here—*somewhere.* We came with him by boat. The Yankees are after him and they'll send him back to prison if they find him."

"And us—we escape weeth zee *capitaine*." Lila said.

"Da cap'n is heah? Thank da Lord!" Roscoe's eyebrows shot to the heavens.

"Hesh up Roscoe! Din' yo heah da woman say ta hesh up?"

"Oh lawdy, Delilah!" Roscoe shook his head. "Der gonna be trouble 'bout dis!"

Much mumbling came from the workers as they considered this new and dangerous predicament.

"We don't want to get you in any trouble, but is there any way that one of you can get to the house to see if the captain is there?"

"Hey, Rufus!" Delilah called to the small crowd. "Tell Rufus ta get his sorry body heah!" Delilah ordered.

A small dark head peered from the crowd and stepped center.

"You go on and tell da Missus I gots hurt and needs a little help. Don' you say no word to dem two soldiers. Go on, now."

Rufus ran off, his skinny legs carrying him swiftly across the yard. Summer and Lila watched with baited breath for the little fellow's return. Soon, they spotted Rufus leading a woman across the yard. She was dressed in a full black skirt made fuller by a wide hoop, and a black blouse buttoned clear up to her neck. Pagoda sleeves draped from shoulder to wrist. Her graying hair was parted in the middle, as was the fashion of the day, and pulled back off her face, secured into a chignon.

"You must go back to the boat," the woman said as she approached the group. "My son wishes it so. He will come to you."

"My name is…"

"I know your name. And yours," she said, turning to Lila. "Now go, before the soldiers see you and my son is taken again. Go!" The woman in black stared sternly at Summer, leaving no recourse for conversation.

"Come on, Lila." She sensed that Lila was about to come back at the woman with a few French expletives.

"But zee *capitaine*!"

"Mrs. Ruiz is right. We're putting the captain in danger."

"*Señora Ruiz*, if you please," the woman said, with black eyebrows arching over dark piercing eyes.

"*Señora* Ruiz," Summer nodded in farewell, her patience with the woman growing thin. She took Lila's hand and they stepped back into the thick and prickly growth.

"She eez not a nice person," Lila said, looking behind and giving Señora Ruiz a look of her own.

"She's worried about her son, I guess." For the captain's sake, Summer wanted to give his mother the benefit of the doubt.

Lila grumbled a reply, and the pair battled their way back to the sailboat in silence, aside from a few yelps brought about by sharp thorns.

* * *

"I don't like the looks of that sky." Summer took a bite of left-over catfish. Dark clouds had gathered and now the western sky was black and ominous, blocking out any chance of viewing the sunset. "Sure looks like a storm to me."

"Where eez zee capitaine? Why does he not come for us?"

Indeed. They were hungry and soon they would be wet, too. The boat rocked gently in the murky waters of the Mississippi as they ate their meager supper.

"I want to be in zee house, even if zee woman is a *sorcière!*"

"A what?"

"A *sorcière.* You know, a weetch."

Summer laughed. She had to agree that the woman did not present herself as friendly; but still, considering the dreadful circumstances, they had to give her a chance. She was dressed in mourning clothes, and she hoped nothing had happened to the child.

"Maybe she'll warm up to our charms."

They laughed through mouthfuls of catfish.

"Look at you…zo charming! Your clothing is rags!"

"And you, your hair looks like you stuck your finger in a socket!"

"What?" Lila straightened her shoulders. *"What eez theez zoquette?"*

Oops! It was so easy to forget that these people did not grow up with the same conveniences she had, such as electricity. "Oh…never mind. You wouldn't understand."

Before Lila could reply, a tremendous burst of thunder clapped overhead.

"Oh no, zee storm come!"

Within seconds, torrential rains plummeted the deck cutting like icy needles, but it was the lightning that sent the women running from the boat and into the dense tropical forest.

"Where eez our *capitaine?* How can he leave us like theez?" Lila pulled her tattered skirt over her head like an umbrella, and Summer followed suit.

There, they huddled amidst the thorns and brush as the winds picked up, dropping the temperature a good ten degrees.

"This is ridiculous!" Summer yelled, as the rain was terribly loud making it difficult to hear anything at all besides leaves and branches rustling and shaking overhead. They screamed when a large branch cracked and fell nearby.

When all seemed hopeless—that they would ride out the storm like the creatures of the forest—the captain appeared.

"Where have you been?" Summer screamed.

He was a welcome sight, but she couldn't help feeing angry that he had left them for such a long period of time.

"Come!" he yelled, ignoring the question.

Again, they found their way through the broken patch to the clearing while the winds howled angrily through branches and leaves, hurtling pelts of rain unmercifully at their soaked bodies.

"Shhh…" Ruiz held a finger to his lips and, looking right at Lila,ran his fingers across his throat. "Follow me."

Ruiz hunched as if ducking bullets, and started off across the yard toward the manor house. The women scampered to keep up, crouching low like the *capitaine*. The rain and winds were unrelenting and battered them as they moved swiftly across the grass. At last, they reached a door on the ground level. Inside it was dark, damp but dry, much to their relief.

"Mon Dieu*!*" Lila shook her soaking head of frizzy hair, splattering showers of cold rainwater.

"Hush!" Ruiz ordered. "The soldiers are in the house!"

"How many?" Summer asked.

"Two—but two is more than enough."

"What will we do?" She had been through this before, when the answer was to '*kill them*'. Mick Mason had been good at killing the Yankees[41] and it was still fresh in her mind, having to wrap their bodies in blankets; the bodies buried beneath the rose garden at Magnolia. She did not want to be involved in murder again.

"We will take care of them," he replied.

"How?"

Even in the darkness, she could feel his eyes on her, hesitating to speak. "Do not concern yourself."

---

[41] This event from Book I

Chapter 12

"*Aquí hay ropa seca para ustedes*[42]*.*" Seῆora Ruiz dumped an armload of clothing onto the four poster bed. Standing over the oil lamp that had been set upon the bedside table, she took on a ghastly and oddly shadowed appearance, amplified by a stern face and hair pulled severely into the chignon. The women had been cloistered away in a second floor bedroom where heavy brocade drapes hung tightly shut over French doors that opened onto a large, shared veranda which overlooked the immense pecan orchard.

"Thank you," Summer replied, forcing a smile at the stern faced woman.

A quiet "hmph" escaped Seῆora Ruiz's straight-lined, tight lips as she swung her black-hooped body sharply around to exit the room. Behind her, the heavy wooden door shut with a dull "thud".

"Eet was a pleasure!" Lila said loudly.

---

[42] "Here are dry clothes for you."

"Quiet! Jeez, do you want the soldiers in here? Please control that mouth of yours, we want to make friends with the woman!"

"She does not want to make zee friends weeth us. I tell you, she *eez a sorcière.* She weel put a curse on us. I know theez!"

Once Lila came to a conclusion, it was a difficult feat to change her mind. This observance Summer took seriously; so, giving up any attempt at persuasion, she focused on changing from the wet, dirty and tattered clothing.

"Let's see what the woman brought," she said, twisting the wick of the oil lamp to release more light. The room was dim with the drapes closed, but they had been instructed to not open them for fear the soldiers would get a glimpse and come to investigate.

"Oh *le rouge!* I must have *le rouge!*" Lila exclaimed, holding up a red (and noisy) taffeta skirt. She flung a spattering of items around on the bed until she found a three-hooped petticoat folded in upon itself, therefore lying flat. "Oh, Mon ami, we weel look like zee ladies tonight!" She then quickly grabbed a matching red satin blouse trimmed in yellowing lace, as well as a muslin shimmy and pantaloons.

Summer eyed the remaining scattered clothing on the bed: a three-hooped petticoat; a green, yellow, red and black plaid taffeta skirt; a green cotton blouse that buttoned up to the neck with the traditional pagoda sleeves that ended in a row of eyelet lace at the wrist, and another set of shimmy and pantaloons—and two corsets, their cords spread across the bed in invitation.

"Oh zee corzets! Look!"

Until that moment, they had ignored the corsets, but there they lay as unavoidable remains of the day.

Summer rolled her eyes. "I hate those things. But," she said, reaching for one, "I will tie it loosely."

The women bathed the best they could, sharing the bowl of cold water on the vanity. They helped one another dress, tying loosely the corset cords, and admiring their clean clothes in the full length mirror that stood fixed to an ornate mahogany frame at one end of the large room.

"Eet eez so dark in here I cannot zee!" Lila twirled, the hoop twisting with the motion, but sliding gracefully into proper position when she stopped. "Bring zee lantern!"

Summer obliged, and they each held the lantern for the other to inspect her own reflection.

"Now what?" Summer asked, ruffling her cropped hair. "Do we just sit here waiting for Seῃora Ruiz or the captain to come for us?"

Wait, they did, for a stretch of time that had them pacing the floor, napping on the bed, or simply primping in front of the mirror. Profound boredom overtook the pair until a giggle was heard in the hallway. Ears perked, the women tiptoed to the door, each pressing an ear against its wooden surface.

Tap, tap, tap. The quiet vibration of tapping from door to ear caused them to step back. *Tap, tap, tap.*

Summer was fearful to answer. "What if it's the soldiers?" she whispered, her heart pounding.

"Who eez eet?" Lila asked.

A child-like, high-pitched screech alarmed them.

"Shhhh." The voice came from the person on the other side of the door.

"Who eez eet?" Lila demanded.

"It's jes' me, Dilly, and little Marguerite. Seῃora Ruiz want me to see if you's alright." The woman had obviously been instructed to keep her voice low, as her words came in a hushed tone.

Summer opened the door and stood dumbstruck at the beautiful child in Dilly's arms. Dilly was dressed plainly in a long muslin skirt topped by a muslin blouse gathered around a scooped neckline, and tied with a corded bow at the front. Upon her head was affixed a yellow turban that complimented her pretty brown face.

But the child—the child! Small white teeth gleamed from between pink lips that smiled in amusement at the strange visitors. Pitch black curls framed and fell softly about her cherubic, rose-tinted cheeks. She sat in Dilly's arms as if engulfed in a cloud of ruffles and eyelet. Her eyes, large and brown, were outlined in dark lashes and reminded Summer ever so much of her beloved captain.

"Dis here is Marguerite. She da chile' of da cap'n. Her momma don die right befo' our eyes when she birthin' da baby. Oh we cried and cried for dat po' woman!"

"Come in while you write zee book," Lila said, at which Dilly responded with a confused look.

"Come in," Summer said, ignoring Lila's snide remark and indicated the woman and child to enter.

Dilly followed the gesture and set Marguerite on the floor. The child immediately took off in her cloud of ruffles and eyelet to investigate the room.

"I ain't writin' no book." Dilly said, matter of factly. "I don' know how to write no book. We wasn't allowed to learn writin'—or readin' neither."

"It's okay, Dilly," Summer said, shooting Lila a scolding look. "Tell the Señora that we're okay here, but wondering how long we must stay in this room. We're getting hungry. Can you tell us where the captain is? Where are the soldiers?"

"Da soldiers havin' suppah' wid da Señora. Dey do dat every night. She don' like it but deys da boss now. Dey waitin' fo' da capt'n return." Dilly crossed her arms over her chest and nodded, as if proud to know such details.

"Where's the captain?"

"I don' know dat. Da missus say it bes' dat none o' us knows where he at. I jes' know dat he heah, somewheres." She rolled her dark eyes up and sideways, searching the beyond, and shrugged. "He heah somewheres."

"So, the soldiers are with the Señora now…." Summer asked.

"Yes'm. Miss Margueritte done have her supper already. She goin' ta bed now. Da missus don' let dem soldiers see Margueritte case dey gets any ideas."

"Do they know the child is here?"

"Yes'm. Dey docs, but dey don' see her mos' da time."

"And when do we get get zee food?" Lila asked.

"Soon's I gits Miz Marguerite to bed."

Dilly gathered the child, said her goodbyes, and left the women standing in the dark room that grew even darker with the setting of the sun. "Come on, Lila." Summer grabbed the French woman's hand and opened the door slowly so as not to make a sound.

"Where?" Lila asked in a whisper.

"Let's look around. The soldiers are eating now."

A candlelit chandelier that hung over the large foyer of the big house shed enough light for them to leave their lantern in the room. Ever so lightly, and in bare feet, they tread over the runner that stretched an immense hallway overlooking the foyer.

"Shhh," Summer said, stopping to listen at the top of the grand stairway. "Can you hear them?"

"Yes, ze soldiers!"

The women stepped quietly down a few steps and stopped, ears pinned to the air for sound.

"…you waste your time," Señora Ruiz said. "My son will know you are waiting for him. He will not come."

"Beg your pardon, ma'am, but we will be the judge of that. These are our orders." A deep masculine voice spoke amidst the tinkling of silverware.

"We don't have to be so nice, you know," said another male, his voice a notch higher and nasally. "We've ransacked every plantation nearby. You're just lucky that the Federal Army wants him so badly. We could'a done a job on this place, and you and that curly-headed brat would be livin' in them old slave huts with the darkies."

"Ahem," the deep voice responded. "Enough, Sergeant."

As fate would have it, as soon as silence overtook the trio in the dining room, Lila lost her footing on the staircase and slipped. With a yelp, she thumped two steps on her behind before Summer grabbed her by the neck of her blouse. Immediately chairs slid out from the dining table. Summer heard a sword slide from its sheath as well as a rifle cock.

"Oh my God!" she whispered. "Hurry!"

Up they raced to the landing where they stood confused for a moment, not remembering from which direction they had come.

"Up there!" the nasal voice shouted, and the soldier came at them two steps at a time, weapons drawn.

Lila shrieked and grabbed onto Summer's arm. Together they ran—the wrong way—all the while hearing the Señora yelling at the soldiers in Spanish.

Then, to Summer's horror, she heard Captain Ruiz's voice loud and strong. "Gentlemen! Stop!" The soldiers came to a halt halfway up the staircase and turned. The women also stopped at the sound of his voice. They still had a partial view of the foyer, and from where they stood they could see the Señora's full black hooped skirt, the rest of her figure obstructed by the bannister. Ruiz was not in their line of vision, but the two soldiers were in view.

"This is not good," Summer whispered to herself, and, looking to Lila, saw that the French woman's face was white as bakery flour. All was still.

"Are you looking for me, my friends?" Ruiz asked nonchalantly.

With her heart pounding wildly, Summer moved closer to the bannister to get a look at her lover who stood stately at the bottom of the stairs, his hands crossed and folded beneath a jacket. He looked like his old self; his eyes twinkled in mischief while he stood as if he had not a care in the world. My, how her heart thumped! If worse came to worse, she would fight the soldiers. She would push them down the stairs—anything to save Ruiz!

"You're under arrest!" yelled the deep-voiced soldier as he and his companion hurried down the stairway for the capture. But before they reached the bottom stair, Ruiz pulled two pistols from beneath his jacket and fired both.

Lila screamed, while Summer watched each man double over and cry in pain. The sound of the firing resonated throughout the big house and in the distance, Dilly shrieked, and little Marguerite wailed. Summer stepped to the top landing but cringed; she had lived through his before and it was difficult to watch the scene play out again.

The soldiers, far below her, staggered; one desperately reached for the bannister with a bloody hand while the other bounced against a wall, blood spewing against the flowered wallpaper.

"Mon dios!" cried the Señora, and raced to her son's side.

One by one, the soldiers toppled to the landing and were still.

"¿Qué hemos hecho[43]?" The Señora made the sign of the cross and covered her mouth with her hands.

Ruiz put an arm around his mother and leaned his chin onto her head. *"Es necesaria, madre[44]."*

"Lo se, lo se,[45]" she whimpered.

* * *

Once more, as she had at Magnolia, Summer helped to bury dead soldiers. With a heavy heart she tucked a blanket tightly around a still body. She and Lila rolled each soldier into a blanket until he was tightly wrapped in his own cocoon. Ruiz carried each cocoon to a wagon pulled by the one remaining horse. The women did not ride the wagon, or see where Ruiz and two male slaves had dug the graves. It was done; two young men would never return home. They would lie forever in a land foreign to them, away from all they loved. Summer wiped tears from her eyes as she watched the lone horse pull the wagon away toward the unfortunate soldiers' destinies.

---

43 *"¿Qué hemos hecho"* What have we done?

44 " *"Es necesaria, madre."* It's necessary, Mother.

45 " *"Lo se, lo se."* I know, I know."

Chapter 13

What is unlucky for some, is lucky for others. Due to the tragedy of the soldiers' deaths, the women were now free to roam the grand house in the open, at least until other soldiers arrived, or until they came up with a plan.

"I am thinking!" Captain Ruiz strongly replied when Summer questioned him on the next move. He had not yet come up with an answer.

In the interim, Summer tried her best to cozy up to the Señora. She offered to help in the kitchen, as many servants were sent to work the pecan fields. She offered help watching Ruiz's beautiful child, a job she enjoyed thoroughly, while Lila begrudgingly aided in laundry day with Dilly.

"I am not a laundress!" she complained to Summer. "I am a…a…a woman of opportunity! Theez eez a job for ze esclaves!"

"And I'm not a cook, Lila, but I'm cooking. I'm not a maid, but I'm cleaning. This is only until the captain comes up with a plan for us."

"Ze capitaine wants to play weeth his bébé. Ze capitaine wants to spend ze time weeth his mama; theez eez all zee capitaine wants to do."

"Can we blame him?" But, she, too, was discouraged. Her captain was all but vacant from their lives these past few days, only seeing him at meal times. The lusty physical unions she and Ruiz shared on the journey were becoming a memory; she ached for him, and only after a week! He could have come to her as she now had a private room of her own, but to date, he had not. Finally, on the eighth night of their stay at Bella Vista, she felt him slip beneath her bedcover.

"My Verano." He nuzzled her neck, tickling her with the thick, black beard that now adorned his face. "I love you, Verano."

She should have scolded him for ignoring her. She should have questioned him, kicked him from her bed for his arrogance. She was not a whore. She had risked life and limb beside him, and not just now, but in Nassau, as well as a dangerous ship pursuit into the Gulf of Mexico[46]. But, she was powerless; she allowed his lips to engulf hers. She allowed his hands upon her breasts. She allowed his hands to travel wherever they desired—and they did. She gave herself to him willingly and knew that as long as she was with him, she was his.

"Where have you been, Ruiz?" She asked later while lying in the crook of his arm.

"You think I have done nothing, but I have done everything. I have contacted my friends in New Orleans. We will go; you, me, Lila, Marguerite and my mother. We will take Dilly as well."

"But…how? What happens when the soldiers are discovered missing? I don't understand…."

"It is arranged. I am sending my mother, Marguerite and Dilly to Buck. They will be safe there."

"And how do you intend to accomplish that?"

"I have many friends, Verano. They have made arrangements. I want you to go with them."

"No!" Summer leaned on an elbow. "No! I will not leave you."

"That is what I think—that you will not go. I do not wish you to go, my love, but I want you to be safe."

"I *am* safe with you. No need to worry about me; there is nothing can harm me."

He raised his eyebrows. "No? And why is this?"

---

[46] These events occurred in Book II

"Because I am your angel, my love. I am here to help you." *If he only knew....*

* * *

The group of escapees donned the plainest of clothing for their journey. Clothes were traded with the slaves, a trade the workers found quite pleasant. A hooped petticoat was traded for a muslin skirt. A fine silk blouse was traded for that of a worn, faded calico. A gentleman's jacket was traded for that of a stable hand, and on and on until the servants looked quite like the gentry, and the gentry as a rag-tag group of misplaced farmers. Ruiz left instructions for the remaining workers to disappear, to go off on their own. They objected vehemently, as they could be considered runaways if caught, and the punishment could be severe.

"You are right, my friends. Please be safe and keep our home safe until we return."

The lone horse was harnessed to the family carriage, but this was of great concern for it was not a farmer's wagon. Though it was large enough to accommodate the group, the carriage of a family of means was sure to bring attention, while carrying a family of much less distinction. Summer insisted on sitting next to Seŋora Ruiz to keep Lila from creating more angst between the women. Therefore, the captain sat in the driver's seat with Lila beside him, while Dilly held onto Marguerite in the rear seat, which faced backward and delivered a view of Bella Vista as it diminished beyond the pecan trees, and the Spanish moss drapped live oaks.

"Perhaps you will return soon, when the war is over." Summer said, in an attempt to raise the spirits of the weeping Seŋora,

"Perhaps," the woman replied, wiping away a tear with a laced, monogramed handkerchief.

Other than the intercourse of few words, the group rode in silence throughout the journey, broken only by Lila's occasional blurt of excitement over the prospect of returning to her own element.

"Le Vieux Carré! I return to you! Oh, Zummer, finally we break zee chains of theez journey. You weel be zo 'appy!" Lila twisted around in her front seat to relay this news, and Summer couldn't help but smile at the childlike softness of her face in the excitement. The happiness was nearly catching, or would be, were it not for the sad, stern woman sitting beside her.

"It will not be the same, you stupid girl. There is a war. Have you forgotten?" Ruiz scolded. "The city is infested with Yankees. They are the *enemy*."

"For you zee enemy; for me, zee money!" Lila broke into peals of delighted laughter that intermingled with—and evaporated into—the humid air alongside the Mississippi. The bumpy, old dirt road followed the turns of the great river as it snaked toward the old city. Nearing twilight, they finally reached the edge of the city, and turned inland so as to avoid interaction with the Federal forces portside.

"You must be quiet now," Ruiz warned Lila. "We must get to my friend without the soldiers stopping us." He guided the tired mare through the narrow cobblestone streets of the French Quarter while they held their breaths in the fear of discovery of their masquerade. Summer couldn't help but stare in awe at the unique architecture. People of all colors roamed the shops, gathered on street corners, or watched them pass from the second story wrought iron balconies that overflowed with planters full of colorful flowers and vines. The captain was definitely correct; the soldiers were everywhere. They walked in the streets at every block, stepping aside to let the carriage pass.

"Wait here," Ruiz said, having pulled into an alleyway between two dwellings. He left the women and child to sit in the carriage while he disappeared into a side door of the rose-colored building on their right. Marguerite became very bored and fidgety and squirmed in Dilly's arms as darkness enveloped them.

"Dis chile' don' want to sit heah no more, *Seῆora.*"

"Give her to me," Summer said, climbing from her seat and onto the alleyway.

The Seῆora nodded approval, and Dilly set the child into Summer's arms.

"We'll walk a bit," Summer said, and took Marguerite the short distance to the street, where again she was enraptured by the sights and smells of the city. The quarter was alive, and she understood now why Lila was so anxious to return; the energy was catching. As she and Marguerite walked hand in hand to the corner, the child pointed and giggled at the few passing carriages. A small group of women of color stopped to exclaim Marguerite's beauty, for even in the worn calico dress, she was as a china doll and worthy of such attention. As they began their return to the alley, an approaching soldier set her heart to racing. *I have put us in danger!*

"I haven't seen you before, ma'am," the soldier said, lifting his cap to show a mop of dark hair.

"Oh…I…well, I don't come out often. The child, you know; she keeps me busy."

"Is she yours? Why she's a pretty one, isn't she," he said, bending to inspect the girl at eye level. Marguerite smiled her charming smile at the man. "Why, she doesn't look a thing like you with all those black curls. Black eyes, too."

Automatically, Summer reached to touch her pale, blond hair cut unusually short for the times, and hoped the soldier would not inquire. She was grateful the little girl could not speak yet, and what few words she could say, were in Spanish.

"She belongs to a friend—a friend who must work."

The soldier eyed her suspiciously. "Oh…I see. And are you a working girl?" he asked, his demeanor changing dramatically from courtesy to the edge of lewdness.

Before she could answer, he pulled paper money out of a pocket. If you are," he said, leaning close to her face, "I can give you money."

"I beg your pardon, sir, but I am *not* for sale. Now, excuse us." As she sidestepped to pass him, he stepped also, blocking her path.

"Come on, now. Wouldn't you like to make some money?" He waved the bills before her eyes.

"You're insulting me, *sir*. Get out of my way."

"Ahem."

The man turned to see Lila, who even in her dowdy clothes managed to strike an inviting pose.

"You make a meestake, soldier. *I* take zee money. Theez eez my *nourrice*[47]. Now go, Madam. Dépêcheez-vous![48] Zee bébé needs her zupper!"

Summer was all at once relieved and terrified. *I've put us all in danger!* She cast a questioning glance at Lila, who stared her down, eyes big and nodding for her and Marguerite to make haste back toward the carriage.

"Why did you leave?" Ruiz asked, as she handed Marguerite to Dilly. He was furious. "We make it here safely and you—you bring this danger to my child and to us!"

---

47 "*Nourrice*"Nanny

48 "*Dépêcheez-vous!*" Hurry! Hurry!

Summer was embarrassed and ashamed at being reprimanded by her lover, and her attempt to swallow choking tears was in vain.

"¡Cállate![49]" the Seῆora said, but Summer had great difficulty in muffling her sobs as they sat in the wagon, in the dark alley, waiting for Lila's return.

¿Por qué esperamos para esta mujer? Es un problema![50]"

"Because she has saved my life." Ruiz replied. "I would be dead if she did not save me, and you should be grateful."

"Hmph!" the Seῆora replied, crossing her arms. "¡Es el problema!"

"Where *is* she?" Summer asked, recovering from her breakdown and now terribly concerned for Lila's safety.

"She is working. She will return soon, or we will leave. There is a boat waiting for my mother, Dilly & Marguerite."

"You can't just leave her!"

"Why not?" Ruiz asked "This is her home. There is no need to worry about Lila."

"She is not worth waiting for," the Seῆora spat.

"*Un poco mas*—a little longer," he replied, and sighed heavily.

Minutes later, having given up on Lila, and in the process of backing the carriage out of the alley, Ruiz halted when Lila magically appeared with spry steps and a smile on her face. "*Regardeez! Veuilleez écouter!*" she exclaimed, waving two bills while she climbed into the carriage. "We have money! We can eat!"

"Oh, mi Dios! I will not live on contaminated money!" The Seῆora said in total disgust

"Mother, we have no other money to spend. I had only a few gold coins, and with those I paid for your safe passage."

Again, they traveled in silence through the narrow streets which now appeared to have doubled in population as more and more people of color—people of all ages, from infant to the elderly—seemed to fill every space of sidewalk and street

"Mon Dieu*!*" Lila exclaimed. "What eez happening here?"

"The slaves who have been given freedom, they come here. They have nowhere to go," Ruiz said looked over his soldier at Summer. "You see? This is why our slaves stay, because they have a home."

---

[49] "*¡Cállate!*" Be quiet!

[50] "*¿Por qué esperamos para esta mujer? Es un problema!*" Why do you wait for this woman? She is a problem!"

After reaching an area at the far edge of town, and with the Mississippi on their right, Ruiz guided the horse along a dark, dirt road that ribboned ahead beneath an overgrowth of leafy trees. Their venture ended on another dark narrow road that lead to a small clearing alongside the river. There, a sloop waited at the edge of a dock worn well by time. With barely a sound, Ruiz walked his mother to the man waiting on the dock. Dilly walked slowly behind, the child in her arms.

"Hurry!" Ruiz said.

"I ain't goin' on dat boat!" Dilly replied.

"You *are* going. You will be safe, and you will care for the Señora and Marguerite. Do you understand, Dilly?"

Dilly cried softly, which brought Summer to the pier. "Dilly, don't be afraid. There's a man there, a Señor Buck. He is a friend and will take good care of all of you. You must go, it isn't safe here."

"But Miz Summah, I ain't never been on da water! I can't swim!"

"You will not need to swim, I promise. Now go!"

"Do not frighten Marguerite any further!" Ruiz warned. "You will be well rewarded for this, Dilly. There is nothing else for you here."

Marguerite began to cry.

"*¡Ven conmigo!* Come!" the Señora grabbed Dilly by the elbow and led her to a gangplank where a sailor waited.

"Take good care of my family, Caron! I hold you responsible."

"You know I will, Alejandro," the sailor replied, helping the women on board. "They are safe and sound with us."

"Pass the message to Señor Buck that we will come for them when the time is right."

"Will do, Ruiz. Farewell."

"Vaya con Dios," Ruiz whispered as he and Summer watched the sloop disappear into the river traffic, for even at night, like the city, it did not sleep.

"They should be fine," Summer said, hoping it was true.

"Marguerite is only a small child. She does not know me even now. When will I see her again, Verano?"

They watched in silence until the sloop was indiscernible against the night.

"Come," he said, taking her hand. "We have much to do." They walked back to the carriage where Lila waited, impatient to return to her Vieux Carré.

Chapter 14

"Look at theez mess!" Lila proclaimed from the third floor balcony of the apartment she had managed to finagle from her previous landlord.

It had been a tough battle for the rooms, as the landlady had assumed that Lila would not return from prison. Her old rooms were rented out, but Lila bribed the woman with one of the bills she received from the soldier she had sold her services to, and promised there would be more to come. This newly procured "apartment" consisted of two small rooms that would have to suffice, without another choice, as bedrooms. Lila took first bids on the lumpy cot in the larger room, telling the others that it was her right as she was a former tenant and had managed to procure the rooms in the first place. Summer slept on another lumpy cot in the smaller room, and Ruiz claimed the faded, flowered—and certainly filthy—throw rug that took up nearly all the floor space in the cramped second room. Cooking facilities were nonexistent, and toilet facilities were shared with the other unfortunate tenants in a water closet in the hallway. The only saving grace of the new accommodations was the balcony, which allowed them a few extra feet of living space. All in all, Summer was relieved that they would not be sleeping on the sidewalks below with the rest of the bedraggled folks.

"Look at theez, *capitaine*!"

Summer and Ruiz both joined Lila, who leaned on the ornate but rusting cast iron grillwork of the third floor balcony, viewing the scene below. Gas lamps illuminated the many meandering bodies of freed slaves and poor whites that had come to New Orleans seeking food and work. Children and babies cried as mothers huddled against buildings or sat slumped on the filthy uneven sidewalks away from the moving tide of humanity; there was nowhere to go. There was no shelter, no work, and no food.

"This is unbelievable," Summer sighed, feeling pangs of guilt. After all, *she* had a place to sleep. The women and children on the streets had no comforts. "I can't look," she said, turning her back to the grillwork. "This is a nightmare."'

"Move along! Git. You can't stay here!" A booming voice caught their attention, and they peeked over the balcony to see a small group of soldiers on horseback breaking up the hoard of folks filling the street.

A moan from the masses resonated from below. "Ain't got nowheres to go, soldier!" one brave soul shouted, followed by a woman's voice. "Where we goin', cap'n? Where my chillen' gonna sleep?" she asked, and that followed by more of the same.

"Listen!" the soldier's voice struggled to be heard over the chattering crowd. "Shut up and listen!" You're going back of the town[51]—toward the levy."

"Where dat?"

The other soldiers had split up and were herding the people who stood on the sidewalks and the women with children, into the street.

"You follow us. Come on, now. Listen to me! You can't stay here, understand? You are going to the back of the town. You can camp there."

"This is what it has come to," Ruiz said, stepping away from the balcony. "The Federals free the slaves and look, they are sent to the swamps to starve and die."

---

[51] *Back of town*, or 'Backtown', where freed slaves and Negroes were forced to live in the outskirts of the French Quarter, and historically where jazz was born. Today it is referred to as 'Gert Town'.

* * *

Later, Lila, whose main goal in life was to rack up money in whatever means available, sailed in on a wave of excitement, as she had extracted a few of her fancy clothing items from the landlady's closet. The back of her long skirt dragged behind, while from the front she carried a mixture of fabric and hoops, all hugged dearly to her chest, her face obscured behind the circles of whalebone. "That woman! She theenk she can have everytheeng what belong to me! I tell her I return for my jewelry, my shoes, my stockings and *everytheeng* she take! Where eez zee capitaine?" she asked, tossing the armload onto the lumpy cot.

"The captain has gone to look for work—I think. He didn't say, just said he'd return, and left."

"Hmph. And you? You do not look for work?"

Is there a need for a paralegal secretary? Will I even be here long enough to hold a job? "Of course I can look for work, but where? Who has money to pay these days?"

"Zee soldiers, of course!"

Summer face flushed. "There is no way in this world that I will do what you do!"

"No?" Lila looked shocked. "Ha! That eez a joke, no? You cannot do my job. You cannot make zee money like Lila do. You are not zo…attractive."

Summer crossed her arms over her chest. "Oh no? Do you think there is something wrong with me that I can't attract a man? Why, I attracted one a few days ago if you recall, thank you," she said, remembering the soldier who had offered her money.

"Look at you," she said, circling Summer. "A mousie-mousie. You have no bosom. You have no hair. You have no—how you say—savoir-faire."

What? I can certainly savoir-faire you out of the ballpark." *She hoped.*

Perhaps it was boredom, or the fact of being stuck in a time warp in New Orleans, or the fact that Ruiz was so pre-occupied elsewhere these days, that caused her to do it. "Savoir-faire, huh?" She gathered a red skirt with matching bodice from the pile on the bed. "I'll show you "*mousie-mousie*"!"

Though stained around the bottom of its skirt from Lila's walking of the dirty French Quarter streets, and squeeezed into the bodice, considering that Lila was of smaller construction than she, the complete attire was quite complimentary. Summer was not graciously endowed, but she did cut an attractive figure. Her small breasts, due to the tight squeeze, swelled gracefully above the bodice showing enough cleavage to bring attention from the masculine eye. The skirt matched that of the bodice, with the black lace scalloped midway down the skirt, the scallops topped with black satin bows, and many of which were missing. The hoop gratefully hid the frayed and stained pantaloons beneath the ballooning skirt. She questioned the fact of Lila disregarding her pantaloons completely.

"Why for? They only get in zee way," was her nonchalant reply when questioned

Once hooped and inspected by the other, the women maneuvered the staircase to the ground floor and out into L'Allée d' Orléans. One end of the street was blocked by St. Louis Cathedral, which Summer pointed out to her companion. "Look, there's a church. How can you sell yourself with a church in plain sight?"

Lila shrugged. "We want to eat, do we not? Would God rather I steal from people who have notheeng?"

Summer weighed the thought. "Yes, we have to eat, but I will not…cannot…you know… with any men."

"Ha! You tease, theez eez it? You tease ze men and then what? They give no money for tease, you know."

"Then, I will send them to you, since you are so very careless with your virtue."

"You insult me! I let ze men lovey-lovey me so you can eat, and yet you insult me!"

She has a point.

They had not moved an inch from the doorway of the three-storied house that had become an apartment building during the difficult days of war. Already an unkempt trio of men stood eyeing them from outside a tavern on the corner of L'Allée d' Orléans and Bourbon streets, which was only a stone's throw away. Summer nonchalantly attempted to ignore them, but the streetlamp shone light enough for lurid stares to send shivers up her spine. A group of men, and such men as these, congregating and staring lewdly, was not a good sign for a woman at night in a narrow street, dressed provocatively and flaunting her wares. A sudden shame overcame her; that she should challenge Lila in the first place; it was ridiculous! Why try to attract men if she wasn't willing to follow through? *Why am I here in New Orleans anyway? There must be a reason....*

The men made her jittery. For the first time since her journey began, she wanted *home*. She wanted to wake up in her bed at Magnolia, safe, pregnant and with Guy beside her; *I want my life back!* But, here she was standing in a narrow street in 1864 New Orleans at night with a prostitute, and leered at by men who made her skin crawl.

"Look at them, Lila. This is dangerous." she whispered "How can you allow yourself to do this?"

Ignoring Summer totally, Lila yelled, "You can lookie-lookie, but there eez no touchy-touchy without zee money-money!"

"What are you doing?" Summer was horrified and tried to hush the French woman.

"What eez eet *you* do? I am working!" Lila whispered gruffly.

The men, perhaps considering the expense of *two* women, meandered back into the tavern.

"Come, we go to zee port." Lila linked arms with Summer. "Come! Move zee feet or go and hide. We cannot stand here all zee night! Zee money does not come to us!"

"Just so you know, I am *not* having sex with strangers."

"I weel do it myself. You are useless, Zummer."

Lila was lovely in a yellow gown with its puffed sleeves set off the shoulder. Her breasts ballooned at the top of the bodice practically to the point of exposing nipples. The French woman had tamed her wild reddish curls into a mass of swirls pinned to the top of her head with hairpins procured from the landlady, and pinched her cheeks to the color of red apple. Surely the landlady was aware of Lila's profession, but the promise of money brought no criticism, only encouragement, for these were hard times. In contrast, Summer's short crop was topped by a small bonnet of netting, ribbon and feathers, which had been retrieved from the landlady's stolen stash.

As Lila led Summer to her "place of beenez", as Lila endearingly called it, other women of the night strolled by the cathedral in the direction of the port. Lila was greeted with unkind remarks from some, as the small tribe of prostitutes made their way to what they surely hoped would be a profitable night. Lila appeared undisturbed by the snub, sticking her nose into the air while promenading alongside and past her hecklers.

"They sure don't like you, do they?"

"They are jealous because Lila take their beeznez. Zee men like Lila best," she said, loud enough for some of her competition to hear

As they reached the dock and began their promenade, Summer's anxiety level rose. She cringed at the catcalls and obscenities from the sailors. Soldiers gathered at every angle of the eye, shouting orders to the stevedores, or smoking and talking with their counterparts, many, of course, leering as the women passed. Lila seemed to have her standards as far as Summer could tell, as she had not yet sold her favors though she had ample opportunity.

The port was incredibly busy, surely a sight that would stick in the mind for quite a while. The smell of sweat off the backs of black and white alike permeated the humid night air as the endless labor continued, loading or unloading the immense ships. Blocking out the whistles and catcalls, Summer focused on the ever-expanding scene of soldiers, sailors, slaves and magnificent hodgepodge of ships moored dockside. Masts jutted high into the sky at every view, their rigging, masts and sails all a-jumble and docked so closely together it was difficult to decipher which rigging belonged to which ship; it was a wonder that they didn't collide and damage each other on a daily basis. Ships were anchored further off shore as well, visible only by lanterns shipboard that rolled with the gentle current of the Mississippi this night. Flags were visible flying from the dockside ships, and most represented unrecognizable countries, but in all the flutter of foreign flags, the American flag waved majestically from a pole set at the dock, a sight that was a comforting in this strange journey of hers. She wondered how many stars were on the flag, but certainly had no time to count between the waving flag in the gentle breeze of the night, and Lila, who nudged her along, anxious to drum up business.

It was inevitable, with the large selection of men available, that Lila would finally consent to sell her favors.

"...and how much you pay for Lila?"

"Let's see," the soldier said, reaching into a pocket and pulling out a wad of bills. Lila's eyes nearly threw sparks at the sight of such a thick roll of Yankee notes so near to her sticky fingers.

"twenty-five cents," the man said.

"No, no, no!" Lila shook her head of curls, her lips pursing into a dainty kiss with each "no" uttered. "Lila *special.* Lila give you good lovey-lovey. One dollar."

At this point, Summer stepped away, curious to watch Lila make a deal, yet not desiring to be included in any way shape or form with the institution of prostitution.

The soldier looked the temptress up and down. “Seventy-five cents, and you’d better be good *lovey-lovey* for that price.” He glanced at Summer. “I can find someone for your friend.”

Lila shot her a snide glance. “Oh no, monsieur, my friend is…uh, how you say?” She whispered into the man’s ear.

“Oh, that’s too bad. She’s a pretty little thing. Well…” he said, glancing again in her direction. “She has a mouth, don’t she?”

Summer’s eyes nearly flew from their sockets. “What? What did you tell him, Lila? Whatever it is, I’m not doing it!” She was boiling mad. “I told you…” she began, but Lila hooked onto the man’s arm and wandered away, once looking back over her shoulder to part with a sly grin. Summer wondered where in the world in this jumble of humanity, Lila planned on giving the soldier his seventy-five cents worth of “lovey-lovey”.

Now what? Do I wait? Do I go? Standing in the port at night alone in this century— or any century—was not a good idea.

“Hey, sugar. What ya got for me?”

Summer turned to face a burly, middle-aged, bearded, grizzled man perhaps off one of the ships.

“Huh?”

“Come on, sweetheart. I got Yankee notes, good as gold. What ya got for me.”

“No…nothing. I have nothing!” *This was a dumb idea, this savoir-faire thing.*

“Don’t look like nothin’ to me.”

She turned away, hiked up the skirt and, at a dainty trot, prayed she knew her way back to the apartment.

“Hey!”

Horrified, she realized the man was following close behind.

“Hey, Yankee notes is good money!”

“I’m not a working girl,” she said, hurrying along as fast as her feet would carry her, loaded down in clothes as she was. She crossed St. Ann Street toward the cathedral

“My money is good!” the man said. She felt his grip on her arm. “My money is good, whore.” He jerked her to a stop.

“Get your hands off me.”

“You too high and mighty for a working man’s dollar?”

"I told you, get your hands off me. I'm not a…a…*I'm not!*"

"Come on," he said, pulling her back across St. Ann Street to the ornate three-storied dwelling that stretched over one whole city block..“You's 'cavortin' with whores so you must be one of 'em."

"'Ey mon. Let da missus go."

The voice was deep, loud, and very authoritative. Enough so that both Summer and the man stopped their wrestling to see who owned the voice.

"Let da missus go."

Summer was surprised when a woman, a black woman, of considerable breadth and girth, stepped out from the shadows of a doorway. She wore the typical attire of women of color on the streets of New Orleans: gathered skirt, apron, blouse and tignon. She presented quite an imposing figure, standing with her arms crossed over her tremendous bosom.

"Shut up, nigger, this ain't your business," the man growled and then spit in the woman's direction to stress his point.

The woman raised her eyebrows, exposing the great white orbs of her eyes. "It my business, mistah. You go on now, or you be boo-coo sorry."

"You gonna make me?"

"You bet," she said, approaching the duo. The closer she came, the larger she appeared, until she stood towering a head over the accoster and possibly twice his width. "Leave da missus go," she warned, fists on hips, head bent over his.

"Shit niggars. Shit whores," he mumbled, obviously defeated, and wandered off toward the dock.

"Oh, my God." Summer collapsed against the nearest wall. "Thank you so much. I was getting scared."

"Whad you doin' dressin' like dem whores and prancing 'round da town. You ain't no whore like da man say." The woman hovered like a giant black shadow. She squinted, the white orbs morphing into beady black piercing needles. "I know what you is…," she tapped her temple. "You sees tings."

I…I used to," Summer replied, a bit taken aback.

"You does, and dis ain't yo place."

"No, it isn't."

"Where you come from, girl?"

"Georgia."

The woman stood back, scrutinizing the smaller woman before her. "You ain't from no Georgia. Whad yo' name?"

"Summer. What's yours?" she asked, all the while barely conscious of the foot traffic that stepped around them as they conversed beneath the iron balcony apartments.

"I'se Mama Dolly."

Summer stifled a grin. *Mama Dolly?* The woman did not resemble a doll in any sense of the word, yet it was difficult to shake loose the feeling that the woman knew her somehow—knew all about her. *She's reading me...I know she is*. It was impossible to turn from the woman's eyes.

"You gots some mystery der, girl, but Mama Dolly gonna figger it out." These words the woman uttered low and guttural, and with conviction.

Summer nodded nervously. "I must go. I don't want any more trouble from men."

"I come wid you. You be safe."

Perhaps the woman could read *her*, but could she read the woman? Just how safe was this stranger, this giant Mama Dolly, with arms thicker than a weightlifter?

"We go dis way." It was impossible to do anything but let the woman lead her, as Mama Dolly had hooked her thick arm through Summer's thin one, pulling her along across St. Ann toward the church.

"How do you know where I live?" she asked,

"I knows, like you knows tings. Ain't too many white folks can see tings. You's a special one; I know dat."

As the odd couple strolled down Chartres Street it was obvious to Summer that all of the people they encountered crossed over to the other side of the street to avoid Mama Dolly and her companion. Turning right onto L'Allée d' Orléans they nearly collided with the three men who had earlier leered at the women from the corner of Royal Street. The men quickly stepped into the middle of the road, not once looking at Summer in the way they had earlier.

"Dey knows not to mess with Mama Dolly," the woman said, sensing Summer's wonder at the odd behavior of the nighttime population. "I tole' you you's safe wid me."

Mama Dolly stopped at the door of entry to the apartment building. 'Here you is, safe home. Don' you wander 'roun dis place at night, less you have Mama Dolly wid you."

Strange woman, strange night, she thought, looking up at the giant shadowy figure. "How on earth could I find you?"

"I sees. I knows. Call my name, I be der." With that said, she left Summer standing at the doorway and disappeared around the corner of Royal Street.

* * *

Summer carefully climbed the stairway, which was black as pitch at this hour, and having no lantern, had to feel her way to the apartment hand over hand on the railing and then the walls. "Oh my God," she said aloud, when the knob didn't turn; *Lila has the key!* She knocked lightly, hoping Ruiz was back from his mysterious venture and, at the same time, hoping to not wake the crotchety landlady.

Tap...tap...tap, again. It had been such a bizarre night, all she wanted was to get out of the restrictive clothing and relax. To her relief, the door creaked open, enough for lantern light to flood out into the hallway. Ruiz stood in his nightshirt looking none too happy as his eyes roved over her body top to bottom. He opened the door and turned away.

"What is my little American doing out in the Quarter at night, and dressed like a whore? Did you not think to leave me a note so I would not worry?"

"Well…what was my captain doing all day and all night? Did you not think to leave *me* a note?"

"I am on a mission; it is my business."

"And what is the mission? You just escaped from prison, for Pete's sake. Are you anxious to return? Are you anxious to be executed? What are you *doing*, Ruiz? We never see you—*I* never see you."

"Verano." His voice had softened. He set the lantern down on their small dining table and drew her into his arms. "*My* Vernano. It is better you do not know what I do. This is war."

"I'm here to help you, Ruiz. You make it difficult."

"Why do you always say you are here to help me?

"I got you out of prison didn't I?"

He pulled her tighter, finding her lips with his. "Yes, yes, my love. You have helped me, and now you do not need to help me further."

If he knew…if he knew that she was stuck here from another time, what would he say? *Should I tell him?*

"Ruiz…" He covered her lips again with his own while his hands expertly undid the row of tiny buttons on the bodice back. Her breasts, small as they were, popped like springs from their confinement; she could breathe again. Never leaving her lips, and by vague lantern light, he walked her backward into the small room they shared, their shadows plastered against the wall like a silent movie. She could never refuse him; she knew it... *he* knew it...and again, as so many times before, they shared their love in wild abandon, never giving a thought that Lila could walk through the door at any moment.

Afterward, Ruiz fell asleep, his stocky body nearly filling the small cot upon which she normally slept alone. *He knows how to shut me up, doesn't he,* she thought, nearly falling to the floor trying to rise from the narrow ledge of cot he had left her.

The lantern on the table now dimmed further. She approached, still booted up as Ruiz had not had time to undo her boots in that lustful moment; she had performed the sexual act in skirt, hoop and boots and, therefore, stood clutching the loose bodice to her breasts. Not knowing whether to raise the wick or let it die, she stood mesmerized by the flame. After all, Lila should be returning soon, or at least she hoped she would.

And just why am I worrying about that snotty little whore? But there was no denying it; she *was* worried about the snotty little whore. She shivered, thinking of the lewd remarks and leering men at the dock. Anything could happen to Lila!

The door creaked, and Summer jumped.

"Why eez theez door not locked? Do you want us to be robbed?" Lila had returned.

"Sorry, we forgot. And just where have you been all this time? Oh, never mind; you've been selling your body to strange men in dark alleyways. Why did I ask?"

"Huh!" Lila spewed, and threw a wad of bills next to the dimming lantern on the table. "Food. Money for food, inutile femme![52]

Summer sighed. "I don't want to fight. I'm just glad you're back safely. Captain is back too. Goodnight, Lila." She stopped at the doorway to her room. "And, Lila...thanks. I know you work hard. I just worry because your work is so dangerous. Do you know you can catch serious diseases from these men, these strangers?"

Lila looked totally exasperated. "Of course! You think I am stupeed?" She reached into a hidden pocket in her yellow gown and pulled out a strange object setting it on the table.

---

[52] *"inutile femme!"* ungrateful woman!

"What the heck?" Summer leaned over the object, which lay shriveled and quite ugly next to the lantern. "What is it?"

"It eez a condom.[53] Do you not know of theez things?"

"Good lord." She stepped away from the table. "Of course I know of condoms, but I didn't know you had them in this cen…." She caught herself.

"Theez was expensive."

"You only have one?" Summer asked, incredulous.

"I just tell you eet was expensive. Of course I have just one. How many do I need, eh?"

"How many men did you do business with tonight?"

"Let me zee…u, du, trois…quatre…cinque…"

"Oh, Stop! Lila, this is dangerous. You can't use the same condom for every man! It's unclean. You will catch a disease, or spread a disease."

"Zummer, I cannot buy a condom for every man; nobody does theez! Vous êtes fou!*"*[54]

"So, what are you going to do with that?" she asked, nodding toward the limp condom.

"I weel wash eet, no? Eet will be clean for tomorrow."

"Oh, my God. I give up. Goodnight, Lila."

---

[53] The first rubber condom was produced in 1855 by Charles Goodyear. Condoms made from animal intestines and other materials have been used for centuries.

[54] *"Vous êtes fou!"* You are Crazy!"

Chapter 15

Captain Ruiz was extremely cautious when leaving the apartment lest he raise suspicions from the countless Yankee soldiers who occupied the French Quarter at this time. Instead of the dashing figure that had captured Summer's heart (and caused many a woman, young and old, a swoon or two), he now took on the persona of a street bum. A dirty hat of battered felt, dogeared and spotted, sat tightly onto his head, the brim pulled low to hide his eyes. His dark hair hung scraggly below his ears, and not in his usual pomaded comb back style.

"Phew!" Summer pinched her nose, while dangling by one hand, Ruiz's newly acquired but old-and discarded-by-someone brocade and silk vest. "This smells! You won't be making any friends, I can tell you."

"I do not need friends, Verano. I need the Federales to leave me alone."

"And you shall get your wish wearing this thing!" She held the vest out while he slipped his muscular arms through the armholes.

"Thank you, my love. I do not know when I will return."

"And *that* is exactly what worries me. What are you doing? Why can't you tell me?"

"It is better that you do not know. This is war, Verano. Men must take action."

"You really worry me."

"And you, my pet, worry me. Do not be seen on the docks with Lila or you will have trouble, and I will not be there to protect you."

"Aye, aye, captain…*my captain!*" She wrapped her arms around his neck, the brim of the hat bumping her forehead, the putrid stink of the vest wafting up her nose. "Oh, Ruiz, I wish I didn't love you."

"But you do, my Verano! When this war is over…."

"Hush." She put a finger to his lips. She could not let herself think of a future with him; she already lived in the future. She would have a wonderful husband in the future. She was pregnant in the future. She had a life to live in the future. Just the same, she could not bear to think of the day when she would be ripped from Ruiz's arms, away from the war, away from Lila, away from all that she had experienced in this strange adventure into the past.

"Go," she whispered. *Go before I cry….*

* * *

It did not take long for her to slip down the stairs after Ruiz left. She would follow him. How could she help him if she had no clue of what he was up to?

He walked quickly, his shoulders hunched, hands in pants pockets. Summer scurried to keep him in view, but kept close to the buildings in case she needed to step into a doorway should he turn to look behind.

He did not look behind, but kept a steady pace, a man with a purpose, a direction, and the direction took her right back to Lila's hunting ground. The dock was a hustle-bustle of activity, noise, and smells even in the afternoon light. The clip clop of horse's hooves on more than one occasion caused her to step lively to the side.

"Move, woman!" men shouted from behind. She was certain the horses and wagons would run her right over without a second thought; there was big business on the docks, and everyone had an agenda, a dollar to make. A lone woman in daylight at the docks was just another hooker and deserved her fate.

"Hmph!" Summer raised her skirt, her head bopping this way and that and bustled through the crowds attempting to keep Ruiz in sight. "Damn!" He was gone, but then a moment later she caught a flash of his yellowed muslin shirtsleeves and quickened her pace. She was vaguely aware of remarks from sailors and soldiers, but ignored them totally as she sped by the moored ships, their flag-flying masts bright against a deep blue and cloudless sky.

Finally, the frantic pace was over; Ruiz had stepped into a tavern at the far end of the dock. Summer arrived out of breath, even though her corset was lying on the cot back at the apartment and had not restricted her breathing.

The pub door hung wide open, exposing an overwhelming odorous mixture of tobacco, urine and beer to any who stood in its threshold. She glanced up at the large wooden sign overhead. "*Le Blue Mermaid,*" it read in chipped, white scroll. To verify the name of the tavern, a roughly painted mermaid held a starfish over each nipple while a blue mane of hair flowed gracefully about her head, and matched in color her finned lower half.

Summer peeked into the open doorway. It was necessary to search multitudes of faces throughout the noisy, dark and smoky interior in order to spot Ruiz, which proved not an easy task considering the density of the smoke.

"In or out, woman?"

She turned to a gruff looking character. "So sorry," she said, stepping aside.

"Come on in, sweetheart, I'll buy you a drink."

"No thank you." She took another step backward.

"Suit yourself," he said, passing through the doorway.

Again, she searched for Ruiz in the crowded pub; and then, through the haze, she caught sight of a yellowed muslin sleeve, the rest of his body obscured by other patrons. His back was to her, but he sat at a table with two other men, and she positioned her head to where she could see the stranger's faces. One man was Spanish, as defined by the blackness of his straight hair and darkened skin. The other man was bearded, fair haired, with wide shoulders and, considering how his head sat well above the others, a tall man.

"What are you up to, Ruiz?" she whispered.

"Well if it ain't the whore from the other night!"

With horror, Summer turned to stare into the face of the man who had accosted her the night she had foolishly ventured out with Lila.

"Leave me alone," she warned, backing away from the doorway.

"You don't need to drum up business in there when you got me out here. I still got my two bucks, ya know."

"And I told you that I am not a prostitute, so leave me alone."

"Uh, uh. Not this time, lady. Your nigger ain't here to butt in." He took hold of her arm. "Lookie there, a nice alleyway; nice and dark for us," he whispered, his rank breath nearly choking her.

She shook her arm hoping to break free, but instead was pulled toward the narrow alleyway between Le Blue Mermaid and the Baron's Ale tavern.

"Help! Help!" she screamed, frantically trying to shake herself loose. She dug her heels into the wooden planks of the dock and screamed again, but the man was far stronger than the heels of her boots.

"Mama Dolly!" she yelled, remembering the woman's instruction to call when she needed her. She couldn't—wouldn't—call for Ruiz and jeopardize his safety. "Mama Dolly!" she screamed again, praying against hope that the woman would show, and now, just inches away from being sucked into a dark alley by this unsavory character.

"Hold it, mister!"

Unbridled relief enveloped her at the sound of a masculine voice

"Hold it right there."

It wasn't Mama Dolly, but a Yankee officer!

"Let the lady go."

He did. "She's just a whore. Ain't this what she does? I ain't done nothin' wrong."

"The woman is screaming. Unless you want to be arrested for attempted rape, I suggest you remove yourself from the dock."

"Ah shit," he said. Damn whores. Damn Yankees...uh, no offense officer." He lumbered away, foiled again in his attempt to procure a little entertainment.

Summer fought back tears. "Oh, thank you—thank you! This is the second time that man has attacked me."

"Pardon me, ma'am, but if you are not here for business, you'd best get off the dock. This is not the place for a lady, and you may not be so lucky next time."

"I realize that, officer...Officer...?

"Captain McAllister, ma'am." He tipped his wide brimmed navy blue officer's hat, adorned with the gold braiding and tassels that fluttered with the breeze. "And with whom may I have the pleasure of speaking?"

"Oh!" The question threw her for a loop. Surely she couldn't give the officer her real name. After all, the Federal army was on the lookout for Ruiz. Suppose she was known as an accomplice? "It's, uh, Miss Baron," she said, taking the name from the "Baron's Ale" sign. "I was just taking a stroll. You see, I'm visiting from far away and…," she reached up to touch the ribbons of her bonnet at her throat and realized she had left the apartment without it! Instead, she ran her hand over the short crop of blond hair. "Oh," she giggled nervously. "I've forgotten my bonnet!"

"Perhaps you will enlighten me as to what you were doing outside the Mermaid?"

"Oh, I was just curious. We hear so much about the French Quarter, you know; and it was such a charming name for a tavern. I suppose I was looking for a blue mermaid!" A high-pitched laugh escaped her lips. "I had better get back to the apartment," she added, feeling very silly in her behavior.

"I'll accompany you," Captain McAllister extended his arm. "This way you will return home safely without further trouble."

She had no choice but to hook her arm through his, or surely he would grow suspicious. As they turned to walk back toward the square, they came face to face with none other than Mama Dolly, who stood blocking their path.

"I tole' you, jes call my name," the woman said—or did she? Did she speak? Did her mouth move? Summer could not recall hearing Mama Dolly's voice, but more the sense of "*feeling*" it.

Officer McAllister did not question the large woman, but flicked his wrist in a rude signal for the woman to move aside.

Mama Dolly complied, her black eyes boring deep into Summers'. "Jes call my name," the woman said without speaking, and Summer nodded in recognition of the message.

"Perhaps you could answer some questions." Officer McAllister asked as they strolled through the busy dockside crowd.

Summer's guts were a'jumble. *What in the world is happening? First, that awful drunk shows up again. Then, the strange appearance of Mama Dolly who speaks without opening her mouth. Then, an officer with "questions".* Nerves quivered within as they strolled back toward Jackson Square. "You have questions for me?" He was not about to let her loosen her arm from his. He held tight as they walked along. This time, no soldiers or sailors called to her.

"Do you know a Captain Ruiz?" he asked, as nonchalantly as if he were asking of the weather.

Her heart fell, and her knees trembled. It took a moment to muffle the shakiness in her voice. "No. I can't say as I do know a Captain…Captain who?"

"Ruiz. Alejandro Ruiz."

"No, I do not, sir. What makes you believe I would?"

"Captain Ruiz is a criminal. He escaped from prison, which was not an easy task considering the prison sits on a small island in the Gulf of Mexico. He escaped with two women, one a prostitute, and the other a slight blond woman with a crop of very short blond hair and no previous record of existence. The woman gave her name as Summer Woodfield."

Oh shit!

"You quite resemble the description of the blond woman."

"There must be a mistake, sir. My name is Sarah Baron. I come from Chicago. I'm a Yankee, like you."

"What happened to your hair, if I may ask?"

"I sold it for money, sir. This war has been difficult for everyone."

"Indeed it has, Miss Baron."

They turned right onto St. Ann Street, which was a jumble of activity. Women of color balanced baskets upon their heads calling out their wares. Small horse drawn carts offered fresh calas,[55]as well as the horses depositing steaming fresh mounds of manure, piled like small hills in the street. The sights, sounds and scents of freshly brewed coffees, fried beignets, the calas, and fresh horse manure, blended into an odorous atmosphere that at once was both quite pleasant and putrid.

Leaving the busy square, they traveled up St. Ann in silence, turning left onto Royal Street. Captain McAllister seemed to know where they were headed.

As fate would have it, at the corner of Royal_and L'Allée d' Orléans, Summer caught sight of Lila talking with a sailor. At the same moment, Lila caught sight of her and quickly turned her back to avoid eye contact.

"This is my street," Summer said, trying to divert any attention to the business dealing across the way.

---

[55] Fried rice balls, a common vendor food in New Orleans at the time

"I know."

"You know?"

"We're keeping an eye on you, Miss *Baron*, along with the woman you board with. If you are who you say you are, you have nothing to worry about. However, let this be fair warning; if you are involved with Miss de Peau or Captain Ruiz, you will be punished to the full extent at their capture and arrest. Good-day," he said, tipping his hat.

* * *

"Why do you disobey me?" Ruiz was furious. Lila had apparently told him of the Yankee officer who had escorted Summer home.

"Look at it this way, Ruiz. If the soldier had not escorted me, then you would not know what peril you are in at this very moment—and you too, Lila."

"And you as well, Zummer."

"And me, as well," she lied. *But not me.* She could not tell them that she was from another place and time; their fates were not her fate. "They're looking for you, Ruiz. It's time you fessed up. What's going on? Where do you go? Who were the strangers in Le Blue Mermaid?

"They are patriots like me," he said. "We make plans."

"Plans for what?" How could she tell him it was futile to make any plans against the Union?

Ruiz paced the room, stopping at the French doors that led out onto the balcony. "¡Maldita sea! I cannot even stand out there without worry of Yankee spies!"

The dogeared felt hat lay on the small table, leaving his black hair, slightly graying at the temples, to hang from his head like a shaggy lampshade. His broad shoulders and muscular, compact figure only tore at Summers' heart as she watched him compute the situation. *Your efforts are futile, my love!* She so desperately wanted to say the words. Then, perhaps, he would disappear up north, or to Nassau—anywhere—just to be safe until the war was over.

Lila sat on her cot, elbows resting on knees, chin on hands. "Mon Dieu"! You have brought us trouble, Zummer! I do not wish to go back to Fort Jefferson. I want to stay in Le Vieux Carré and make zee money."

"Let me help you, Ruiz. Tell what it is you are up to with your friends."

"We plan to blow up the ships of the Federales that are anchored off the dock," he said flatly. "There are many of us. We will blow the ships. It is the best we can do at this time."

"Blow…and then what? When? Are you crazy? This town is full of Yankees! Where will you hide? They already know you are here! You can't do this, Ruiz. You can't kill all those soldiers."

"No?" he turned to her. "No? They have destroyed my home, my family, my livelihood. They have destroyed *us*, the people. They have taken away our worth. They have taken it all away." His arms flew into the air in exasperation. "We have nothing. Look at the starving Negroes who fill our streets now; there is no work, no food, no home. They cannot live."

"And when do you plan on doing this horrible thing?"

"Tonight."

"Ruiz," she said, approaching, touching his arm. "Ruiz, you will not win." Tears threatened. She understood the pain he felt; she had seen it first hand, all that he spoke of. It was true, but this was a war he could not win, not him, not his friends, not by blowing up the few Yankee ships in the Mississippi. It was lost, and she could not explain it to him. She could not let him murder more soldiers in a hopeless attempt to win a winless war.

"And what about *us*, Ruiz? What about me? what about Lila? If you blow up the ships, what happens to us? They will execute you, you know. This is insane! I cannot watch you die—*again!*"

"I go make zee money," Lila said, rising from the cot. "If zee capitaine blow zee ships, we will need money for escape." Lila fluffed her hair in the one mirror that hung by the apartment door. Her small hands maneuvered her breasts within the confines of the bodice until she was pleased at the way they swelled alluringly above the lace trim. "Au revoir!" she said, blowing a kiss, and left.

"I go too," Ruiz said. "I meet my friends." He grabbed his hat from the small table, only to meet Summer, who stood blocking the apartment door.

"No, you don't go!"

"You do not understand these things. Move away. I must go." He attached the sorry felt hat to his head.

"No!" she yelled, hot tears rolling down her cheeks. "You can't go— I won't let you!"

He grabbed her by both shoulders. "Verano, I must go!"

She reached for the collar of his muslin shirt, clenching it tightly in her fists. "Don't go—please don't go. They'll kill you…."

"Stop this!" he ordered, shaking her with hands of steel. "Vernano, move aside!"

She sank. She let go the collar and sank as if melting onto the floor. "It's hopeless, Ruiz," she sobbed. "You must trust me…it will get you nowhere. You cannot win this war."

"Stop, my love," he said, his demeanor softening as he settled to the floor with her. "I love you, Verano. Please do not cry, and do not stand in my way. I do what I must do."

"And I do what I must do, Ruiz. You can't go."

"And how will my little American stop me?" He asked raising her chin with a finger.

She knocked the hat off his head with such power it flew across the room. "Like this," she said, and pulled him to her, her lips reaching his. She held tight until his arms wrapped around her, laying her back onto the floor. Off came the vest, the shirt, the bloomers, the simple blouse of her simple attire and even the corset. Off they came until clothes scattered about them like a haphazard picture frame.

Was it desperation? Was it love? She could not think of anything but his body upon hers, strong, muscular, compact and so dear to her that her heart broke even through their passionate union. He entered her as what he was, a strong, virile and desperate man trying to survive desperate times any which way he could.

Afterward, they lay side by side upon the floor seeing nothing above them but the chipped ceiling. "You cannot stop me, Verano," he said, raising his arms to tuck behind his head. "I don't know why you say we cannot win this war. It worries me that you think this way."

"It worries me that you think otherwise," she answered, turning onto her side to place a hand over his heart. "Your heart is beating and I want it always to be so."

"It will always beat for you, Verano."

"What is this?" Summer asked, rising up on an elbow. Below the dark fluff of the hair of his armpit was a mole, a heart-shaped mole.

"Ruiz, you have a heart on your arm!"

"Yes, my love. "It is a sign of my family. My daughter has it also."

"How poetic is that?" She leaned over and kissed the heart-shaped mole of the man she loved so desperately in this time.

* * *

He was gone. Her love could not hold him, and she was left lying on the floor, staring at the chipped paint of the ceiling. Day was fading and twilight coming on. Soon she would light the lantern and pray that Ruiz would return to her, that he would have given up the insane plan....

Knock, knock, knock.

"Who is it?" she asked, reaching for her blouse.

"Captain McAlistair, Miss *Woodfield.* Open up."

Chapter 16

"Oh, mon ami, how nice of you to join me!" Lila sat on a wooden bench in a dark cell on the second floor of the Cabildo.[56] Enough light from the briefly opened cell door allowed Summer to view Lila sitting on the bench, her back propped up against the wall. Her breasts still plumped over the lace trimmed bodice, neat and tidy, as if she had just left the apartment and walked straight to the jail cell of her own accord. It was a short walk as the Cabildo was only two blocks away from the apartment. Upon Captain McAllister's knock on the door, Summer had scurried to retrieve her clothing and redress after the desperate, but passionate, romp with Captain Ruiz. Captain McAllister arrested her and marched her down

[56] The Cabildo in the French Quarter was originally a French government building. When the Spanish gained power, it was their Capital House. In 1803 the Louisiana Purchase was signed in this building. The Cabildo also served as a prison. It is now a state museum.

L'Allée d' Orléans to a small cobblestoned alley that led directly to the Cabildo.

"How long are we to remain here?" Summer asked, as Captain McAllister began to close the wooden door.

"Until one of you ladies tells us where to find Ruiz, or we find him ourselves. Either way, you are both in serious trouble." The captain glared at the petite woman slumped against the wall of the cell. "Especially you, Miss de Peau. You *do* realize it's against the law to break out of prison?"

"Aller sauter dans la rivière,"[57] she spat in reply.

"Have it your way." Captain McAlistair tipped his hat and left.

"Great." Summer sat on the bench next to Lila. "What now?"

"Notheeng."

"I guess not. No prison breaks, anyway," she said, scrutinizing their small cell. "Not even a window! I'm so afraid that Ruiz will get caught. His plan is foolish; there is no winning this war."

"And why you say theez? Eet eez not yet over."

"Take my word for it, Lila; it's over. The South is lost."

"Humph! I do not like when you talk like theez, Zummer. Zee capitaine does not like eet either. Why he love you, I do not know."

The prison was not only dark, but damp and humid. "This is disgusting and inhumane!" Summer lamented after several hours of pacing. "When are they bringing us food and water?" The ammonia rising from the toilet bucket was beginning to burn their eyes; and judging from the diminishing light, what could be seen from the miniscule spaces of the door frame, darkness approached. Scratching sounds in the walls put them on edge; an ominous prelude of what could come in the darkness.

"I thought for sure we'd have some sort of contact from the captain by now." Summer was at her wits end; her eyes burned, her stomach growled and she was terrified for Ruiz. "Wait a minute!" She jumped to her feet. "Mama Dolly!" she whispered.

"Mama Dolly? You call Mama Dolly?" Lila asked in a voice edged with anxiety.

"Do you know Mama Dolly, too? She said to call when I needed her."

"Mama Dolly eez hoodoo*!*"

"So? What does it matter—and what is hoodoo anyway?"

---

[57] *"Aller sauter dans la rivière"* Go jump in the river!"

"Ze magic, Zummer. '*la magie noire'*. Ze black magic! Do not call!"

"Don't be ridiculous!" she said sharply. "We have no one else to turn to, in case you haven't noticed. And just what do you mean by 'hoodoo'. Is it the same as voodoo?"

"Voodoo, hoodoo, eet make no difference. You make more trouble for us if you call Mama Dolly!"

"Could we possibly be in *more* trouble than we are now? Mama Dolly!" she called again, only louder just to aggravate Lila.

"Stop eet!" Lila ordered, whacking Summer on the behind.

"I'se here." The deep voice came from somewhere within the cell. Summer spinned a circle, looking, but saw nothing. "Where are you? I can't see you!"

"What are you doing? Who do you talk to?" Lila was bewildered. She stood and imitated Summer's spin. "There eez nobody here. You are crazy!"

"Don' fret. I'se here." A quiet knocking alerted them to the cell door.

Lila gasped. "Trop tard! Trop tard!"[58]

"Thank God, you're here!" Summer exclaimed. She couldn't *see* Mama Dolly, but she knew it was her on the other side of the door.

"How did you get past the guards?" Summer asked, directing her voice through the crack between door and frame.

"I have many friends."

Indeed, she must! Summer could not imagine how the woman was able to pass through the guards and the small courtyard to the steps that led to the second floor and their cell without being stopped.

"Do you know Captain Ruiz?" Summer asked.

"I am trapped with a crazy person!" Lila suddenly yelled. "Help!"

Summer turned at this outburst to see Lila standing on the bench flattened against the wall, her eyes saucer-sized.

"Shut up, Lila, you'll bring the guards!"

"Who do you talk to? I hear *notheeng!"*

"I can't explain it," Summer whispered loudly. "I'm not crazy, so be quiet!" She again turned her attention to Mama Dolly. "Do you know Captain Ruiz?" she repeated.

---

[58] *"Trop tard! Trop tard!"* Too late! Too late!"

"I know da captain, he safe now, but trouble come. I bring you some calas. I give to da guard. He bring dem to you when I go. And some rum, and someting else—you see."

"What is it?"

"It keep you safe."

"Thank you, Mama Dolly." She heard the woman shuffle away. "You can come off of there," she said to Lila, who still stood on the bench smacked against the wall. "Good news! Mama brought us some calas and rum."

"I hear notheeng like that, Zummer. You talk to *nobody*."

Within moments the key turned in the lock.

"Mama Dolly brung you ladies this." The guard stood in the doorway allowing a dim flood of light to enter their cell. "What do I get for giving it to you, Lila?" he asked, holding onto a kerchief covered basket.

"Food!" Lila exclaimed. "Dépêche-toi!"[59] I take care of you later!" she told the guard, who begrudgingly turned the basket over to the ladies.

"How you know theez thing, that Mama Dolly bring zee food?"

"She told me. I can't explain it, so don't ask."

Within minutes, the tasty rice balls had been consumed. The rum warmed their bellies and made the darkness of the cell, now fairly black as midnight, a bit more endurable through the haze of alcohol. The scratching noises that now escalated within the walls blended into the general atmosphere, and the women took no notice.

"I feel darn good," Summer said. "Sleepy even." She then peeked into a red flannel bag that had arrived with the rice balls. "This must be the other thing Mama Dolly was talking about, but it's so darn dark in here I can't see it."

Lila yawned. "Zee Mama put something more than rum in zee bottle."

"Hmmm," Summer murmured and drifted off with her head on Lila's shoulder, and the flannel bag tucked into the waistband of her skirt.

As the women dozed silently, slumped against the wall, head upon head upon shoulder, the rats scurried about the cell, tipping over the toilet bucket, and scattering across the women's laps, climbing the walls and running in and out of the prison cell through mysteriously hidden

[59] *"Dépêche-toi!"* Hurry up!

passageways. The women slept on, and were oblivious to the merry-making in their cell.

* * *

"Oh, mon Dieu!"

Summer woke to a start. Lila stood in the middle of the cell frantically scratching at her head through her thick, frizzed red hair. It was not long before Summer lit from the bench, groaning at a stiff neck and sore back from spending the night in a sitting position, and clawing at her own short mop. She itched *everywhere.* "Something is biting! What's going on?"

"Les puces! Zee fleas!"

"Fleas? What?" Summer practically shrieked as she jumped from foot to foot, hoping the action would somehow alleviate the problem. "Let us out of here!" she yelled, hoping a guard or at least *someone* would come to their rescue. "Help!" she screamed, as Lila practically tore the bodice from her own body.

"What the hell is going on here?" A different guard in Yankee blue appeared unnoticed as the women slapped and scratched at the invisible fleas.

"What do you theenk! Zee damn fleas. Let us out of here!"

"You know I can't do that, Lila."

She knows him, too? "Who is this, Lila?"

"Eet eez Sammy, a friend."

I can imagine what kind of friend. "Sammy, this is cruel and unusual punishment. You have not supplied us food and water, and now we stand here being eaten alive by fleas. I insist that you open this door and let us out immediately!"

"I can't do that, Ma'am. Not without orders from the captain."

"Well go find him, and right now! *Hurry!*"

"I'll do my best, ma'am."

"He'd better return soon," she said, reaching beneath her skirt to satisfy an itch from the insufferable pests. "They can't treat us like this —give us no water, no food and then infest us with fleas."

"But of course zey can; we are zee enemy, remember?"

"Not in my time; they can't treat us like this."

"Maybe Mama Dolly made zee fleas come."

"Of course not. Don't be ridiculous. Mama Dolly is going to help us, you'll see."

"What eez eet she give you there." Lila pointed to the red bag partially tucked and forgotten in Summer's waistband.

"Oh, let's see. It's some kind of bag. What the heck?"

"It's gris-gris![60] She put a curse on you, Zummer!"

Summer shook the bag, which made dull thudding noises as items inside collided against each other. "Don't be silly. Why would she do that? She brought us food and drink, didn't she?"

"Et eez a spell—a curse! And she bring us drugs in zee rum. I remember notheeng of zee night. Oh, mon Dieu! What weel happen to us?" Lila sank onto the old bench resting her forehead in her hands.

"Ouch!" Summer whacked at a flea that had nipped her on the neck. "Let's keep our wits, Lila."

BOOM! BOOM! BOOM! Three explosions shook the cell and rattled their eardrums.

"What eez et?"

"I don't know, but whatever it was, it must have been big." A cacophony of shrieks from the outdoors indicated an event worthy of alarm.

"Unless it…oh no! What if Ruiz is blowing up ships?" She turned wide-eyed to Lila.

"Then it eez good, no?" Lila smiled.

"No, it is *not* 'good'. They're going to catch him and kill him, I know!"

Over the commotion, they didn't hear the key in the lock of the cell door, and jumped when daylight flooded the interior of their cell.

"Bless you Mama Dolly!" Summer said when she recognized the large, turbaned shadow.

"Hurry now, b'fo da soldiers come on back. Dey all lookin' at what dat big noise is 'bout."

"How the heck did you get the key?" Summer asked. *How does she do it?*

"It jus' be. Dat's all. Les' go, now." Mama Dolly said, waving them through the door.

The women followed their liberator down the stairs and straight out the Cabildo entrance. There was not a guard in sight, just folks running toward the pier, and the sharpened voices of exclamation over

---

[60] Gris-gris: a voodoo charm made of natural objects such as roots herbs, snakeskin, bones, stones, animal parts etc….

the event that had happened only minutes ago, the cause of which Summer was certain.

Chapter 17

"What's happened?" Summer asked as they hurried along the sidewalks, first up the small cobblestoned alley. Then right onto Royal Street and left onto L'Allée d' Orléans, passing their apartment, and still whacking at the fleas that now joined them on their new journey.

"Yo' cap'n, he blow up a Yankee ship.

"Oh, I just knew it!" Summer said through gritted teeth.

"A ralenti! Please slow!" Lila huffed, her yellow, hooped skirt clutched into her small fists, her boots tapping noisily along the sidewalk. "I cannot breathe!"

Mama Dolly stopped in her tracks and turned to the straggling women. "You want dem soldiers to catch you's again? Dey's gonna be lookin' for you two." The mere appearance of Mama Dolly's face drawing near as she scrunched her black eyebrows together, her eyes narrowed into piercing slits, was message enough to curtail any whining.

"No," Summer whispered, shrinking back as she scoured the parameter to see if any soldiers had magically appeared from anywhere. "Keep going!"

Again, they followed the woman all the way up L'Allée d' Orléans, passing folks of all color and walks of life, who raced toward the dock to inspect the cause of the explosion. After several blocks they stopped at a large square where, literally gasping for air, the women were able to rest a moment and catch their breaths.

"Where are we?" Summer asked.

"Dey call dis "Congo Square."[61]

"Where are we going?"

"Wid me. Hurry now."

Off they went again, trying to keep pace with Mama Dolly who did not seem to have the least bit of an issue with oxygen intake, a surprising fact considering her size.

The architecture now changed dramatically from the quaint balconied townhouses and shops of the Quarter, to the squalid, rough, unpainted clapboards, shacks and lean-to's of the freed slaves and displaced Negroes that had poured into the city. The two white women following behind Mama Dolly like baby ducks were an oddity that garnered many stares and comments from the meandering Negroes.

"Mon Dieu, why are we in theez place?" Lila squeaked. "We do not belong here, Mama."

Again, the large, black woman stopped in her tracks. "You are wid me because you are wid *her,*" Mama Dolly said, nodding to Summer, and then pressing a finger into Lila's chest. "She special, and you are *noting.*"

"Hmph," Lila replied, her entire body conjured instantly into a shrug of dislike.

Once more, the women followed Mama Dolly into a neighborhood of the roughly hewn diminutive shacks until they stopped at one in particular, a dingy wooded clapboard. Mama Dolly opened the latch. The door creaked open, sending a not-unpleasant odorous mixture of herbs and extinguished candles wafting up nostrils. Inside, she lit a lantern, spreading a warm yellow glow into the small one-room dwelling. Summer immediately spotted a square table off to one side, balanced

---

[61] Congo Square: An open area in today's Louis Armstrong Memorial Park that was established in 1817 as a meeting place for African Americans to socialize and dance on Sundays.

under one leg by a wad of cloth. On the table were various objects which must have been used in the making of the gris-gris bag, which was still tucked into the waistband of her skirt. Against another wall was a small cot covered in tattered blankets and a lumpy flat pillow. A wood-burning stove sat front and center against the back wall, its smoke pipe wrapped in rags at the crude ceiling opening in an attempt to keep out the heat, or cold, and mosquitos.

"Where are we and why?" Lila asked, doing one small turn around to soak in the new environment. There was plenty to take in, as the walls were covered in a strange assortment of religious items, such as crucifixes, crude paintings of Jesus and the Holy Mother and many cloth dolls with large button eyes. Interspersed between the religious objects and renderings were odd items that had no recognizable meaning to Summer.

"You's here, in da Backtown, safe," Mama Dolly replied. "Don' give me no sass."

Two stools shoved beneath the wobbly table beckoned, and Summer took one, placing herself aside the strange items. "What is this?" she asked removing the sack again from her waistband.

"I make it to keep you safe."

"It's not a curse, then?"

"No! No curse! We keep you safe, special lady. You have de vision and tonight we see da Queen at da Bayou."

"Oh, no! I do not zee Queen!" Lila paced the small quarters, her arms gesticulating wildly. "You no make me go, crazy lady." She stopped her pacing to stand defiantly in front of the tall woman, who appeared nearly thrice the size of the French woman as viewed from Summer's perspective.

"I do not care what you do!" Mama Dolly exclaimed, shooing Lila away with her large black hands. She walked to the small table and retrieved a bottle of "potion", as she called it, to kill the fleas. It was oily and reeked of an undiscernible odor, but Mama Dolly insisted they rub it over their entire bodies and through their scalp. It miraculously worked, and the women were relieved of their biting companions.

Mama informed them that they needed new clothing due to the flea infestation. From a badly dented trunk she rummaged through an odd and colorful assortment of clothing, tossing pieces onto the floor when she was satisfied she had found the correct item. Closing the trunk and gathering the bundle from the floor, she tossed it onto her bed.

"Come on, dis ain't got no fleas." From there, she delivered to each woman, the clothing she was to wear. This was not an easy task because of the size of Mama Dolly compared to the other two. However, when they were finally dressed, with Lila complaining loudly having to leave her pretty yellow working garments behind, they were ready to face Backtown dressed much like Mama Dolly, but in skirts that were tied around the waist with colorful strips of fabric in order to keep them from falling off, muslin blouses, and the signature colorful tignons.

* * *

Lila, who had decided there was safety in numbers, and Summer, followed Mama Dolly through Backtown, Aside from their white skin, they blended into the other inhabitants who appeared to be heading in the same direction as they. When they reached a slow moving body of water, they saw that many Negroes had also arrived at the spot and more were beginning to gather.

"Where are we?" Summer asked.

"Dis da Wishin'Spot,"[62] Mama Dolly said proudly.

"What happens here?" Summer asked, trepidation seeping into her voice.

"You wait; you see."

Countless Negroes of all ages continued to gather along the bayou's banks as the three women stood waiting. *Waiting for what?* Summer wondered, but it was not good to press their leader.

"I haven't had a vision in a long time, just so you know." Summer wanted to be perfectly clear on that matter, considering that the woman thought she had exceptional powers. The only new and strange experience (aside from the magic of time-travel) that she could think of was the bizarre occurrence of Mama Dolly speaking to her without opening her mouth.

"You gots da vision, girl. I knows it, and da Queen gonna know it too. You see."

"Oh!" Lila exclaimed when a horse and carriage pulled nearby delivering a young white woman, nicely dressed in her hooped green

[62] Wishing Spot: A place along the St. John Bayou where voodoo Priestess, Marie Laveau, held many spiritual and exotic ceremonies.

satin attire, and a gentleman of equal superior fashion. "They must not see me!" she whispered, stepping behind Mama Dolly.

"Why not? What now? I suppose he's is a *'friend,'* like the jailer?

"Monsieur Fontaneau; he is why I go to prison! I steal from him!"

To avoid trouble, the three women moved further away from the newly arrived fashionable couple.

Summer was perplexed when a few more white people appeared at the site, and she prayed that no soldiers would also appear to jeopardize their new-found freedom. "Mama Dolly, why are there so many white folks here?" It seemed strange, surrounded by the black crowd as they were, that white women, especially, would come to whatever event was about to happen.

"Dis is da Wishin' Spot.' Dey come for good luck, or to shoo da bad luck away."

"As long as the soldiers don't come...."

"Dey busy wid what da captain done."

"I need to see the captain. Can you take me?"

"Not now. When da time come."

A sudden hoopla spread throughout the crowd, which divided in such an exact manner that Summer thought perhaps it had been rehearsed. From the center of the newly formed aisle came a handsome and statuesque, light-skinned woman of color. Atop her head she wore an eye- catching tignon, bright red in color and decorated with flowers and jewels that sparkled with reflection from the setting sun. Most eye-catching, though, was an immensely long, thick-bodied snake which hung from the woman's shoulders. Its forked tongue flickered in and out of its serpentine head, which bobbed to and fro, side to side, eyeing the crowd through slanted eyes.

"Da Queen." Mama Dolly whispered in a voice that changed from deep, and husky, to soft and breathless. Summer glanced at her and saw quite plainly that she was totally in awe, her demeanor had changed dramatically.

"Mon Dieu! Zee woman is crazy!" Lila whispered from behind Mama Dolly's huge form, as she was still very nervous about being spotted by Monsieur Fontaneau. "Zee snake, eet eez alive!"

The crowd fell silent as the Queen and her snake passed. There was no denying it; the woman was Backtown royalty. As she strolled majestically through the parting path, her snake moved slowly about her head and neck, and the crowd, which had grown quite large, stood hushed. The quiet made Summer nervous. She knew little of voodoo and nothing of hoodoo. *What next?*

In this pause, Summer observed that the Queen was finely dressed, though not in the fashion of the day; no frills or petticoats or hoops. Instead, she wore a long skirt of purple fabric, topped by a plain cotton blouse with long, billowing sleeves secured at the wrist. The blouse fully covered her chest and was pinned with what appeared to be a fetish of sorts at the neck. Atop the blouse she wore a long and flowing multi-colored vest which stopped short at calf length, and looked to be of a woven fabric. Its colors were richly dyed, eye-catching, and embellished a figure that demanded respect.

Summer and Lila both jumped when the beat of a drum broke the hush of the crowd. The Queen, who had reached the edge of the still waters of the bayou, suddenly came to life. Her reserve and stateliness disappeared immediately upon the drum beat. The crowd had left an open circle in which the Queen entered, gyrating erratically, swinging the snake over and about her head and singing loudly in a foreign tongue. As the drum beat heightened, a man entered the circle. His pants hung loose, tied at the waist, while a linen vest sat unbuttoned over his bare, muscular chest. In his hands he held a live rooster that flapped its wings hysterically with the commotion. The man's skin glowed and glistened from a fire which now flamed in the middle of the open space, a fire that seemed to appear mysteriously. As Summer was so busy watching the gyrating woman and man, she did not notice when the fire was set.

The crowd roared when a machete knife appeared in the man's hand as mysteriously as the fire had appeared, and off came the rooster's head in one fell swoop. Summer and Lila screamed at this unexpected move, while the Queen's voice rose in crescendo as the rooster's headless body, still flapping its wings, fell to the ground amidst an enlarging pool of blood.

This action appeared as a green light for the crowd to join in; they did. Hordes of bodies filled the space until only the very tip-top of the Queen's tignon was visible to the eye. Mama Dolly disappeared into the crowd as smoothly as if she were a mist, which brought to mind the fact that the woman was quite agile for her size.

With Mama Dolly now gyrating with the rest of the crowd, Summer and Lila stood exposed; two white women sticking out like sore thumbs amongst the much larger number of Negroes. As the other whites were few, and mainly on the other side of the crowd, the women were semi-blocked from their view by the dancers, and hoped the dreaded Mr. Fontaneau would stay to his side. However, when the crowd parted again, it parted in their direction, putting them in the spotlight!

The Queen came forward, moving to the beat of the drums which had now increased significantly in volume and tempo. She held the snake high above her head as her hips and bare feet melded with the beat. Terrified at the thought of the Queen and her snake approaching in such a fashion, yet paralyzed by the woman's glistening eyes that locked into hers, Summer struggled in vain to turn away, to run, but an invisible force held her. The woman and snake came at them, ominously shadowed by firelight that shot strobes of orange flashes upon the faces in the crowd, faces that glistened of perspiration in the heat of frenzy. The sounds were deafening; a cacophony of drums, of wailing, of sporadic bursts of shouts from the electrified crowd. The Queen had pulled the back of her skirt between her legs and tucked it into the front of her waistband, thus creating pantaloons and enabling her to keep with the beat of the drums and distinguish the steps of her energetic dance.

The escalating beat reverberated in Summer's head like the sound of the blown Yankee ship: BOOM-BOOM-BOOM! The Queen came closer, holding Summer prisoner with her piercing eyes, dark, moist and deadly serious. The jewels of the red turban sparkled in the firelight. Closer and closer she came, her feet pounding to the rhythm. Summer stood steady, frozen in place. She was vaguely aware of Lila tucked in behind her, clutching the back of her blouse. Finally, the Queen was inches away—the snake's tongue flickering wildly—and yet she could not move.

The Queen's eyes bore down upon her. "I see you, white lady. I know you, white lady. I know what you is, white lady. You come from far away to dis place!" BOOM, BOOM BOOM!

Lila screamed, running backward as the snake slithered from the Queen's shoulders onto Summer's.

Mama Dolly now stood beside the Queen, gyrating as well, moving to the drumbeat.

"We know you, white lady." The women spoke in unison—only without moving their lips! It was the eyes…the eyes spoke!

The vested, bare-chested man now appeared, and from his mouth came discorded ranting. He held the rooster's now severed feet in front of Summer' face as he jumped and twirled. She didn't flinch; she couldn't move. The snake wrapped its body around her neck and held her there while the voices from unmoving lips continued to rant.

"We know you, white lady. You come from away to dis place!"

Chapter 18

"No!" Leave me alone!"

"Wake up, Summer! Wake up, you're dreaming!"

"Huh? Where's Mama Dolly?" she asked through lids heavy as sandbags.

"Wake up. You were having quite the dream; scared the pants off me."

"What?" she asked, vaguely aware of her body being shaken. *The hoodoo!* She shot up to a sitting position and was surprised to see Guy sitting at the edge of the bed. "Wait…" she looked around the room, Aunt Ada's old room, and realized she was back at Magnolia in their bedroom, hers and Guy's, not hers and the captain's small shared room in New Orleans. "Orleans!" she shouted, causing Guy to leap off the bed.

"Orleans? Hey, wake up. You're dreaming, hon."

"You're right," she said, throwing the covers off and stepping to the floor. "So sorry, I really need some aspirin." In the bathroom she opened the vanity, her hands shaking as she took the aspirin bottle off its glass shelf. "Oh, my God—New Orleans!" She whispered to the mirror.

Her cropped hair stood in odd spikes in her reflection. "Bed head, to boot." Running her hands over the swell of her belly, she realized she really was back. "I'm home, my little ones." But this she said with an aching heart and the gnawing feeling that things were not quite settled in New Orleans. It was fuzzy in her head. Was it a dream, or had she really time-traveled again?

As the day wore on, breakfast, lunch, dirty dishes to wash, the usual work, the previously vague memory of New Orleans grew stronger. Around three o'clock in the afternoon, the nagging memory came full blown. "Captain Ruiz!" she said aloud, and quickly climbed the stairs to the nursery. The attic door was shut; all was quiet. Taking a breath and counting to three, she turned the latch to find—*nothing!*

What's happening in New Orleans? She sat on the third stair hoping the captain would appear, then hoping he wouldn't. "Don't come to me!" She spoke the words to the empty stairwell. "It's best you don't come, so don't come, Ruiz. I can't keep doing this." But her heart was heavy. The memory was too new, too recent. She wanted to rip the captain from her heart. She felt her belly and was ashamed that she could sit on the attic stairs, a soon to be married woman to the most wonderful man in the world, and cry over a man who lived over a century before, not to mention a man who just blew up a Yankee ship…a criminal!

* * *

"You don't seem yourself. Are you feeling okay?" Guy asked at dinner that night.

"I know, and I'm sorry. Maybe it was the dream, I haven't felt very good all day."

"Summer…I hate to ask this, but… you weren't traveling again, were you?"

A knot of dread joined the twins in her belly. "No…of course not," she lied, hoping she sounded convincing.

"Good," he replied, but raised an eyebrow and eyed her suspiciously.

She stood and walked to the back of his chair, wrapping her arms around his wide, muscular shoulders and nestling her head next to his. "I'm not going anywhere, just staying here and getting ready for our wedding. Lots to do before then!"

As the days passed and preparations for their big day approached, Summer could not shake the sad and desperate feeling that bad things were happening in New Orleans, and that she wasn't there to help the captain, or even crazy Lila, the annoying prostitute. Time travel was so confusing! *Is anything happening, or is nothing happening?* She questioned this, and hoped that nothing was happening, that time had marched on into the next centuries; that what once was, was done, finished, buried. Perhaps, sometime after the wedding, she could do a search on genealogy sites and find mention of Ruiz and his family. Did the Yankees catch him? Was he executed? *That* thought shot a pain through her heart. Yes, she would definitely do a search *after* the wedding, not before...*not before*. She would devote the next days to Guy and the babies...*I will not think of Ruiz!*

* * *

"You'll look gorgeous!" Jesse said admiring the wedding dress hanging from the guestroom door.

"And you too," Summer said, knowing that Jesse would be stunning as always. She was to be the maid of honor and because the color was perfect against her ebony skin, Summer had chosen a lovely chartreuse evening gown.

"I love my dress, gal!"

"I know you do, and you'll look like a million. Maybe you and Raymond will be tying the knot soon?"

"I think Raymond is stuck in the mud, afraid of marriage." Jesse sighed. "Well, at least we have one wedding to look forward to and your baby as well."

"*Two* babies."

"What?

"It's *two* babies. Twins. Can you believe it? When I sin, I sin big."

"There's no sin in babies, gal! I can hardly contain my joy...*two* babies, imagine that!"

"We're excited."

"*You're* excited? I'm having two little cousin babies coming. I could do a dance right here and now; one baby for you, and one for me!"

"You're funny."

"So, what are they, boys—girls? Boy and girl? What...what?"

"We're going to be surprised."

"Alleluia! The old-fashioned way. Wait till I tell Raymond."

"I guess we'd better get ready for the dinner."

Preparations had been made for a catered rehearsal dinner to be held in the Magnolia dining room. Leaves were added to the table, which was beautifully set in white linen and lace to accommodate ten people. On the guest list were Blaine Ascot (Best Man) and his date, Amelia Hunt, of another neighboring plantation. Her family, too, had once been planters of stature in the community, owning many slaves and producing much rice and cotton in antebellum Blue Bell, Georgia. Jesse's boyfriend, Raymond, would be in attendance, as well as two other lawyers and their wives with whom Summer had little social experience.

A centerpiece of roses fresh from the garden was displayed artistically, accompanied by baby's breath and ferns. The catering company had done a magnificent job selecting the roses and greens from the gardens of Magnolia, which Guy kept in impeccably good order. Summer tried to erase the thought of the Yankee soldier bones buried beneath the beautiful rose bushes.[63] Yes, they had a lovely grave, but they never made it home to their loved ones. A shudder ran through her as she thought of Mick Mason, who killed the soldiers and forced her to help bury them in the garden. There was so much history in this place which spoke of both pride *and* sorrow.

How nice it was to sit and be waited on by the catering staff. Dinner was a scrumptious six-course affair topped off with brandy and coffee in the parlor.

"150 years ago, I would have been waiting on you." Jesse whispered into Summer's ear as she viewed one of the hired help pouring brandy.

"It's fine with me if you want to," Summer whispered back, and the women giggled.

"And Raymond could be the butler…." The giggles continued. "I can just see him in white gloves, a starched cotton shirt…Y'sm, Mistress Woodfield is at home but she busy birthin' da babies…."

Peals of laughter could not be contained, and Blaine's date ,Miss Amelia, who throughout dinner had put on enough stuffy airs to outshine even Summer's nemesis, old and buried Elizabeth Woodfield[64], sent a cold, disapproving look to the women.

Summer immediately put on a straight face.

"Amelia, would you care for a tour of the house?"

---

[63] This event occurred in Book I

[64] Elizabeth Woodfield, a character from Book I.

"Why…I suppose so," she said, lifting her body from a leather chair. The other two women, who came with the two senior law partners, declined the tour, complaining of bad hips and knees.

"Would you care to start with the old slave stairway?"

"Certainly not! I'm well aware of the central stairway. My home has it too."

"Oh well, I suppose it does. Come see the improvements then. You know, the place was a disaster when I first came here."

The second floor tour passed with little comment from Amelia Hunt, which Summer found to be extremely impolite. She and Guy had worked very hard to improve the second floor rooms, repainting, fixing and replacing old and broken windows, repairing trims, and refinishing the wooden floors.

By the third floor, Summer was fed up with Miss Amelia who clearly had no interest in the tour, *or* in Summer and Jesse.

"And this is the room of the slave nanny, Ruth, back in the day." Continuing through Ruth's old room Summer placed her hand on the knob to the nursery, and suddenly froze.

"What are you waiting for? Open the door." Jess said, having nearly crashed into Summer on her abrupt stop.

She wasn't sure what stopped her, but stop her it did. Before she had a moment to consider the reason, the door flew open sending a blast of frigid air into the three women. Summer gasped, but not from the frigid air that left her momentarily breathless, but because Captain Ruiz stood before them in all his glory! With hands on hips, he stood cocky and defiant in his costume of white shirt with billowing sleeves, black knee boots, and his hair, slightly graying at the temples, pomaded and combed back away from his face, hanging nearly to his shoulders.

"Where have you been, Verano? I need you. Come to me."

She was speechless. Could the others see him? Could they hear him? Feel his presence? She half expected Miss Amelia to ask who the heck the dashing stranger was, but instead Miss Amelia had taken several steps backward and was white as a sheet. "Is there a window open? I didn't realize it was so cold and windy outside."

Jesse, too, though not as white as a ghost, stood wide-eyed behind Summer. "What in the world was that about?" she asked, arms wrapped around her shivering torso.

"No…no windows." Summer tried to collect her wits. "Perhaps a window in the attic is broken," Summer offered. A poor excuse, as Miss

Amelia had now joined the two women in the doorway and peeked into the old nursery room.

"Isn't that the attic door? It's closed."

"I guess it's just the mystery of an old…old house."

"Perhaps you have a ghost," Amelia said, matter-of-factly.

"And this concludes the grand tour," Summer said bluntly, forcing a smile, eager to leave the situation as quickly as possible. As she reached for the knob of the nursery door, it slammed shut on its own causing all three women to jump backward.

"My, oh my. You must have an *angry* ghost," Amelia said, as they left Captain Ruiz behind.

"Amelia," Summer stepped next to her as they descended the grand stairway. "Would you mind not mentioning the uh…uh…"

"Ghost?"

"Well, we won't go so far as to say it was a ghost, will we? I would just appreciate it if you wouldn't mention it to Guy. He's worried enough about my 'condition', you know. I don't want him thinking—*heck I certainly don't want him thinking, period!*—that anything is amiss with the place. You can understand, can't you?"

"Certainly, Summer. You have my word I won't mention it to Guy, but I can't wait to mention it to Blaine! Besides, we Georgians figure there have to be a few ghosts in these old places, anyway. I have a few myself."

Later, with the party over, Raymond, Jesse, Summer and Guy stood in the doorway waving the visitors off.

"Maybe she's not as bad as we think," Jesse whispered.

"That was a close one." Summer replied, keeping her voice low and out of earshot of Guy.

"Was that your captain who blew the door open?"

"It was. He was standing right there in front of us! Gosh, this really makes me nervous. At least you two couldn't see him."

"Are you crazy? I'd love to see him!"

"What's all the whispering about?" Guy asked.

"Just girl talk. There's a wedding tomorrow, you know!"

* * *

Summer threw aside the covers. Guy slept beside her, lightly snoring; and as much as she wanted to resist, she simply could not sleep without first visiting the nursery. *Is he still there?* Obviously Ruiz was trying to find her again, but why now, the night before the wedding? Over the past two weeks, she had tried her best to block him from her mind and concentrate on Guy and the wonderful life they had planned with their two little bundles of upcoming joy. How could she, though, with the thought of Ruiz in trouble and searching for her?

She used the slave stairway, creepy as it was, to reach the nursery. At least she had a flashlight this time and didn't have to worry about burning herself up with a lantern or candle as in times past.

"Ruiz?" she called in a whisper, once she opened the nursery door. There was no cold blast to greet her this time. Opening the attic door to nothing but a musty stillness, she sat on the third tread, the flashlight beaming upward to the slanted stairway ceiling as she set it next to her. They, the spirits, had always reached out to *her,* not she to them. Perhaps she couldn't summon Ruiz; perhaps it didn't work that way. After all, what was she but a hapless victim of the spirit world? She had to play by *their* rules, not hers.

After a while in which Ruiz did not materialize, she decided to head to bed before Guy realized she was gone.

"You've come, Verano."

A hot flush ran through her as she stood and turned, flashlight in hand to shine brightly on the *other* man, the man she loved in a different place, in a different time. Ruiz!

"I need you, Verano. I could not find you...."

The flashlight dropped from her hands, thudded down the last step and rolled across the nursery floor.

She turned to watch it roll, terrified Guy would hear it; but when she turned back to the captain, he was gone! *All* was gone: the stairs, the attic, the nursery, there was nothing, just blackness....

Chapter 19

"She wakin' up, Mistah Fontaneau!" The voice came from a faraway place. *Guy must have invited Mr. Fontaneau to the wedding. Oh, oh, Lila won't like that!* She opened her eyes slowly, as if they were set upon by weights. *My wedding day! Our wedding day,* she corrected herself, running her hands over her expanding belly only to the realization that her belly was flat. Her eyes flew open. "My babies!" she screamed, bringing a pudgy black woman running to her bedside.

"You gots no babies here, miss. Hold on, now. Mistah Fontaneau! She awake now!"

I must be back in New Orleans. Alert now, Summer realized her head was sunk into the middle of an overstuffed goose down pillow in an elegantly carved four-poster bed and covered with a lace edged spread. *Oh, my God, where the heck am I? I can't disappear on my wedding day!* Her stomach did flip-flops as she rose to a sitting position and realized with horror that her clothes were gone, and she wore a cotton nightgown tied with a ribbon at her neck and arms covered to the wrist. She eyed the black woman who was eyeing her back.

"Dat Mistah Fontaneau slow as a slug today," the woman said, and then shuffled about the room, pretending to straighten items that looked like they needed no straightening at all.

"Who are you?" Summer asked.

"Why, I'se Dancie. I keep house fo' Mistah Fontaneau. Who's you?"

"My name is Summer Woodfield. Why am I here? Where am I, anyway?"

You's in Mistah Fontaneau's home. He bring you from da Wishin' Place".

The Wishing Spot! The Queen, Mama Dolly, Lila—where is Lila?—and the fancy couple...Fontaneau!"

"Holy Smokes!" She threw the lace-edged spread off and stood. "Is there a bathroom, Dancie?"

"If you mean da water closet, y'sm. Come wid me."

Summer followed the woman out the bedroom door and into a wide hallway. A few steps away, Dancie opened the door to a very small, dark room. "Da water closet."

No wonder they call it a closet. "No light, right?"

"Ain't no light and I don't have no candle. It's daytime."

Summer closed the door behind her. She had to think. She sat on the strange commode and hoped there weren't any spiders hiding below the lip, or rats, or anything that appears much more terrifying in the dark; it was black as night in the small room. *Mr. Fontaneau's home. Why? How? What happened to Lila?*

With only a wooden door between her and the hallway, a man's voice, certainly Fontaneau's, reached her ears.

"Have Miss Woodfield dress and meet me in the library."

"Yes Sah. She be down lickety split. Soon as she come out a da closet, I help her get ready."

"Thanks, Dancie."

Footsteps disappeared down the hallway. She was relieved that she didn't have to meet Mr. Fontaneau face to face wearing a nightgown. What in the world happened to put her here?

* * *

"Wow!" Summer twirled while viewing her reflection in the standing mirror. The oval-carved mirror frame was just as luxurious as every other piece of furniture in the room.

"You's lookin' mighty nice!" Dancie said proudly, having taken 45 minutes to dress her charge.

Aside from the usual undergarments, including the restrictive and tightly laced corset that Summer fought wearing, she was embraced in yards and yards of beautiful red silk that fell lightly over a four-hooped crinoline. The bodice hugged tightly and a bit low cut and risqué for daytime. *Beggars can't be choosers!* Indeed she was dressed from head to foot; knitted stockings were held up by lace garters, and feet slipped into leather slippers.

"Where's yo' hair, gal?" Dancie asked when she ran the brush through Summer's short crop.

"Where I come from, we can have short hair."

"I never heard of no place like dat where a white lady can walk about wid no hair."

"Take my word for it, Dancie. It exists."

"You's ready gal. Les' go."

Summer followed Dancie down a gracefully curved, elegantly carpeted stairway with a highly polished oak banister from which her hand slid as swiftly as if it had been buttered. Butterflies fluttered in her stomach as the time of truth was upon her. *Who is Mr. Fontaneau, and why am I here? How did I get here?*

Dancie knocked on the thick mahogany door. "She's heah, Mistah Fontaneau!"

After a few nervous seconds, the door opened and there stood Mr. Fontaneau, a dandy if ever she had seen one; a complete contrast to Captain Ruiz. He was taller than she, and as impeccably dressed as she remembered from the Wishing Spot the night before. *Was it the night before?* She could never answer such a question, as time travel was completely unpredictable.

They had apparently caught him off guard, as he was buttoning a tan linen frock coat over an elaborate brocade vest.

"Miss Woodfield, such a pleasure!" He bent at the waist and waved her through the doorway with a sweep of his arm. "Thank you, Dancie, and please bring us tea." With Dancie gone on her errand, the two of them were uncomfortably, on Summer's part, alone.

"Please sit." He indicated a high-backed velvet chair in front of a fireplace that was not lit, as the weather had been quite warm and a fire was not required.

"I'm afraid you have the advantage, Mr. Fontaneau. I have no clue as to how I got here, or why I'm here. How do you know my name? What's happened to my friends?"

"If you recall," he said, sitting in the chair across from her, "we both happened to be at the Wishing Spot for the Queen's rather energetic performance."

"I do remember that much."

"When the crowd parted and the Queen made her advance toward you, I caught sight of Miss de Peau, the little thief, and you, Miss Woodfield. I know who you are, and I know that you, Miss de Peau *and* that thief Ruiz, all escaped from Fort Jefferson, though I can't imagine how you managed to do so. Horrible place, stuck out in the Gulf as it is."

"You've been there?"

"No, I can't say I have, but I have certainly heard enough stories….well, that is beyond the point."

"The point? Just what is the point?"

"The point is, that I'm very interested in contacting Ruiz."

"Why is that?"

"Let's just say we have some unfinished business."

"I don't understand how having me here is going to help you with your unfinished business with Captain Ruiz. I don't know where he is, and he doesn't know where I am."

"He will, Miss Woodfield. Trust me."

Trust him? I don't think so! "What's happened to Li…Miss de Peau?"

"I'm not interested in Miss de Peau. There is nothing that will reform the little whoring thief. What I want is Captain Ruiz."

"I told you, I don't know where the captain is."

"No matter. He'll know where you are soon enough, though he may have a bit of trouble getting here considering the number of soldiers searching for him. Blowing up the Yankee ship was a foolish act that only cinched the noose around his neck."

Summer cringed, a slight twitch that did not pass unnoticed by Mr. Fontaneau.

"That is correct. Your lover is a criminal, and he is headed for the gallows."

Control yourself. Don't let this pompous ass get to you. "I disagree," she blurted. This is war, and the captain has done nothing but protect his right to defend his country and livelihood. The Yankees —*forgive me, my homeland!*—have done the same all across the South; they have burned, pillaged, raped, and virtually destroyed all in their path." It was not a lie; she had lived it!

"This war is lost, Miss Woodfield. Though I agree with you in your patriotic babble. After all, I am a Southerner; but this war is lost and Ruiz is doing nothing but digging his own grave. And for what? It's over; the life we knew is over." Mr. Fontaneau lit a pipe and sat quietly in thought. For a moment, Summer thought the man was going to cry.

"What do you want from him?" she asked softly, cutting into his obvious state of despair.

He looked up through the opaque and sweet-smelling cloud of pipe tobacco and said, "I want my gold."

His gold? Does he mean our gold? The gold I risked being shark bait for? "Why would Captain Ruiz know anything about your gold?"

"Oh come now, Miss Woodfield. Don't pretend you don't know anything about the gold that Ruiz stole from Carlos in Nassau![65]"

"Why would I?"

"Miss Woodfield, I have friends in many places. They keep me informed, and I know very well that Ruiz absconded with my gold. I also know that Carlos—you do remember Carlos, don't you? You do remember that Carlos chased the Diablo Volante into the Gulf of Mexico?"

How the heck, in a world without satellites and internet, could he possibly know about the sea chase? Did one of Carlos' crew survive?

"Miss Woodfield?"

Summer's mind had drifted off, back to the battle between the sloops. She could not remember seeing any survivors; not even her precious captain. There was no one left but she, Cherry and Buck—and the sharks.

"I guess you have me painted into a corner, Mr. Fontaneau. Yes, I remember. And, I remember Carlos saying it was *his* gold. There was no mention of you."

"But of course not! Carlos was a thief, a pirate, as is your lover, Captain Ruiz. It was *my* shipment of cigars. Cigars made from *my*

---

[65] This event occurred in Book II

tobacco. It was precious cargo, and all is lost. I do not intend, in these stressful times, to lose what fortune I have left."

Summer sat speechless. Her head hurt; she was confused. This pirate-blockade-running-time-travel-gold-treasure-Civil-War-life suddenly sat heavy upon her shoulders. Her breath came short, due, no doubt, to the tightness of the corset. She stood, trying to catch a deep breath, but it wouldn't come.

Mr. Fontaneau jumped to his feet. "Dancie!" he yelled. "Bring the salts!" He rushed to Summer's side and caught her just as she felt herself falling, bright stars flashing in a black sky.

When she woke, she could breathe. She opened her eyes to Dancie holding a foul-smelling concoction beneath her nose. She was still in the library, but lying on a settee with Mr. Fontaneau still in his chair.

"Feeling better?" he asked.

"Much," she said, attempting to rise, and then realizing with horror that her red silk bodice was missing! The corset had been loosened about the white cotton chemise, which sat exposed about her naked shoulders. "Oh!" she squeaked, frantically searching for the missing piece.

"Relax," Mr. Fontaneau said. "Dancie tied the corset much too tightly. I have instructed her to not do it again."

Summer came to a sitting position and pulled a portion of her ample skirt up to cover the top of the chemise and loosened corset.

"Relax!" he said again. "I have seen many women with much less on than you wear now." He smiled wickedly.

"I'm sure you have," she replied, remembering the fancy woman who had accompanied him to the Wishing Spot, and then there was Lila who assuredly must have done "beenez" with the man in order to steal his money. On second thought, surely this man of obvious culture and class, did not need to pay a woman for favors.

"How do you know Lila?" she asked, curious now that she was half naked (or so felt) and held prisoner, waiting for her lover to be trapped by the dandy, Mr. Fontaneau.

"Miss de Peau, the little urchin. I procured her for a friend who had taken a fancy to the dirty wench. We brought her here to the house where she entertained my friend throughout the night. In the morning she was gone, along with my friend's money. She also managed somehow to lift several items of value from my home along with money I had locked in a desk drawer. She is a sneaky little rat."

"So you had her arrested."

"I did, and she was sent to Fort Jefferson. Now the little whore is back in Le Vieux Carré. However, I suppose she has had punishment enough, and I am not interested in the whore anyway." His eyes bore into hers. "I am solely interested in the return of my treasure. Do you understand, Miss Woodfield?"

"Yes, I understand. But do you understand that I do not know where Ruiz is, and I certainly do not know where your gold is, either." She rose, holding the loosened corset against her chest. Spotting the red bodice on a chair, she grabbed it, and then paused at the library door. "Do I need your permission to return to my room?"

Mr. Fontaneau had risen at her standing, a social politeness long embedded into the minds of southern gentleman.

"Of course not," he said. "You are free to roam the house, but you are not free to leave."

We'll see about that….

Back in the opulent bedroom, she opened the French doors which led to the typical balcony surrounded by wrought iron railings. She had no idea of her exact whereabouts in the Quarter or, was she still in the Quarter? *Yes,* she assured herself as she glanced up and down the narrow cobblestone street to see that all the adjoining buildings were of similar construction, all having the ornate wrought iron railings that so distinguished the city. Horses trotted beneath, their hooves clip-clopping musically across the cobblestones as they pulled their carriages along behind them. From other streets, vendors called out their advertisements of calas, beignets, breads, flowers, and vegetables; a veritable parading supermarket. She remembered the starving days at Magnolia when the planters suffered so, while here, in this city, some folks were able to maintain a lifestyle, or at least have food on the table. While here, she and Ruiz had depended on Lila to keep them fed. Looking back on it now, it did seem a lot to put on the poor French woman, but Lila was eager to practice her chosen profession.

Thoughts of Ruiz and Lila broke her moment of reflection. *Where are they? Is Ruiz safe?* Her anxiety level rose quickly to a sharp peak, at which time she blurted the name, "Mama Dolly!"

A passerby looked up at the sudden outburst from above, and Summer shrank back from the railing. *Stupid me! Is that woman really going to show?* "Mama Dolly!" she called again, only softer, deciding that at least calling the woman would not hurt, just in case what Mama

Dolly had told her was true, that every time she called her name, she'd be there.

Summer stepped to the balcony again, and peeked over. No Mama Dolly. *Darn.* Then, just as she was turning to return to the bedroom, she caught sight of the woman's unmistakable figure rounding a corner; and there she was.

Mama Dolly stood one moment beneath the balcony. "Later girl," she said. Or did she? It seemed that she and Mama Dolly were able to communicate without speaking; an accepted revelation that was simultaneously frightening yet functional.

"Later?" Summer asked, with nary a sound leaving her lips.

"Later," Mama said, soundlessly, before nodding and lumbering off down the street.

What a strange world I'm in.

Chapter 20

After a sumptuous but spicy concoction of shrimp and rice for supper that night alone in her room, Dancie helped her change into her pilgrim (as she thought of it) nightgown and wondered how she would get to sleep. It had not been a physically challenging day. Instead, it had been mentally challenging wondering and waiting for Mama Dolly's meaning of *'later'* to materialize.

She had not seen Mr. Fontaneau since the library meeting, as he had a mysterious appointment elsewhere. She knew this by having overheard him instruct Dancie to keep track of *the woman*, and to not *let her leave the house.* After her supper, Dancie lit the bedside lantern, and left, leaving her to lie wondering and waiting.

* * *

She woke with a start, realizing that she had drifted off. "Wha..?" *Mama Dolly!* The covers flew as she ran across the floor to the

French doors, opening them wide. A sweet and gentle breeze fluttered her nightgown as she peered over the railing.

"I's here!" Mama Dolly spoke the words with her eyes, her mind, or whatever it was, Summer understood. "You catch dis." The woman tossed the end of a rope upward, but Summer missed. Thanks to the gaslights on the street, she was able to see fairly well, and when the rope was thrown again she grabbed and held on.

"Tie it to da railing." Mama Dolly instructed.

Summer peeked over the balcony, visually measuring the distance from where she stood on the balcony to the ground, and shuddered. "You want me to climb down this rope?"

"De only way. Hurry now."

"I'm in a nightgown!"

"Don' matter. Tie da rope and climb b'fo' someone see!"

Summer, having little knowledge of knot tying, hoped that her freelance-loop-de-loop knot would hold. She glanced up and down the street and realized it was oddly vacant from both foot and horse traffic, and she was free to make her harrowing escape.

"I don't know about this," she said, warily swinging a leg over the balcony. "I've never done anything like this before."

"If you wanna see yo' cap'n, you get dat leg over and get yo' body down heah."

Mama Dolly was clearly losing her patience, and Summer didn't miss the agitation in the woman's voice, or head, whichever way it was they were communicating.

Slight as she was, her body felt heavy as lead when she finally surrendered to the rope. Swinging wildly below the balcony now, she prayed the railing would hold. Her legs kicked the air in panic as she tried in vain to walk her hands down the rope. She simply did not have enough upper body strength to carry her weight; and instead of moving like an athlete, she mainly slid, her hands burned by the rough hemp of rope. Pain caused her to let go five feet from the bottom, and she landed hard on her feet, and then fell to her behind. She wanted to cry from the frustration and pain, but Mama Dolly was not going to let her succumb to weakness.

"Les' go!" She pulled Summer to her feet and took her by one sore hand. Though totally lost as to where they were in the quarter, Summer gladly let the big woman lead her along, occasionally ducking into narrow alleyways if a pedestrian came their way. Luckily, the hour was somewhere between midnight and dawn, making the roads fairly devoid of traffic.

After a time of racing through streets and alleyways, in her nightgown and bare feet, she recognized Congo Square, which they passed through quickly, and eventually arrived at Mama Dolly's front door.

"Zummer!" Lila rose from where she sat on a stool and ran to hug her counterpart. "You are alive!"

"And you, too, I see."

"Zee Mama has taken care of me."

"Jes cuz you's Miz Summah's friend," Mama Dolly clarified.

"Humph! You love me, Mama…I know eet's true." Lila pursed her lips together and planted several kisses into the air.

"What now?" Summer interjected. "What about the captain? Where is he? What happened after the explosion?"

"Dem soldiers lookin' everywhere for dat man. Dey even come to Backtown, but he ain't heah. I know dat for sho. Where yo gris-gris, gal?" Mama Dolly asked, realizing that there was no place for the red flannel bag of good luck to hide on Summer's night-gowned body.

"Oh, no! It must be back at Mr. Fontaneau's!"

"Dat no good! Dat fo' good luck!"

"I'm sorry, but they had me so confused. Why did you let that man take me?"

"Chile, if da white man wanna take da white woman, da black woman ain't got noting' to say 'bout it. He come over and scoop you up and off you go."

"And where were you, Lila?"

"Mon ami, surely you do not theenk I can help. The man put me in zee prison!"

"Mr. Fontaneau says he isn't interested in you anymore."

"Wha'd he want den?" Mama Dolly asked.

"He wants Ruiz, and we have to make sure he doesn't get to him before we do."

* * *

Mama Dolly laid the crude, small black coffin on the front steps of Mr. Fontaneau's apartment. Before that moment, and back at the large woman's one-room shack, Summer and Lila had been privy to a spell put on the coffin which required much spouting of foreign words in a cacophony of fluctuating and erratic decibels. Mama Dolly rattled bones, threw chicken feet onto the table where the black coffin lay, rolled her eyes to the back of her head, sang strange verses, sprinkled mysterious powders over the black box until, finally, she plunked herself down onto her cot, sweating and breathing heavily.

"Mon Dieu! Zee curse will not come to us, weel eet?" Lila asked, her eyes huge in mortification.

"De curse is for dat Mistah Fontaneau. He gots da good luck gris-gris, and dat not good. Now he gots da bad curse, and dat curse bigger den da good luck gris-gris." Mama was clearly exhausted after her energetic fervor over the black coffin, but within minutes she was ready to deliver the box to its intended victim.

Before leaving the shack, the women were given a change of clothing. Lila reluctantly removed her yellow dress, with which she had gladly replaced the previous Wishing Spot attire, in exchange for the dowdy skirt that was yards too large at the waist, and therefore tied with a sash. The blouse, as well, was far too large and it was necessary to pin it at the neck with a frightening-looking pin representing a voodoo god. Lila was not happy, and nearly in tears from her frumpy new attire; especially when her signature curls were hidden beneath a stained tignon. "Theez eez zo ugly, Mama!" she cried.

"If dem soldiers sees yo' hair, dey will know it's us, and dat ain't gonna happen."

Summer changed into similar attire as well, only without complaint. In the dark, the women could pass as Negroes, as long as no one saw the colors of their skin.

* * *

`Satisfied that the black coffin had been properly cursed and delivered to Fontaneau's doorstep, Mama Dolly led her wards toward a road that appeared to Summer to head away from the Quarter.

"Where are we going?"

"We's goin' to see da captain."

"You know where he is?" Relief flooded through Summer's veins. She desperately wanted to see Ruiz, to make sure he was alright, and to scold him for his foolish act which had put them all in more danger than they were in already.

"Oh," Lila moaned. "What weel become of us? I love Le Vieux Carré and now I cannot live here weeth zee soldiers looking for you. You mess my life, Zummer!"

"What? I did not mess your life, Miss de Peau. You messed your own life with your disgusting career of prostitution and thievery!"

"Humph!"

"Hesh up," Mama Dolly ordered as they walked along a dark road, the city lights fading behind them. "White folks," she muttered, disgustedly.

Chapter 21

"How far do we have to go, Mama Dolly?" The women were totally exhausted as it seemed they had walked for hours and hours. The sky was dark when they began their journey, and now the sun headed for high noon.

"You wanna see yo' cap'n? Den hesh up and move along."

"Along", required following the woman through dense brush, sometimes along a dirt road, but often hiding in the vegetation if an approaching wagon were heard. They were so off the beaten path that not one fancy city carriage had passed. Still, at any unusual sound of traffic Mama Dolly had them camouflage themselves into the brush with who knew how many snakes and biting insects. Surely they were exposed to more critters than they cared to imagine.

"Why are you doing this for us?" Summer asked, as nothing had been asked of her in return for all that the woman had done for them.

"Cuz you gots da vision, gal," Mama said without looking back.

"*Qu'est-ce?* What vision? What does she zay?"

Summer ignored the question and plodded along behind Mama Dolly. The day was warm, and mosquitoes buzzed mercilessly about their heads and bodies drinking their blood, and causing Summer to wonder if they were being exposed to mosquito-transmitted diseases. Sweat rolled like rivers from faces and armpits, spreading damp blotches on the worn fabric of their blouses, creating an odiferous aura about the trio.

"Humph! Eet eez not fair you do not tell me what vision Mama speaks of," Lila huffed, cursing now and then at the mosquitos or sharp brambles of the roadside growth.

How could she answer? Mama Dolly and the Queen had recognized something in her; they knew she was not of this time. As for having vision, the only vision she wanted was Ruiz standing safely in front of her! Maybe he had a plan, but could they go anywhere safely? *Was* there anywhere to hide? At that moment a glittering through the trees caught her attention. *Water!* "Is that the river? Is this where we're headed?" she asked, hoping it was, as she was exhausted and Lila certainly had no qualms at disclosing her displeasure every few seconds.

"Dat da lake." Mama said. "Da big lake Ponchartrain."

"Won't the soldiers be looking for him here?"

"Dey might, but dey won' fin' him."

Summer smiled. *Sly captain.* He *was* sly; he was a criminal in the eyes of the Yankees; he blew up a ship and most likely killed the men onboard. He stole gold from Mr. Fontaneau. He was a rascal, a thief, a criminal, yes, but he was a patriot, and her heart thumped in anticipation of being in his arms again.

"If we can find him, why won't they?"

"Dey gon' be too scared, gal!"

* * *

Scared? Mama Dolly's statement didn't make sense until the brush and vegetation of their path led into what Summer could only describe as a Cypress swamp[66]. The trees grew tall, eerily draped in Spanish moss, some nearly reaching to the shallow waters that the women now gingerly tread. Through the cypress knees,[67] white egrets

---

[66] The Great Cypress Swamp of Lake Ponchartrain existed until heavy logging in the early 20th century destroyed the Cypress forest. It never regrew.

[67] Cypress Knees: Woody projections from the cypress trees

fished in abundance, quietly lifting their stick legs from the water, to step ever so silently forward so as not to disturb their prey. Birds called and flapped their wings at the trespassers, sometimes swooping in front of the three women as they wove through the swamp, ever watchful of snakes and alligators. It was not Summer's first journey into mystical swamplands, as she was so reminded of the fateful journey with Cherry and Buck, and her time with the Florida Seminole. But there were no Seminole here.

"Where do you take us, woman?" Lila's voice broke the natural quiet of the swamp. Birds shrieked, splashed and flew up through the trees. Croaking frogs stopped singing and the swamp went dead silent, aside from the relentless and hungry mosquitos that buzzed around their heads.

Mama Dolly stopped in her tracks, turned, put her hands on her ample hips and scrunched her brow. "Hesh up! I take you to da cap'n jes like I said!"

"And where eez zee capitaine? He eez in theez disgusting place? My shoes are full of zee mud!"

"It's okay, Lila. Calm down. We don't need an argument in the middle of a swamp with everything else that's happening. My shoes are full of mud too, if it's any consolation." Summer turned to Mama Dolly who looked as if she were ready to smack Lila's head off her shoulders. "Are we almost there?" she asked.

"Yes," Mama Dolly hissed, and after giving Lila a foreboding looked, turned and continued forward holding the front of her skirt out of the water.

Distant conversation wove through the swamp like a snake. When it reached their ears a hint of laughter and indiscernible words hushed and spiked in a raucous masculine melody. Summer stopped to stand still amidst the cypress knees and parent trees. She held the front of her skirt above the water to preserve whatever bit of dryness she could salvage. "Listen! Is it Ruiz?"

Mama Dolly continued to trudge ahead. "It is," she answered, her voice cracking through the forest like a whip. "Come on now, don' tarry. Dis ain't my kinda ting to do. I don' like lookin' for dem snakes."

---

that form roots which form from the bottom of the tree to stand above the water level of swampy waters. It is thought that the knees oxygenate the trees, but that hypothesis has not been scientifically proven.

*Splash....splash....*her large feet marched into the seemingly stalled, and seemingly endless, shallow waters of the forest.

"Mon Dieu, mon Dieu!" Lila moaned, trailing behind and constantly swearing in French beneath her breath. Occasionally she let out a long tirade in which Summer would swear she heard the names of Mr. Fontaneau, and that of Captain Ruiz.

At last, just when it appeared they would march through the swamp into eternity, the sun lightened their world as the number of trees diminished slowly until there were no trees to hold them; and the women stood on a lump of dry land overlooking the massive expanse of Lake Ponchartrain.

"Merci mon Dieu!" Lila released her skirt to rest her small hands on her narrow hips. "We are here...but where?"

It was then that Summer realized the voices and laughter of men had vanished completely. Had they walked this long journey for nothing? She turned to Mama Dolly who also stood perplexed at the lake's edge.

"We's heah!" Mama yelled, with no reply but that of the birds of the forest that squawked and flapped their wings as they navigated to a more secluded feeding ground. "Where is dat man?"

"Verano!"

As if conjured, Summer turned to see the captain step from the soggy path from which the women had just come. Behind him, were the two men Summer had witnessed the captain speaking with at Le Blue Mermaid.

"Ruiz! Do you realize how much trouble you're in? Every soldier in the city is searching for you." She ignored the two scraggily characters standing beside the captain; she did not like the way in which they scrutinized and leered behind the captain's back.

Albeit, the women presented quite a sight. Waters of the swamp stained their skirts thigh-high, topped with blouses filthy and damp with sweat. But, she supposed, women were women whatever the condition, and these characters were not gentlemen.

Mama Dolly wiped her brow. "Der you is. I'se brung da lady to you, now I go."

"Shouldn't you rest a bit first?" Summer asked, sincerely concerned as the woman surely had to be exhausted after such a journey.

Mama Dolly looked around. "Ain't no place to rest," she said, and disappeared back into the cypress.

The land was simply a narrow strip from which the Ponchartrain gently and occasionally lapped. The men had built a small fire pit which now was nothing but an ashen pile of charred bits of wood. Woolen blankets lay rumpled over low growing brush, presumably (and in vain) to dry in the damp and sultry air.

"You are in so much trouble, Ruiz! What will happen to us now?"

"Relax, my Verano," he said, folding his muscular arms around her waist, pulling her to him. "I have missed you," he whispered, resting a stubbly, bearded cheek against her own. "There is a plan, so do not be so concerned." Once released, she stepped back, folding her arms over her chest, partly from exasperation, and then partly due to the two men whose eyes drifted to rest upon her breasts.

"A plan," she echoed. "And just what is the plan?"

"Yez, tell us." Lila had been so quiet that Summer had forgotten her for a moment. "What eez zee plan?"

Ruiz turned to the French woman. "Why do you not go with Mama Dolly?"

"I...I worry, like Zummer. Eef you no like me to worry for you, then I weel not! Hmph!" She, too, crossed her arms over her chest in defiance.

Ruiz waved her away. "Go entertain my friends."

"Captain! Don't encourage her!"

Lila glanced at the two men and smiled. "Only if zay have zee Yankee dollar." She approached the men, every move integrated into her best sultry walk. "Have you zee money?"

"No tengo, Lila," the Spaniard, Alvarez, said.

Summer shot Lila a look of disapproval. *Does she know everyone?*

"Me either," said the other man, reaching into his pockets.

Lila sighed. "Zee? You have poor friends, my capitaine!"

Ruiz led Summer a distance away from the trio. "If I tell you everything, then you are part of it. Trust me, Verano, I will take care of you—-and her," he said, nodding toward Lila. "Now tell me about Fontaneau."

"I was under the impression that the gold belonged to Carlos. But Mr. Fontaneau says the gold is his, and he wants it bad, Ruiz."

"The gold is *mine.* I work for it. Carlos was a thief and tried to cheat us both, me and Fontaneau. I deliver cigars, Carlos doesn't pay."

Summer looked out at the Ponchartrain and thought for a few moments, computing the situation. The sun now beat down upon the group at the edge of the lake, pumping up the humidity. There was not a dry body present. "So, Fontaneau sends his cigars to Nassau in your boat, you deliver, and Carlos doesn't pay. You steal the gold from Carlos..." Summer wiped the sweat from her brow.

"It was mine to steal!"

"....and so Carlos chases us from Nassau to the Gulf of Mexico, the ships sink...everyone is dead except for Buck, Cherry and you—or so I think—and the gold is lost." She looked out at the Ponchartrain, again wiping the sweat from her brow and shading her eyes from the relentless sun. She wished for sunglasses, or at least a hat.

"Well," she said, looking back at Ruiz. "Buck and I retrieved the gold, so in truth, finders keepers. Seems to me the gold is ours, Buck's and mine. After all, we braved sharks to retriever it. What do you say to that?"

Ruiz appeared very surprised at her question. "You do not love me, Verano? You would take my gold?"

"What about Fontaneau? Seems to me if you do a job for someone, *you* get a cut of the money, and the owner of the cigars should have his due share coming to him. *That* is the honest way, Captain Ruiz."

"You betray me, Verano!" Ruiz walked a short way down the strip of dry land, putting distance between him and the others. He muttered in Spanish as he walked, his hands hooked together behind his back.

"What eez zee problem?" Lila asked, having appeared suddenly at Summer's side.

"It's personal, Lila."

"What concerns you, concerns me. We are together, you remember."

"Not in this instance." Lila was getting very nosey.

When finally Captain Ruiz returned to the damp and ragged group standing at the edge of the Cypress swamp, he pulled Summer aside.

"You are right, my love. Scoundrel that Fontaneau is, he does deserve to know what happened to the gold. But, what do I do? Do I tell him that you retrieved the gold? Do I take it from Buck and the baby to give to Fontaneau? Do I give him my share?"

A conundrum. She sighed. It was true. Could she honestly take gold from Buck, Buck who had risked life and limb to retrieve the gold? Could she deny Cherry's child a future? Could she deny the Captain his reward? "Oh!" She blurted, stamping a hot and muddy foot onto the only bit of dry land visible for miles. "I'm so tired of this! Why am I here?"

This is the past! She turned so she would not look into his eyes, as they had already registered alarm at her sudden outburst. The sun beat hot and heavy, cooking the air to nearly unbearable humidity as the sun rose higher in the sky.

"What is wrong with you, Verano? Do you not love me? Do you not wish to be with me?"

"Oh, Ruiz, I'm sorry. I...I guess I'm just hot and tired and wet to the bone. Forget what I said; I want you to do what feels right to you. I've never met Mr. Fontaneau before now. You know him personally; you know his character. Who am I to tell you how to handle your affairs?"

"Ah, my love. Now you use your head, and now I must ask you to do something for me."

"What?" she asked, a hint of suspicion in her voice.

"Go back to Fontaneau. Tell him that Ruiz says the gold was lost when the ships sink. It is true, no?"

"Go back?" She pointed to the cedar swamp. "Go back through there? Through the swamp? Ruiz, I have no clue how to get back and besides, I am not going alone."

"I send you with Otto." He nodded to the wide shouldered, muscular white man.

She shivered. "No! I will not go with him! Why, look how he looks at me. He must think I'm a whore, like Lila."

Ruiz must have sent a signal to the man behind Summer's back, as Otto suddenly cut his gaze from her and directed it to the far shore.

"He knows you are my woman and that I will cut his throat if he harms you."

* * *

Three hours later, Summer was grateful for the shade of the Cypress forest as she trudged again through the swamp waters, her skirt held high to prevent the water from seeping up to her waistline. Otto, broad shouldered and muscle-bound, walked ahead, a large pistol tucked into his waistband. It was a sight that reminded Summer of the old pirate movies she had watched growing up in an uneventful lifetime ago in her parent's home. Feeling quite puny and vulnerable in the company of this burly stranger, she tried hard to concentrate on the instructions Ruiz gave her to convey to Mr. Fontaneau. These instructions she had to remember in her head, as none of the motley crew on the shore of the Ponchartrain had a scrap of paper, never mind a writing utensil.

Otto did not so much as say a word to her the entire journey through the swamp. Once in a while he turned to make sure she was behind him, but other than that, they made their journey in silence with only the sounds of the swamp birds to keep them company.

When they arrived at a dirt road, Otto signaled her to stay hidden while he checked for signs of human life. Again, he signaled, this time for her to join him. "When I tell you to hide, you move fast," he ordered. She scampered to keep up with his wide strides.

"Oh, you have such a nice way of speaking," she said, snidely.

He stopped dead in his tracks. "Don't be smart with me. I'm a fighter, not a nanny to silly women."

"For your information, I am *not* a silly woman." She said this to his back, as he had continued the trek down the dirt road toward the city.

"How are we supposed to get to Mr. Fontaneau's without being seen?"

"Just follow me and shut up. I ain't supposed to talk to you."

"And a good thing, since you're not a very nice person."

Otto stopped again to lean into her face. "You're good for one thing, woman, and that's fuc….

"Stop it!" Summer cut him off. "Okay, I'll shut up. Just get me to Fontaneau's and the sooner the better."

Chapter 22

"Stop!" Otto broke her stride with an extended arm. The alleyway between the townhouses was darkly shaded from the sun which now had sunk so low as to disappear behind the townhouses across the narrow street from Mr. Fontaneau's. She leaned against the coolness of brick, exhausted from the long journey.

"What is it?" she asked, forgetting the "no talking" rule. The journey from Ruiz to Fontaneau's lavish town had taken several grueling hours, darting into bushes and trees when a carriage approached on the dusty road from the lake. But here they were, sandwiched between two buildings, hidden from the many carriages that clip-clopped along the fashionable street.

They shrank into the dark alley when pedestrians passed, which was far more often than desired. Summer looked longingly at the lovely hooped skirts that swayed from scrupulously groomed women whose laughter tinkled into the darkness of their hideaway. She was filthy, smelly and tired beyond comprehension. Still, she had a message to deliver.

"Soldiers leaving," Otto whispered. "They come from Fontaneau's". Putting his large hands on her shoulders, he turned her around, nudging her down the alley to the back of the townhouse. "We go in this way."

Wearily, she followed him up the few steps to a backdoor, which he pushed open with more force than necessary. From behind his massive frame, she heard a startled shriek, and then Dancie's voice.

"Mr. Fontaneau!" Der's a stranger heah!"

Summer quickly peeked her head around Otto. "It's okay, Dancie. It's me, Summer."

Dancie stared at her a few seconds before relaxing her weapon, a broom held over her shoulder ready to attack. "Dat really you, Miz Summah?"

"It's really me; it's okay."

"Where you been? Mistah Fontaneau, he madder n' da devil on Sundays when you dis'pear."

"Well, I'm back and I have a message for Mr…."

At that moment, Mr. Fontaneau burst through a doorway holding a pistol, cocked and ready to fire.

"Hold it!" Summer shrieked. "It's me!"

Mr. Fontaneau stopped in his tracks, but kept his pistol pointed at Otto.

"I've returned the woman," Otto said bluntly. "Captain Ruiz's orders."

In comparison to the filthy duo, Mr. Fontaneau was again dressed in his dandy attire of smoking jacket and trousers, which made apparent the horrid condition of the travelers now standing in his kitchen.

"So I see," Fontaneau said, keeping the pistol aimed at Otto. "You sit there." He nodded, pointing the pistol to one of the two chairs at a table. Otto obliged.

"And you, Miss Woodfield. Dancie, take her upstairs and clean her up."

"We need to talk," she said, as Dancie led her by an arm through the doorway.

"We will talk when you look presentable," Fontaneau answered.

Summer had no alternative but to follow Dancie up the grand stairway to the room she had occupied beforehand.

"You stay heah, Miz Summah. I'se gonna fetch you a hot bath."

It was a heavenly idea, though she did wonder what was transpiring downstairs. Otto was certainly not a conversationalist, nor likely to give out any pertinent information. But, she was much too tired to worry about it and lay on the bed, so glad for this wonderful comfort. It did not take long for sleep to overtake her.

* * *

"Ah, lovely. Turn around. Let me appreciate the entire vision." Mr. Fontaneau twirled his index finger and Summer followed suit. The corset was tight, of course, and pushed her breasts into fleshy swells above the yoke of the blouse, which also confined her chest into a tightly immoveable space. *No wonder women were subservient in those days! Who could breathe in this outfit?*

"Aside from your hair, which we agree is missing, you are quite the attractive young woman!"

"Thank you," she said. "But I would feel a lot better if I could breathe." Just the thought of less oxygen caused an involuntary gasp for the umpteenth time. The corset and tightly buttoned blouse stopped an inhale very short of satisfaction. "I may faint, you know, just so you're aware when I keel over into the soup bowl," she said.

"Oh, Miss Woodfield," Mr. Fontaneau said, throwing back his head to expel an exaggerated laugh, "you are greatly amusing." He then held out his arm to escort her to dinner.

Shock did not quite describe her reaction to the two Yankee officers sitting at the elaborate dining table in Mr. Fontaneau's dining room; she was stunned! One was none other than Captain McAllister who had imprisoned her and Lila in the Cabildo!

The men stood. "Good evening, Miss Woodfield, so nice to see you again." The captain gave a slight bow as she passed on the arm of Mr. Fontaneau, who delivered her to a chair next to his own seat at the head of the table, placing her directly across from the two officers.

"Hello Captain McAllister," she said, struggling to keep calm under the façade of her smile. "And so good to see you again—under different circumstances, of course."

Once seated, and to avoid looking directly at the officers, she scanned the table while the men took their seats.

What next? Whatever it was, would surely put Ruiz in even more danger.

"May I introduce First Lieutenant Briggs," the captain said, at which time, Lieutenant Briggs raised briefly again from his seat with a slight nod of his head.

With introductions complete, a moment of embarrassing silence passed in which Summer felt totally scrutinized. She busied herself taking a sip of water from a goblet, only to discover it was wine. After a few more sips, she felt fortified to break the silence and face the situation head on.

"I assume you gentlemen are here because of the dreadful event at the harbor?"

"You assume correctly, but have you dismissed the fact that you and Miss de Peau willingly escaped from your jail cell at the Cabildo?" the captain said.

"Might I remind you that I, at least, was incarcerated for no other reason aside from the fact that I know Captain Ruiz? Is that a crime?"

"And might I remind you, Miss Woodfield, that you also aided two known and incarcerated prisoners in escaping Fort Jerfferson?"

"And do you….."

"Wait, wait, wait!" Fontaneau cut in. "Let's get to the point. Miss Woodfield," he said, turning to face her. "We know that you are in cahoots with Captain Ruiz, a dangerous blockade runner, pirate and thief," he added, anger welling in his voice. "We are here to make a deal with you; if you lead us to Ruiz, you will gain your freedom, free and clear."

"And if I don't?"

"Then you will remain here with me, in my home, until you do."

Or until I vanish…. "You have not given me a chance to speak to you in private," she said, her voice lowered but not escaping the ears of the officers. She did not miss the look that passed between them.

Mr. Fontaneau cleared his throat and rang a small brass bell that rested on the table next to his place setting. Dancie appeared within seconds, dressed in what Summer assumed was her "company" attire; a deep blue skirt fronted with a crisp white apron tied neatly into a bow at the back; a muslin blouse tucked into the skirt, with sleeves that billowed slightly and buttoned at the wrist. She carried her matching blue tignon topped head proudly as she scurried to and from the kitchen bringing dishes of sumptuous local fare: a jambalaya of Andouille sausage, shrimp, meats and vegetables which smothered a bed of rice; warm bread, oysters, and crayfish also accompanied the meal, and to finish, fresh beignets, served hot from the kitchen, along with chicory coffee.

At the end of the meal, through which Summer remained silent as the men spoke of all but the current predicament, apparently avoiding the subject under Mt. Fontaneau's sudden change in demeanor, he whispered in her ear as the officers rose to take their brandy in the library. "We will speak later," he said, a hand on her shoulder, his warm breath raising the hairs of her neck. As he slid the large pocket doors between the dining room and the library shut, he eyed Summer who remained seated at the table. "Later," he mouthed before shutting her from view.

She wasted no time in tiptoeing to the closed doors to set her ear against the beveled dark wood. All was silent aside from the tinkling of glasses.

"What's you doin'? Dancie asked, none too quietly. She had slipped into the dining room unnoticed.

Summer put a finger to her lips. "Shh!"

Dancie shook her head. "White folks," she said, lifting dishes from the table. "Never know what dem white folks are gonna do or why dey's doin' it in the firs' place." She gave Summer a scolding look and exited the dining room to deliver her load to the kitchen for cleaning.

Free of Dancie's accusing eye for the time being, Summer pressed her ear harder against the door.

"...will get the information from her," Mr. Fontaneau said.

"We have every right to take that woman into custody," Lieutenant Briggs objected.

"We do, Fontaneau," the captain agreed.

"And did I not give you gentlemen a fine offer for this bit of time? Ruiz hand delivered?"

Silence.

"All I ask is for a fraction of time. Ruiz owes me a fortune and I plan on retrieving it. You will have your reward, and now I demand mine."

"This is highly irregular and would not sit well with the general were it discovered. Several good men are dead because of Ruiz, and we will have him; he will pay for his crimes, and we need that woman to lead us to him."

"I want what is mine, gentlemen, and that is all. I could care less of your generals. As for your good and dead men, we have good men dead at your hands as well, so do not think I have the smallest amount of pity for your losses."

"Very well, Fontaneau," Captain said. "Seventy-two hours. That's what you have. After that, with no results, we will be here to take Miss Woodfield into custody."

"That is good, my friends."

Summer leapt away from the door as the sounds coming from the library now indicated that the clandestine meeting was breaking up. She hurriedly turned, only to run into Dancie who stood with arms on hips.

"You's a nosey gal, ain't ya?" Dancie whispered." I don' know wha'd all dis hesh hesh bizness is, but you best be getting' outta dis room if you don' want Mistah Fontaneau to knows yo's creepin' 'round listenin' to his private conversations."

With those words, Summer departed the dining room, the front of her hooped red statin skirt held high as she raced up the staircase to her room. Out of breath at the top landing, the large meal, the stress of the situation, and her compressed lungs caught up with her. The last she remembered was an empty, useless gasp for air before she collapsed to the floor.

* * *

Someone tapped her cheek. It was Ruiz, and he was safe! A peaceful warmth overcame her, and she basked in the realization that all was well again. But then, the continuous tapping of her cheek became annoying. She waved his hand away. "Stop it, Ruiz, I want to sleep," she murmured, but the tapping continued, pulling her from the safety and warmth of that wonderful place until she was forced to open her eyes to scold him, to make him stop the annoying tapping.

Grave disappointment confronted her as Mr. Fontaneau came into focus. He was sitting on the edge of her bed and tapped her cheek one more time. "There you are. You fainted dead away. The corset was apparently pulled too tightly in the first place. It seems to me that you should be quite accustomed to the apparatus, but it's just another mystery surrounding Miss Summer Woodfield—why she doesn't quite fit into our way of life— but you sound like a Northerner and that could explain it."

"Huh?" she muttered, slowly becoming alert. It was all still fuzzy. "Oh yes, the corset. How can anyone wear those things? Surely a man invented it." She sat up, with the help of a slight pull from Mr.

Fontaneau. It was then she noticed her bodice was missing, as well as the corset, and, to her shock, the black coffin sat at the foot of her bed!

"What is that?" she asked, playing dumb.

"I think you know very well what that is, considering you are an acquaintance of Mama Dolly." Summer's camisole hung low upon her chest—just low enough to barely hide her nipples—and Mr. Fontaneau did not ignore an opportunity to run a finger over the slight mounds of her released breasts.

"Stop that!" she said, slapping his hand away.

Fontaneau's pleasant expression turned suddenly dark and frightening. "Do not think that a voodoo-spelled coffin will keep me from catching Ruiz." He stood, leaning over the bed until his face was a breath away. "Keep your friend's spells away from me, or perhaps she will find the tables reversed."

He stood straight, abruptly stepping away from the bed as Dancie entered the room with a small glass containing an amber liquid.

"Drink up, Miss Woodfield and join me downstairs in the library for our little chat." He left the room, with Dancie waiting to serve the amber liquid to her patient.

Summer swung her legs over the side of the bed and reached for the glass. "What in the world happened, Dancie?"

"Yo' fall to da groun'. I heard dat thump thump and sees you lyin' up der in a heap o' red satin."

"I couldn't breathe, that's why. Those corsets should be outlawed!"

"Well I don' know nuttin' 'bout dat 'cept I'se happy only you white womens gots to wear dem tings."

Summer held the glass to her lips. *Wine? Brandy?* She swallowed it in one gulp and coughed. "What *was* that?"

"Jus' a little laud'num for da nerves."

"Good grief, he's doping me," she said, but when the laudanum hit her belly, the warmth she had felt while in her dream state, that wonderful peaceful place, returned.

When she was able, she stood and Dancie dressed her again in the red satin blouse only this time, not tying the corset as tightly as before. Glowing inside from the laudanum, she traveled the stairway, ready to make a deal with Mr. Fontaneau.

Chapter 23

"So," Mr. Fontaneau said, one arm resting on the marble mantle over the library fireplace. Beside him, a gold leaf edged rose painted clock ticked away the minutes as Summer sat straight in the velvet chair, watching the man as he absorbed Ruiz's offer. "Let me get this straight; Ruiz wants a ship delivered to him at his place of hiding?"

"Not exactly his place of hiding; he has a particular spot in mind."

"And where is this?"

"The point at Black Bay."

"What?" Fontaneau's eyes grew wide. "Ruiz is crazy, a fact that I have always known, of course. Why else would a gentleman from a good family become such a criminal?"

Summer's eyes narrowed. This dandy character was speaking of her lover, her man in this century! "I beg your pardon, but Ruiz is not a…a criminal. He is simply defending his country. I would think you'd be doing the same instead of sitting on the fence as you are. You didn't mind his line of work when you sent your cigars off with him."

"I do not need to explain myself to you, Miss Woodfield. Now, just why should I deliver a ship to Ruiz? I can't think of one good reason, unless he has my gold and is willing to give it up."

"No, he does not have your gold, but he has a very good offer."

"I doubt that, but go ahead. What is it?"

"His plantation."

Mr. Fontaneau went silent, scrunching his immaculately plucked eyebrows together in thought. "Did I hear you right? Ruiz is willing to give up La Bella Vista for a ship?"

"For a ship, and thirty gold eagle coins."

"Gold coins? Why he already has my gold coins! The man has lost his mind!"

"He says that the plantation is worth much more than a ship and thirty gold eagles. I am just the messenger, remember?"

"And what about his mother and daughter? What of their futures without the land?"

"He knows he can't return, and if he can't, his family cannot remain without a man to run the plantation. This is what he tells me; he is finished here."

Fontaneau moved to his massive desk, obviously deep in thought. The library was so silent that the ticking mantle clock was the only sound heard.

"Does he have a deed?" Fontaneau asked.

"He says you are to draw up the legal papers and he will sign when you bring him a ship. He also says you are a crook, not to be trusted, and that you must not bring Yankee soldiers of any rank with you."

"Ha! The pot is calling the kettle black!"

"Are you agreeable to this?"

"I never jump into a deal without thought. I will let you know," he said, excusing her.

She rose, her red satin slippers gliding across the Persian rug to the heavy door where she stopped and turned. "What has happened to Otto?"

"He will be available when I send for him."

"But where is he?"

"Miss Woodfield, you are far too inquisitive. It is not your concern where that barbarian is. Instead, why don't you concentrate on the little ball I'm holding this Saturday night?"

Ball? I haven't heard of any ball.

"Could you tell me what day it is today?" She hated to ask, but it was entirely necessary.

"Thursday."

"Thursday? I can't stay here for a ball on Saturday night!" she blurted. "What about Ruiz? What about his offer? The soldiers gave you seventy-two hours."

"To add to all your other attributes, I suppose we can add "eavesdropper" to the list?"

Oops.

It does not concern you now, anyway."

"I object, Mr. Fontaneau! This most certainly does concern me. Am I your prisoner?"

"Of course! Do you think I would let you go? The Federals are watching me, just as they are you. I told them I would turn Ruiz over to them, but now you have presented me with an offer, an attractive offer. I need time to think on this matter. Let's just say you are my collateral."

* * *

"Collateral!" Summer stared at herself in the dressing table mirror. "Oh Ruiz, I can't get to you; you'll wonder what's happened to me!" Of course her reflection did not have an answer to this predicament, but, then, an idea came to her. *Mama Dolly*, of course! Why hadn't she thought of it before?

She opened the French doors that looked out onto the street. The night was humid, but not too hot; damp not too chilly. A breeze fluttered her nightgown about her bare feet. She closed her eyes letting the breeze ruffle her cropped hair, and concentrated. *Mama Dolly... Mama Dolly... please hear me...please come to me....* She looked below at the passers-by. The street was always active, day and night, but no Mama Dolly. She waited, repeated the chant again and again, but still, Mama Dolly did not appear.

After a while she gave up the chant, closed the window and returned to her room. Climbing into the four-poster canopied bed, so elegantly draped in fine fabric, she pulled the eyelet coverlet up to her chin and drifted off to sleep.

She could not be sure of how long she slept, but something woke her. It was not the crickets, nor the howling cats, and not the fog horn that moaned in the distance. As her mind focused from fuzzy thought to sharp clarity, she flung the covers off, ran to the balcony door and opened it with such force she was afraid Fontaneau may have heard it slam against a bureau. "Mama Dolly, you're here!"

A gaslight cast a yellow glow about the woman as she stood on the street below. "I'se here, chile," she said, or rather transported the thought in her uncanny non-speaking way.

"Oh, thank God, Mama Dolly! I can't leave here. You *must* get a message to Captain Ruiz. Tell him I think Fontaneau will accept the deal, but he's holding me here as collateral. Tell him I'm okay, I'm fine; there is no need to worry about me. Fontaneau will send Otto with instructions. Please tell him this!"

Mama Dolly nodded and walked toward the corner of Bourbon. After she vanished, relief flooded Summer. She could relax, at least for the time being. The thought of Ruiz coming into the city to search for her was terrifying; there were too many soldiers, and he was too wanted a man.

Now that the immediate danger had passed, she became curious about the "ball" Mr. Fontaneau had spoken of. Friday passed without any sign of him. She could not inquire of him the status of the offer, and she wondered if he was working on the papers of transfer.

* * *

The gown was beyond her imagination. It lay across the coverlet of the magnificent four-poster, fluffed as cotton candy, looking as a cloud that had lost its way in a summer sky to settle upon this very spot. Its yards of white gathered tulle flounced over rose colored satin. Here and there deeper hued ribbons peeked from crevices of fluff in the form of dainty bows, kissed by tiny rosette blossoms of silk.

"Ouch! Watch it, Dancie!" Summer tried to pull away from the woman but was caught as a fish on a hook by the laces of the corset. "I can't breathe if you pull any tighter!"

"How's you gonna look in dat pretty gown if you don' gots da nice silhouette?"

"Honestly? I don't care. I'd rather breathe."

Dancie begrudgingly let Summer have her way and left the extra inch of breathing space but, still, it was impossible to fully fill her lungs.

"Oh, dis hair!" Dancie moaned. With the corset ordeal out of the way, Summer now sat at the dressing table, the satin bodice securely buttoned. Small puffed sleeves perched alluringly off the shoulder, enhancing her breasts, which appeared smooth as the satin itself in the glow of the many candles set upon the dressing table and spread throughout the room.

"Wha'd we gonna do wid no hair?" Dancie stood reflected in the mirror, the hairbrush paused midair.

Summer smiled with amusement at the bewildering look on the woman's face. "Where I come from, it isn't necessary that we have so much hair."

"Where dat?"

"Chi…Georgia."

"I never heard of no Georgia ladies wid no hair, but if dat's da truth, den I wants to be in Georgia where I don' gots to be messin' wid no white lady's hair."

"Maybe we could pin some ribbons or flowers in my hair to make it look nice?"

"Fo' sho, Miz Summah."

"Why does Mr. Fontaneau have so many women's clothes here? Is he married? Does he have daughters?"

Dancie laughed. "Oh, Lawdy, no! He jes like haven' dem fancy women come to da parties. Dey stay, sometime. Mr. Fontaneau have big parties wid lots o'men and ladies and sometime dey all stay da night." She leaned close to Summer's ear. "An dey ain't married, neither!"

"Oh, my!" Summer feigned surprise. "Well, I hope Mr. Fontaneau doesn't think I'm *that* kind of woman!"

"No…no he don'. He jes want you here so's he can ketch dat rascal Cap'n Ruiz."

"Do you know Captain Ruiz?"

"Why, ever'body know da cap'n, but Mistah Fontanea ain't never gonna ketch him."

Let's hope that's true…

* * *

Hours of preparation passed at a snail's pace before Summer stood at the top of Fontaneau's grand stairway, a stairway not nearly so grand as Magnolia plantation. She stood, a white and pink cloud totally ensconced in the layers of satin and tulle that once lay atop the four-poster bed in her quarters. Another attempt at a full breath failed as she prepared to descend into the throng of strangers below. Voices rose to her ears in a great cacophony of part -going; tinkling laughter, hearty guffaws and a general indecipherable commotion of people at play. The musicians played their fare over it all, a fact that Summer wasn't aware of until she nearly reached the bottom stair where the tones of strings in rhythm occasionally overshadowed the noisy crowd.

"You look lovely, my dear, "Fontaneau said, having waited at the landing. She hooked her arm through his extended one and they made a grand entrance together into a room she had not been privy to beforehand. It was not huge, as the townhouses in the quarter were not built for grand ballrooms. Furniture had been moved against the walls and chairs added from other rooms to accommodate the 30 or so guests. Still, each piece of furniture was ornately made and spoke of opulence.

"There are a lot of Yankee soldiers here," she observed. Mr. Fontaneau, it seemed, was quite the turncoat, and she wondered what his cronies and neighbors thought of his evening affairs with the enemy.

"And, we will not say a word of Ruiz's offer, now will we?"

"Why would I?" Her spirits raised at his comment. *He's going to make the deal and Ruiz will be free!* "As much as you have been charmed by the Yankees, I have done quite the opposite."

Fontaneau smiled falsely at a passing couple. "We won't speak of this here," he said through gritted teeth.

Captain McAllister nodded to her from across the room. "I see the gang's all here," she said, nodding back at the captain.

"A necessary evil, you might say. The way I see it, the war is lost and I always plan to end up on the winning side. Shall we dance?"

Without waiting for a reply, Mr. Fontaneau took her into his arms and gracefully swirled her around the dance floor. He was an adept dancer, no doubt due to his station in life. Having never needed to perform the waltz in her other, and real, life. Summer tried desperately to not look the klutzy fool. *One, two, three...one, two, three...*it reminded her so of the night with Cherry, Buck, Ruiz in Nassau, when she waltzed with strangers while Ruiz argued with Carlos[68]. It was so sad to think that Cherry was gone, and so miserably....

"Where are you, my dear? You seem to have let your mind wander."

Where am I, indeed? While she, ensconced in a cloud of tulle and satin, danced the night away, her beloved captain hung to freedom by the sheer thread of her ability to strike a deal with Mr. Fontaneau. "So sorry," she replied. "I think I need to sit and have a drink if you don't mind."

[68] This event occurred in Book II

"Quite all right," he said, leading her to a lace covered table upon which was displayed the punch, liquor and petit fours. Dipping a cup of punch, he then guided her to one of the chairs which had been set against the wall.

"On second thought, if you don't mind, I think I'll catch some air on the balcony. The corset you insist I wear, interferes greatly with breathing," she said, taking the crystal punch cup from his hand.

"I will join you in a moment."

"Don't trust me, huh?"

"Should I?"

"I don't plan on jeopardizing Captain Ruiz's safety by being fool enough to run off into the night in this outfit. I would not get very far considering I can barely breath, and we are a floor above the street. Yes, you can trust me." Even that short retort was enough to strain her oxygen starved lungs against the restrictive stays of the corset. Dancie's extra inch was not sufficient enough. Not one morsel of food would pass between her lips this night, having learned her lesson; it was nearly impossible to eat with her lungs restricted in such a way.

On the balcony, the air was sultry and not at all satisfying, but a reprieve from her dance floor display was welcomed. She leaned against the wrought iron railing looking back into the temporary ballroom. The music and laughter wafted onto the street below, which itself was very active with carriages, vendors and pedestrians.

In the ballroom, the men outnumbered the women; but it appeared to Summer that the women were quite adept at spending time with each one of the suited gentlemen. They flirted, coyly maneuvering their fans in that secret language of flirtation and communication. Their hooped skirts glided gracefully with each step, and she surmised much more gracefully than she had appeared in the arms of Mr. Fontaneau. As the room was not extremely large, the hoops bounced gently against one another on occasion, creating a symphony of colors moving in time to the sweet sound of the strings. Summer was mesmerized and nearly missed the sound of her name being called.

"Verano! Verano!"

On the realization that she was being summoned—and by none other than the captain himself—she was frantic that Fontaneau would return at this most inopportune moment.

"What are you doing here?" she whispered to the sidewalk, not having focused in on the captain himself. "Fontaneau will be here any moment!"

"You are looking lovely, my love!"

"Where are you?" She moved from one end of the balcony to the other, scouring the walk below but could not see her lover.

"I am above you," he replied.

She crooked her neck but as there was another floor above and the night was dark, she could not catch sight of him. "I don't see you!"

"It is better this way."

"Why are you here? Did Mama Dolly give you the message?"

"Yes, yes, of course, but I am impatient, not only for Fontaneau's reply, but to have you in my arms again, my love!"

"What are you doing, my dear?" Fontaneau asked, looking upward as he entered the balcony with a drink in his hand. "What do you see?"

Summer's heart skipped a beat. "Oh! I—I was looking at the stars, of course!"

Fontaneau squinted, staring up at the night sky. "Yes, they are lovely, but not as lovely as you. Already my friends are asking "Who is the lovely woman in the red gown"?"

"And how, pray tell, do you answer that question?"

"I tell them you are my cousin, but there are several who have asked for your company tonight."

"My co…I do hope, Mr. Fontaneau, that you realize I am not one of your…your…*cousins* of the night, here for delight."

Mr. Fontaneau laughed. "Of course! There is only one purpose for…what was that?"

A small stone had bounced off of Fontaneau's head, sounding a "ding" on the wrought iron balcony, and fell to the street below. He rubbed his head while looking upward toward the roofline. A cat meowed loudly overhead, and Summer let out a sigh of relief. "Silly cat. Are you alright? Perhaps we should return to your party." She quickly hooked her arm into his and led him back into his makeshift ballroom.

Within moments Captain McAllister was at her side. "Would you care to dance, Miss Woodfield?"

"Please be aware that I am not the best dancer in the room, Captain," she said, hoping to discourage him.

"Neither am I, Miss Woodfield, so we will be equally paired."

Having no recourse, Summer accepted his invitation.

"You are a mystery, Miss Woodfield. We have searched and searched but find no record of you anywhere," the captain said as they circled the room. The captain was correct in that he was not the best dancer, and for once, Summer thought she had one up on him.

"Perhaps you have not looked in the right place," she answered.

"And where might that be?"

"Captain, I can assure you I exist. What does it matter anyway? It's not me you're looking for."

"Mr. Fontaneau has assured us that Ruiz will be looking for *you*, and therefore, you are of great interest to us."

"Isn't Mr. Fontaneau's time up tonight? The seventy-two hours?"

"We have extended it one more night. He feels certain Captain Ruiz will be captured."

"Perhaps you put too much faith in Mr. Fontaneau."

"Time will tell. Until then, consider yourself under arrest."

* * *

The party seemed endless. Summer excused herself after a few more dances, some with the male guests who found her attractive, and returned to her quarters.

"You wasn't down der too long, Miz Summah," Dancie said as she helped Summer remove the tedious layers of clothing.

"It was long enough to nearly pass out from lack of oxygen. Besides, the men are quite busy and enchanted with the other ladies. I don't think they'll miss me much."

At last, free of the corset and wearing her nightgown, Summer stepped onto her balcony. The musicians still played, and light from the ballroom below shone yellow through the opened doors. Summer glanced overhead wondering if the captain was still there, but at least an hour had passed since his secret and abrupt visit. She snickered at the stone that surely he had directed at Mr. Fontaneau. Of course he was gone by now. She sighed. She never knew when she would be ripped from this time and place, but she hoped it was not until her captain was safe and on his way to meet his family on Buck Key.

Chapter 24

Sunday dawned hot and unbearably humid. "Does it ever cool off here?" Summer asked, fanning herself with a napkin at the breakfast table the morning after the ball. She noted that Mr. Fontaneau's eyes were a bit bloodshot. She had also been informed by Dancie that a few of the guests had spent the night; but, as yet, it was only she and Fontaneau at the table.

"I can't imagine it being any hotter here than in Georgia, where you say you're from." He took a sip of coffee and set the cup down next to a folder. "I have the papers here for Ruiz, the *blackguard*."

Summer's heart jumped for joy, but she stilled her voice to not give way to her excitement. "Then you agree to the terms?"

"I do, but be forewarned, if you breathe a word of this to anyone, it may be your last breath."

"Mr. Fontaneau, I do not like to hear you threaten me! I've told you that I have no interest in conveying anything to the Yankees. My only concern is that Captain Ruiz leaves this place safely. May I see the papers, please?"

"What? Why should you see the papers? What do you know of legal matters?"

"Plenty," she said, looking him square in the eye. "If you only knew."

"Aha, secrets! Everything is a secret about you. Captain McAllister has not found any information whatsoever of your origin, or existence other than Fort Jefferson, for that matter."

"And it is of no matter. Let me see the papers."

"In the library, please. I do not wish my guests to be party to this transaction."

I'll bet.

Fontaneau raised from his chair, indicating for her to do the same. On the way to the library, they encountered the first of the guests, two young women dressed in silk robes giggling their way down the stairs.

"Good morning, ladies. I do hope you treated my guests accordingly?"

The women laughed, which, Summer assumed, meant that they had indeed taken care of the gentlemen.

In the library, she took a seat across from Mr. Fontaneau, who sat at his desk looking slightly bedraggled in his smoking jacket.

Tough night? she wanted to ask, but refrained. She wondered if he had partaken in any pleasures with the young women. She pushed that thought from her mind and thumbed her way through the papers he had handed her, concentrating especially on the transfer of the deed.

"What about the signature of a witness? I would prefer it to not be one of your cronies…and, a notary. Do you have notaries in these days?"

"*In these days*? Why Miss Woodfield, do you think we are in the time of the pagans? Where the devil is it you are from?"

Wouldn't you like to know. She gave him a secretive smile. "Let's just say I am not a Southern belle with no knowledge of legalities."

"Obviously, and, yes, we will have a notary, to answer your question. It will all be proper and legal."

"How do you plan to explain this to the Yankees, if I might ask?"

"I can be a patient man. One day, the war will be over, the Federals will retreat and we will have our city and country to ourselves again. Then, at that time, I will publicly take over La Bella Vista."

"When will *this* transaction take place?" she asked, waving the papers.

"Three nights from now. Wednesday, to be exact, and close to midnight. There will be no moon as we will need the cover of darkness. After all, I must get a ship past the lookout points without suspicion."

"Has Captain Ruiz been notified? He will need to reach Black Bay."

"Do not worry your pretty head, Miss Woodfield. All will be arranged accordingly."

"And what about me? I would like to be turned over to the captain as well."

"Of course. You will accompany us."

"No soldiers."

"No soldiers, I assure you."

"Do *not* double cross us, Mr. Fontaneau."

"Of course not!" he replied, but Summer did not trust him.

* * *

Now, what is this about? She could barely believe her ears. She had come to the kitchen looking for Dancie, when she heard Mr. Fontaneau speaking in a low voice. Having stopped just before the kitchen entrance, she leaned against the wall hoping to conceal herself, only to have her hooped skirt jut out into the hallway from the pressure of the wall. Silently cursing the hoops, she took a step forward, thus setting the hoop straight. This move allowed her look into the kitchen but also put her in full view with the possibility of being caught eavesdropping. Mr. Fontaneau stood at the back door speaking with someone.

"…are you sure that is the spot?"

"I am not stupeed, Antoine. Am I not a child of Le Veiux Carré? Do I not know zee places?"

Lila? Is that Lila?

"He has the two other men with him, Otto and the Spaniard"

"That eez right."

"Good job, Lila."

"Zo? I do not do theez for notheeng, you know."

"You're a greedy little slut."

"Yankee note only."

"I know," he said, apparently shuffling some paper money. "Here. Now get back there before Ruiz gets any ideas."

Summer hurriedly turned and ran back to the stairway just as Fontaneau appeared from the kitchen.

"Oh!" she said, standing on the bottom stair, acting surprised. "I'm looking for Dancie, have you seen her?"

"She's gone to market. Do you need something, Miss Woodfield?"

Yes, I need to get to Ruiz, you double-crossing turncoat. "No, she said. It's nothing."

Upstairs, she paced the room, racking her brain, trying to make sense of Lila's appearance. *Turncoats everywhere! Oh my God, Ruiz!* Obviously, he was in grave danger. Lila must have revealed his hiding place. Panic seized her; she had to get to him, but how, she didn't know, as the way to his hiding spot was a blur in her memory. She went to the balcony, closed her eyes, and summoned Mama Dolly. *Mama, I need you. Please come, quickly! Ruiz is in danger!*

Minutes passed like hours, until an hour actually did pass. Still, no Mama Dolly. Summer was frantic; she had to escape and reach Ruiz to warn him of the double cross. Her own clothes, filthy blouse and skirt compliments of Mama Dolly, were long gone. She filed through the ladies clothes in the small dressing room attached to her bedroom. *You sure like 'em fancy, Fontaneau,* she thought, as most of the dresses were low cut and obviously meant to seduce: purple, red, green, blue taffetas and satins, nothing appropriate for trudging through a cypress swamp. The dress she now wore was, as the others, much too fancy to make a trip such as the one she had ahead of her. Alas, as she rifled through the dresses she came across a day dress: brown, plain, buttoned to the neck, the long pagoda sleeves hanging limp at its sides. *Who in the world wore this?* Certainly not one of Mr. Fontaneau's pleasure girls. It looked insufferably hot to be worn in the current weather, but she had not yet come across a dress that was not insufferably hot, having no reprieve from the heat with the blessing of air conditioning.

She hoped it would fit; and it did, hanging slightly loose at the shoulders and waist. At least she could breathe, having left the tight corset on the dressing room floor. The skirt was too long without the hoop, but a hoop would do nothing but hinder her travel through the swamp…*the swamp! Mama Dolly!* She rushed to the balcony hoping that

Mama Dolly had heard her plea, but she was not there. *Mama Dolly, I need you!*

It was hopeless. She would have to find Ruiz alone...*through the swamp alone*...it was not an appealing thought. First, though, she had to get out of the house without notice. Hoping Dancie was still at market, she found the servant stairway, slowly opening the door to avoid its creaking. She recalled the first time she had traversed a slave stairway at Magnolia Plantation. It was old hat now, and her feet deftly led her to the bottom floor without benefit of candle or lantern. Opening the door slightly, she realized she was in the kitchen. Dancie was not present, so she tiptoed to the back door, only to find it locked! *Damn Fontaneau!* Soon the sun would be down, and the last thing she wanted to do was to travel through the swamp in the dark!

The house was quiet. She stood still as a statue listening for any sound of her captor, but there was none, only the sound of her breath and the clip-clop of horses from the street. Treading carefully and holding the long skirt up so as not to trip, she left the kitchen and made her way to the foyer, but the front door was locked as well. *Double damn you, Fontaneau*! There had been no reason to attempt escape beforehand, and she had not considered that the doors were locked. But now, now it was a matter of life and death!

The windows! Oh, but she would look suspiciously silly climbing out a front window, even if it were possible, which it was not. Near to tears, she stood in the foyer looking toward all possible avenues of escape; the front door, down the hallway to the kitchen, the windows...but there were only a few, and none accessible without bringing attention to her escape.

As the first tear rolled down her cheek, she heard it—Mama Dolly's voice.

"Cut dat out, Chile. I'se here wid you."

"Where?" she asked aloud and then clasped a hand over her mouth. *Did he hear me? Is he even in this house somewhere?*

"Come to da back door."

It did not jar her at all to hear Mama's voice in her head. It seemed almost natural now, that she and Mama Dolly could communicate in this fashion—telepathically— and thank God the woman had arrived!

She raced to the kitchen to find the door opened a crack. As she pulled it full open, there stood Mama Dolly, big as life, her tignon decorated in a multitude of fetishes and gris-gris.

"You're dressed to kill, I see."

"We gots protection now," she said, pointing proudly to the gris-gris embellished tignon. "Come, now."

"I was afraid you didn't hear me."

"I had to do da magie noir," she said, again pointing to her decorated tignon. On further inspection, Summer realized the gris-gris was a horrid compilation of crucifixes, tiny black dolls with big white eyes and straw hair. The feet of several unfortunate animals were pinned here and there along with crude beads and unrecognizable fetishes

"If anything will do it, that will," Summer said, awed at the spectacle.

"Come on. We gots to save da cap'n."

* * *

As luck would have it, it was twilight by the time they reached the entrance to the swamp and the path to Ruiz.

"The gators come out now to feed, don't they, Mama?"

"Hesh up! I don' wants to think of dat!"

"Well, heck, I don't either but it's a reality, isn't it?"

"It real, alright."

Mama Dolly splashed ahead, and soon was chanting in words Summer could not understand. The woman had cut a long and thick stick with which she probed the waters ahead.as they tromped through the dense swamp growth. Birds squawked and flew at the sound of humans coming. The bullfrogs croaked ahead but fell silent as they approached.

Soon, twilight became total darkness. A large splash now and then caused Summer to shriek, which in turn brought sounds of alarm from the invisible creatures of the night. Often, glowing eyes appeared ahead, causing the women to stop in their tracks to calm their fears. At those times, Mama Dolly chanted louder, splashing her stick into the low waters. The eyes disappeared with a splash that left them hopeful the creature was moving away and not toward. Mosquitos buzzed about them relentlessly; but no matter how much they slapped at the annoying insects, their blood was spent in small pricks felt, but not seen. It was a long and grueling trek that only a fool would embark on in the dark of night—a fool in love with a culprit!

Then in the dark swamp, Guy came to mind and Summer was ashamed, ashamed that her thoughts at present were only to save her lover, her Captain Ruiz. How difficult it was to combine the two worlds.

While she was in this world, this world of the past, she had to live life as it came. She did not ask to be a time traveler, and especially in this strange episode; it had no rhyme or reason that she could fathom. She had found Cherry and brought her home to rest, but why Captain Ruiz? Why this desperate love she felt for him? There was no answer; it had simply happened to her, and she was helpless in its grasp.

* * *

The trees appeared to be vanishing, though it was difficult to tell in the darkness. The sky was moonless, but the faint smell of a campfire made them aware that they were close to Ruiz's camp.

Thank God, Ruiz!

"Git back! We ain't der yet!" Mama Dolly's sudden outburst startled her; she had not realized that she had overpassed the woman in the excitement of catching a whiff of the campfire. The fact that she was wet from swamp water and smelled from sweat, did not discourage her elation at reaching the edge of camp.

A few seconds later, a tremendous splash a few feet behind them caused both women to shriek in terror.

"¡Cállate! ¡Despertará a los muertos!"[69]

Summer barely made out the form of Alvarez, the man who camped with Ruiz. "Oh," she exhaled in relief. "It's you."

"Who dat?" Mama asked, wiping her brow with a sleeve of her blouse.

"It's okay," Summer said. "It's one of the captain's crew."

"¡Venga! ¡Venga![70]", the man said, trudging through the water ahead of the women.

A few steps more and they were at the clearing where a small campfire crackled, lighting the faces of Ruiz and Otto, who stood at the fire with weapons drawn.

"Hold it, Ruiz! It's just us, me and Mama Dolly!" What a travesty of fate if she were shot by her own lover! It briefly crossed her mind that she didn't know what would become of her in the future if she were killed in the past, but she threw that thought aside as the captain stuck his weapon into the waistband of his pants.

---

[69] "*¡Cállate! ¡Despertará a los muertos*!" Shut up! You'll wake the dead!"

[70] "*¡Venga! ¡Venga!*" Come, come."

"Verano*!*" he exclaimed, crossing the distance between them and encircling her in his arms. "What is happening, my love?" he whispered, moving them out of earshot of the others.

"Where is Lila?"

"Lila, ¡Venga!" he said loudly. "Come!", and Lila appeared at the end of the slice of dry land, faintly aglow from the reflection of the fire.

"Oh, Zummer, you scare us. We theenk we are under attack!"

"You should know all about "attack", Lila, you little double crosser!" Summer yelled, as Lila moved toward them.

"What? What eez wrong weeth you?" Lila asked with a nervous giggle.

"Tell him!" Summer demanded, now standing so close to the woman she could feel her breath. "Tell him about your plan, you and Mr. Fontaneau!"

"I swear, Ruiz, I do not know what she talk about. She eez crazy!" Lila said, rushing to Ruiz's side.

"Que paso?" Ruiz asked. "What have you done, Lila?"

"I do notheeng, I swear!" she pleaded.

Summer again approached her. "You and Fontaneau have a plan. I heard you, Lila. You can't deny it. You told Fontaneau where…."

Summer flew backward at Lila's shove, landing on her backside in the lapping waters of Lake Ponchartrain.

"Ouch!" she squealed, as her rump hit a rock on impact.

"I do notheeng!" Lila screeched, running at Summer, who was now trying to lift herself out of the lake.

Before Ruiz could stop the woman, she had leaped at Summer, sending them both in to the water with Summer pinned beneath her, lake water filling her mouth as her head was just beneath the surface.

Lila was then off her, pulled away by Captain Ruiz who had the woman by her hair. "Tell me, Lila, what is it? What did you do?"

Summer sat, coughing and spitting. "She…she…*cough*… told Fontaneau where your camp is! I know she did! He knows you're here with Otto and…and him," she said, pointing to Alvarez.

"Aye, mon Dios!" he yelled, releasing Lila to stand on her own. "Why do you do this to us?" he yelled, throwing his arms into the air.

"Ruiz, she lies!" Lila said, wringing her hands. "I do not know what she talk about!"

"Get out of my sight!" Ruiz shouted, and Lila stepped backward, eyes on Ruiz and the two other men, until she reached the fire where

Summer stood attempting to dry her soaked clothing. The fire was dim and chance of drying was nil.

Lila sniffled. "You lie, Zummer. I know notheeng what you say."

Summer wanted nothing more than to punch the woman. "Traitor…," she whispered, as now the captain and his men were in deep debate as to what to do now that their hiding place had been discovered.

"Huh!" Lila replied, followed by silence.

"We befriended you, and this is what you do after the Captain saves you from a desperate life in prison. You're nothing but an ungrateful spy, a traitor like Fontaneau—and a slut."

Mama Dolly had stood back watching the scene play out before her; but now she stepped closer and closer, white eyes staring at the accused French woman. She came so close, and had such a frightening look in her eye, that Summer quickly removed herself.

Suddenly, Mama Dolly let out a shriek that ran shivers down Summer's spine, and one that stopped dead the men's caucus. With all eyes on her, Lila's the widest of all. Mama Dolly expelled a long string of strange words, swaying, gyrating, turning, twisting, her dark skin reflecting the orange of the dimming fire. All the while, she chanted in her strange, hair-raising sing-song way. Lila tried to step backward, away from the woman who had appeared to have lost her marbles, but Mama Dolly followed her with each step backward, until they both stood at the water's edge, the large black frame towering over the slight one. Mama Dolly now reached into a pouch and took out a short stick with a potpourri of gris-gris tied to it by small cords. It rattled as Mama Dolly shook it in front of Lila's terrified face, the strange chant spewing from her lips.

Not able to take another moment of the wild woman, Lila shrieked and ran to the path that led out of the swamp. "I go! I go!" she screamed, disappearing into the trees.

Mama stopped her chanting and approached Captain Ruiz, who had stood silently watching the spectacle with his cronies. "She gots da bad magie noir dis time. I take her wid me so's Mistah Fontaneau don' know he been found out."

"Gracias, Mama. Vaya con Dios."[71]

---

[71] *"Gracias, Mama. Vaya con Dios"* Thanks, Mama. Go with God."

Mama Dolly patted him on the arm, and approached Summer, handing her the stick of hanging gris-gris. “You keep dis, chile’. It be der when you need it.” She then disappeared into the path after Lila, who was heard splashing through the swamp waters, screaming in the darkness.

Chapter 25

Captain Ruiz paced across the narrowed point of dry land. "I was wrong to trust him. I know him to be nothing but a liar and cheat. May God punish him!"

The men mumbled in agreement. Alvarez stoked the fire as Otto disappeared into the swamp. When he returned, he brought more wood; and obviously wood that was higher above the ground, as surely the damp growth lower to the swamp waters would not burn.

Across the lake a few sporadic lanterns flickered. Summer assumed it was fishermen getting an early start on the coming day. Seafood was a primary source of protein in the Quarter. The shrimp and crawfish filled nearly every dish that she had tasted, as well as fish and pork sausages, spicy and delicious. She was hungry; her stomach growled.

"What do you eat here, Ruiz?" Summer asked, hoping for a satisfactory answer for her gnawing hunger.

At her question, Otto retrieved a basket from behind a bush. He reached in and took out a lump of bread, or biscuit, for all she could tell, and held it against the fire so she could see. "Here", he said, and she took it greedily only to discover it was stale and slightly greasy, but it was sweet and good just the same.

Beignets," he said, and popped one into his mouth.

"Lila brought us food," Ruiz said, taking a lump from the basket.

"What now?" she asked. "What does Fontaneau have planned?"

"I can only think that he has made a double deal, one with us and one with the Federales. Perhaps he plans to have it all, my plantation, and whatever reward the Federales have offered. "

"What about Lila? What will you do with her?"

"Nothing, my love. I do not harm women. Mama Dolly will serve her punishment." Alvarez and Otto laughed at his comment causing Summer to wonder if they had an inkling of Lila's punishment.

"I can't believe she would do this to you, Ruiz She is ungrateful for all you have done for her."

He shrugged. "It is war, Verano. Bad times for everyone. She is a child of Le Vieux Carré and must get by with whatever means she can."

"You are too forgiving. She's put you in serious danger and yet you excuse her actions!"

"Se la vi, Verano. It is war. Now we must find a way to protect ourselves, to find a way out. Fontaneau has no intention of giving me a boat or gold coins. Now that he knows where we are, he will attack, and we will be waiting for him."

Later, it occurred to Summer as she lay next to Ruiz on a wool blanket set over the damp ground, that whatever was coming could be quite dangerous. Again, the thought came to mind of her death, which certainly was possible in this situation. She had been close to death before in the other times in which she had been pulled back into the past, but this felt different; it was frightening. Surely Fontaneau would come armed, *and* with armed friends. But when? Tonight? How could Ruiz sleep beside her with this prospect? How could the other men sleep a short distance away? She did not like it one bit, and spent the night half in and half out of sleep, listening…listening for the danger that was sure to come.

* * *

"This morning, we set our plan to action!" Ruiz stretched his body, standing next to the re-stoked fire upon which sat a camp coffee pot over a rusty grate. Summer welcomed the aroma of boiling coffee, as her night of worry lay heavy on her eyelids. Otto's magic bush had produced coffee, more beignets, and, to her surprise, bacon sizzling in a heavy black frying pan that shared the grate next to the coffee pot.

"Ruiz, I must find a place to pee," she whispered, having raised her aching body off the damp ground to stand next to him at the fire. Her breath tasted like rotten eggs, and she quickly covered her mouth.

Ruiz pointed her to another path cut into the swamp forest, and she left the men, whose eyes she felt on her backside as she retreated. When she returned, the men were huddled around the fire drinking coffee from tin cups. Ruiz handed her his own cup.

"Drink this and be strong. We have much work to do today. He will not come by boat," Ruiz said, quite adamantly. He would have to pass the Yankee lookouts, and he will not gamble his quest for the Bella Vista on the chance they spot him."

Lila would have told Fontaneau the exact spot at which they were camped, and so they gambled that he and his guns would come that way, through the swamplands path. The men, Alvarez and Otto, disappeared into the swamp to set up specific booby entrapments, in case they were outnumbered, which they assumed to be the case.

"Fontaneau will try to make me sign the deed that you were witness to," Ruiz said, lining up a collection of firearms on an overturned tree. "He will have to bring a notary to make it official. Aha! We will not let it happen, will we, my love? We will be waiting for him!"

"How will we escape?" Summer asked. It was one thing to dispel the enemy, but what happened after that? How would they get away from this bit of sorry land?

"Do not worry, Verano. I have friends in many places, and Otto has been to Miguel. You do remember Miguel who helped us escape from the fort?"

She nodded.

"He will bring his boat to the Black Bay, and it will be there tonight. Surely Fontaneau will come tonight for me. Here," he said, handing her a pistol.

"What am I supposed to do with this?" she asked, holding the pistol with two hands. "Is it loaded?"

"Not yet, but you must have it with you. We do not know what that blackguard will do. If he tries to harm you, kill him!"

Summer shrank back in horror. "Ruiz, I can't kill anyone!"

"Not for me, Verano? Not if our lives depend on it?"

She looked at him, and then at the pistol in her hands. It was smaller than the others, but heavy, as well. "I…I don't know if I can hold it steady enough to shoot."

"Then you wait. If he, or one of his companions threatens to harm you, wait until they are close, like this…." He put his arms about her waist and drew her to him, pressing his lips onto hers, hungrily, passionately, until the pistol dropped from her hands, falling to the ground with a dull thud.

"I love you, Verano." His breath was hot in her ear; his beard scratched her face, but she did not care.

"Oh Ruiz," she said, tears threatening to fall. "What if you're hurt…*or killed!* I couldn't bear it!" She trapped his head between her hands. "I love you too much. We have come so far and now this danger!"

"You will not have to bear it. We will do well." His arms tightened around her as he stepped backward, pulling her with him. "I must have you, my love."

She panicked. "Here? Now?" What about Otto and…the other one?"

"They will not come," he whispered. They are deep in the swamp." He pulled her down onto the damp, steaming blanket, but she did not notice it was damp or steaming, she only felt his hands lifting her skirt—his hands running up the insides of her thighs, his hands massaging her until she groaned with want. When his body slipped between her trembling limbs, it didn't matter that the brutal sun beat blindingly down on her with its burning rays. She closed her eyes against it, and pulled him tightly to her, groaning as he entered, giving herself totally and completely. She did not care that Alvarez or Otto could appear at any moment to find them coupling on the blanket. It didn't matter. All that mattered was this moment, that they shared their love here and now. After all, the future was unsure, and this could be the last time.

"Of course," he said, after their passion was spent and they lay side by side in the hot sun. "I do not expect you to get as close as this before you fire the pistol."

She raised herself onto an elbow and grinned. "Silly man." But, she did not wipe away the teardrop that rolled down her check and onto the small piece of blanket that showed between their bodies. "I love you," she whispered. "Let's get back to work so that we can beat the enemy and leave this place."

* * *

"Now, we wait," Ruiz said. The day had grown long and hot. Sweat left its mark on the small group in the way of heavily stained armpits accompanied by a foul odor that could not be waved away.

Summer sat on the overturned log next to the now loaded firearms as Otto built a fire. "Isn't it too hot for a fire?" she asked, fanning herself with the bottom of her skirt. "Should we even have a fire tonight advertising where we are?"

"Of course," Ruiz said. "We must look like what we are, men waiting to make a legal transaction."

She had the jitters, and badly. Her stomach roiled in fear of what was to come, and she fought the urge to vomit, only her stomach was empty. Maybe they had it wrong? Maybe she had misunderstood and Lila was not to blame? *No! I am right; Lila double-crossed us, the little slut.*

The sun sank and darkness fell. The fire crackled as they waited silently, waited for the sound of feet splashing through the swamp, for the flight of frightened birds, for the frogs to stop their croaking. They heard nothing but their own silent curses and the fire. They were prepared at this moment, but would they be well prepared should the waiting drag on and on and on and the enemy catch them off guard? Miguel would have left the boat at Black Bay by now.

The stars did little to brighten a moonless sky. Without the fire they would have sat in darkness; but Otto, through some magic of his own, continued to stoke the fire with fresh, fairly dry branches that spattered, squeaked and hissed upon entering the flames. Again, they dined on beignets, but the basket was nearly empty. Earlier, Otto had roasted a skinny swamp bird he had caught while setting the booby traps for Fontaneau and his men. It was not a feast for four people, but sufficed; the men needed energy for what lay ahead, so Summer satisfied herself with a wing section, not wanting to take food out of the mouths of these soldiers who were so faithful to Ruiz.

* * *

"Wake up!" Ruiz jostled her shoulder and she woke with a start, damp and stiff from having dozed off with her head against the fallen tree. "They've come!" he whispered; and sure enough, Summer heard yelling deeper into the swamp.

"…and none too quietly," she said, rising to her feet.

"They have fallen for a trap," Ruiz said, taking his pistol from his waistband.

A rush of voices in alarm told her that the marauders had certainly run into some form of difficulty. "What now? What do I do?"

"Go to the other cut," he said, nodding his head toward the cut in the swamp in which she had previously used to relieve herself.

"I don't want to leave you, Ruiz!" She grabbed onto his arm, but he shook it loose.

"This is no place for you; now go!" he ordered, and took her designated pistol off the log. "It is loaded. Use it if you must. Do not hesitate!"

Having no recourse, she took the pistol from his hand, tucked it into the waistband beside the gris-gris stick, and left him standing by the fire. Alvarez and Otto were nowhere to be seen. "But you're alone!" she said, turning once more to his silhouetted figure. "Where are the others?"

"Go!" he ordered, and she went, making her way to the little cut which squished beneath her feet in the damp soil. The further in she went, the deeper the water until it was mid-calf. She shuddered, wondering what creatures she would disturb by this nightly haunt. She cursed the vacant moon, which absence made it impossible to see where she was, or where she was going. All that was visible were the occasional glowing eyes, ominous in the darkness; she was terrified.

The cypress knees were a hazard and she nearly fell several times, having bumped into many of various sizes. Frustrated, she stopped and groped for low branches, anything that would permit her to climb above the water. Tears fell in terror from the sounds of men shouting, then shots from the pistols. With hand over mouth to muffle her cries, she trudged through the water until she was stopped short by a thicker grouping of cypress knees. She wove through them only to find herself blocked by the mother tree. Exhausted, she wrapped her arms around the tall cypress as far as they would stretch, hugging the tree to her for comfort, the pistol and gris-gris stick cutting into her ribs.

When a flicker of light bounced against on the bark of the cypress just above her elbow, a wave of relief flooded her. "Ruiz!" she said, turning to see a torch peeking between the trees as it approached. "What's happened?" she asked, unfolding her arms.

With no reply to her question, she removed the pistol, holding it with both hands. "*You must cock it first,*" Ruiz had said.

"I know, silly man," she had replied, but her hands shook so that she wondered if she would be able to cock it and even shoot, should the

need arise. She wasn't sure who approached, but she prayed it was Ruiz, Alvarez, or Otto. "Who goes?" she asked, trying desperately to sound confident and strong.

Again no reply. "Answer or I'll shoot! I have a gun!"

"She's here!"

It was a stranger's voice that reached her ears. As her stomach dropped to her knees—which knocked against one another—she cocked the gun; but it was too heavy to hold with one hand and fell with a splash into the water.

Oh, no! She groped desperately in the water about her feet pulling out the dripping pistol. *Will it still work?* She hadn't a clue.

"She has a weapon," the man yelled.

"Don't kill her!" came the reply. The voice sounded very much like Mr. Fontaneau's.

"Where's Ruiz?" she asked, yelling loud enough for Fontaneau, who was apparently further away, to hear.

"He is dead!" Fontaneau yelled, after a brief hesitation.

No! It can't be! He's lying! The torch was nearly on her now. *What should I do? Wait? Wait till he's closer? Do what Ruiz said....*

"Thud." The pistol had fired, only the blast she had expected did not happen. Nothing happened except the pathetic "*thud*" that came weakly from its barrel. She dropped it into the swamp and, without a second thought, grabbed the gris-gris stick from her waistband. It worked for Mama Dolly, so perhaps it would work for her as well. She slipped behind the cypress tree, and when the torch was close, she literally flew from behind the tree screeching like a banshee, spewing incoherently in a strange language that seemed to suddenly rattle off her tongue naturally. She shook the stick at the stranger, its gris-gris, attached by inches of cord, bounced and rattled in an explosion of hair-raising expletives in the strange foreign tongue. Her feet had taken off on a lively dance of their own, leaping from the swamp waters again and again in a frenzied and bizarre exhibit that was beyond her means of control.

The man with the torch, a short mulatto man, took several steps backward, his eyes big as saucers; but Summer advanced on him, weaving through the cypress knees, leaping and twirling, spouting the gibberish and waving the gris-gris stick. He made a futile attempt to stop her, to gain control of the situation by repeatedly jabbing the torch at her, but she dodged the torch and continued to advance until he finally turned and ran back through the swamp, the water leaving a wake in his rapid escape.

She was exhausted after her crazy antics. Left to her own wits in the darkness, she felt her way to a cypress knee and rested a buttocks cheek on it. *Now what?* Is Ruiz really dead? She had to see for herself, and backtracked to the cut in the swamp only to realize that Fontaneau and the men he brought with him were still there, as she could hear voices in the distance.

"…we have to get him to a doctor," she heard Fontaneau say. "We'll worry about Ruiz later…."

Later? He's alive!

"How could you let a little woman scare you off like that?" Fontaneau yelled.

"Da magic…she done da magic," Summer's accoster replied.

"We'll have to worry about her later, too. We have to get the magistrate to a doctor. Pick him up, Henry."

The magistrate? Ruiz was right, Fontaneau was going to force him to sign the Bella Vista over!

After a few grunts and groans, which Summer assumed came from the injured magistrate as he was lifted, Fontaneau and his entourage, the number of which she did not know, departed. She waited until the sounds of their leaving diminished and the croak of frogs returned before she ventured to the camp.

Nothing. Even in the darkness, she could tell there was not a soul about. "Ruiz? Otto?" She looked further, beyond the craggy bush that hid their food basket, along the gently lapping lake water, and back a ways into the pathway to the road. Satisfied that all had survived, she returned to the camp, scrounged for one of the woolen blankets, shook it out and lay it next to the unlit campfire where she collapsed and fell into a fitful sleep.

Chapter 26

"Oh, God…" she groaned, having woken to another sultry morning, the wool blanket scratching the back of her neck and her body sweltering under the steamy sun. She sat up, trying to collect her thoughts. *Ruiz!* It all came back full force, and she scrambled to her feet. *Where is he?*

"Ruiz!" She called, over and over again, until she had to accept the fact that he and his cronies had vanished. But where? How could he just take off and leave her? Then it came to her…*Black Bay! The boat is at Black Bay!* Elation turned to disappointment when she realized that she had no clue where Black Bay was; she did not know how to get there.

"Mama Dolly!" she called aloud. "I need you!" Instead of waiting for the woman to miraculously appear, as she always did, Summer entered the pathway to the road; she would head to Backtown and perhaps Mama Dolly would meet her on the way.

* * *

It was far easier maneuvering through the swamp in daylight than it had been the previous night during the confrontation between Captain Ruiz and Mr. Fontaneau. After a few wet, frustrating, bug-infested sweltering hours, she reached the dusty road that led to town. There were no thugs awaiting her arrival, and that thought certainly had crossed her mind. Still, she kept to the side of the road, jumping into the brush upon the approach of a carriage. She could not judge the distance to town, as previously she had followed Otto and had been preoccupied with his less-than-charming personality.

"Come, chile!"

Summer jumped and looked around for Mama Dolly, for surely it was her voice!

"Heah!"

"Where? I can't see you."

"I'se heah" she replied, shaking a leafy bush.

"Why are you hiding?"

"Deys waitin' fo' you up ahead. Come on back heah."

Summer did not delay. She slipped into the brush and grabbed Mama Dolly by her thick arms. "Oh, I'm so happy to see you! Something horrible happened last night. I don't know where Ruiz is —at least I don't think I do—for sure."

"I know's. Mama know's all. Da cap'n alright, so don' you worry none."

"This is such a mess. I'm tired, Mama. I don't know why I'm here. The captain lives dangerously, and I keep trying to save him; but it's just one bad thing after another." She started to cry.

Mama Dolly pulled Summer to her soft bosom. "You come from far away, we know dat. But don' fret, chile, it will be good, you'll see. Have da faith and soon you go home."

Bittersweet to hear the words of going home and leaving Captain Ruiz, but a comfort to know that Mama Dolly understood something of her existence, that she came from another place, and perhaps Mama also knew she came from another time.

The women walked through the brush and trees, avoiding the road. Mama's "shortcut", as she called it, was thick with snakes as well as the hungry mosquitos that buzzed and pricked, making the shortcut a hell. At last, hot, sweaty, thirsty, exhausted, and full of bites, they arrived at Mama Dolly's shack in Backtown, where Summer was given a cup full of warm water that Mama poured from a pitcher, and collapsed on the little stool by the table full of gris-gris. It was then that she saw Lila sitting on Mama's bed. "Well, look who's here, double crossing Lila."

"Mama won't let me go until I zay *zorry.* She put zee curse on me—zee black bitch." The last words spat at Mama Dolly who stood solidly with hands on hips.

"You don' get notin' you don' deserve." Mama said.

"Look what she done, Zummer!" Lila then approached the gris-gris table, pulling her wild red hair away from her face.

Summer gasped. "What on earth?"

"Zee mark!" Lila cried, pointing to the image of a snake that appeared to be tattooed from her forehead to her chin, covering the entire right side of her face. "I cannot make zee money like theez!" Lila returned to the bed, sobbing into Mama's pillow.

"Good grief, Mama. How in the world did you do that? Does it come off?"

"It come off when Mama reverse da curse, but not till she make tings right and da cap'n gone safe from dis place."

"Justice well served!" Summer applauded.

Mama then took an empty flour sack, and with a charcoal pencil began to draw a map. "Dis is how you gits to Black Bay," she said. "Da cap'n be waiting fo' you der."

* * *

She stood on the rickety, narrow dock. The tall black man, whose name was (encouragingly) "Lucky Sam", led her silently west, through Backtown, through another section of Cypress Swamp, where, finally, he deposited her at a narrow dock which jutted a few feet out into a lazy bayou.

"He comin'," Lucky Sam said. "You wait." Then, the silent man disappeared back into the swamp, leaving her to stand alone in yet another dismal outfit put together from Mama Dolly's trunk. A plain muslin turban sat upon her head, which soon had created a steamy nest of itching on her scalp, no doubt brought on by the relentless humidity. She swat at the mosquitos, but it was hopeless; they feasted.

Who am I waiting for? Ruiz? She had followed Lucky Sam, as that is what Mama Dolly had told her to do, but now, as she stood alone amidst the flora and fauna of the bayou, she felt desperately alone—and afraid. She had to admit she was terrified. This was not her world, and she felt a sudden longing for Guy, for Jesse, for her magnificent Magnolia Plantation, and for the twins whom she had not yet met. *I'm tired, tired of this strange world...I don't belong....*

A splash broke the silence. Then another, and another. It was not the occasional splash of the small fish that leapt from the water before her, or the sound of frogs hopping into the bayou from their stations on the bank. No, it was a steady *splash...splash...splash.* She turned to the right upon which a tall moss laden tree stood as a ghostly beacon, its dark limbs naked but for the silvery beard of mosses that hung nearly to the water's surface fluttering in any small breeze.

The tip of a small wooden boat showed from behind the silvery moss, and then the rest of the craft came to view. A dark man, his face covered in a woven straw hat, rowed to the edge of the dock, steadying the boat with one large hand that gripped the splintered wood without concern, and the other held high for her to steady herself as she climbed aboard.

"Thank you," she said, the small boat rocking wildly with her boarding. "Who are you?" The silence of her rescuers was getting on her nerves.

"Mama Dolly tell me to come," he said, not answering her question.

"But what's your name?"

He eyed her suspiciously, then grinned widely, showing two rows of large, yellowed teeth. "I'se Noah," he said.

"It's a very appropriate name, in this instance, Noah. You are saving me from disaster."

"Y'sm." Noah turned the boat deftly with a few moves of the oars.

"We're going to Black Bay, correct?"

Noah looked confused. "No...I'se taking you to where Mama Dolly tole' me to take you."

"Okay. I see." She scooted her behind around on the hard plank seat until she felt some semblance of comfort. Noah was silent as he rowed, but unfortunately, she was sitting facing him and so neither of them had any choice but to stare at one another. She smiled, he grinned. After several smiles and grins, she managed, with great difficulty and rocking of the boat, to turn and face the direction in which Noah was rowing. Now, she could appreciate the beauty of the bayou. Herons perched on low branches, watching the water for the small fish that hovered near the bank. They passed several alligators of various sizes sunning themselves on small grass-flattened clearings alongside the river. The gators, unmoving, painted a serene picture, but she shuddered, knowing full well how quickly the serenity could change to a struggle for life.

"Are we near?" she finally asked after what seemed hours of endless bayou, birds, jumping fish, croaking frogs and sunning gators.

"See dat spot der?" Noah nodded across a larger body of water, wider than the slow-moving river, to what appeared to be another dock.

"What is it?"

"Another fellow gonna get you der."

"Ano....tell me, Noah, where am I going and when will I get there?" By now she was melting from the warm, damp air. The sun was merciless, her behind was sore from the hard plank and she had to pee.

"Don' know. Dis my job right heah, to git you der." She had turned in her seat to look at the man, who again showed his rows of large yellow teeth.

"There's no one there," she said, as they approached the dock.

"Der will be."

"Are you waiting with me?"

"No ma'am. Gots to go fishin' fo' suppah'."

Oh joy. Just where the hell am I?

With trepidation, she watched Noah row the old boat back across the water in the way they had come. Again, she stood at the edge of a lonely dock in the middle of nowhere, without another soul in sight. She removed the hot turban, setting it on the dock and then scratched her head rapidly, her broken nails raking across her scalp time and time again, until she had aerated her scalp properly, allowing it to dry.

"Ah...." she said aloud, stretching her arms into the sky. "Hurry up!" she said to no one. "Do you hear me?" she yelled, causing a flutter of white wings to imerge from brush branches in pursuit of a quieter place to fish.

"I hear you, Miss Woodfield."

With horror, she turned to see Mr. Fontaneau step onto the dock.

"Wha...what are you doing here?" she shuddered, completely shocked. This was not what she expected!

"Shall we go?" he held out a hand, but she stepped backward once, twice...and right into the bayou! It was not deep water, and she immerged immediately, standing waist high and soaked through and through. Wiping the water from her eyes, she quickly realized she would make good gator bait if a hungry one were near, or one she had disturbed at her sudden intrusion. She quickstepped to the bank and grabbed onto handfuls of river grass, but quickly released the blades when they cut into her hands.

"Here," Fontaneau said, again extending a hand. "Let me help before you make a bloody mess of yourself."

Reluctantly, she measured the two evils…gator or Fontaneau? It was an easy choice.

The humid air felt refreshingly cool as Fontaneau brought her to a standing position next to him. He looked damp himself, but from the humidity. Sweat rolled down his cheeks and onto his fine white cotton shirt. He pulled a handkerchief from a pocket and wiped his face. "You are more trouble than you are worth, Miss Woodfield," he said, folding the handkerchief and returning it to his pocket.

"Then why don't you just let me be?" she asked, wringing water from her skirt.

"I need you. Simple as that."

"How did you know I'd be here?"

"I told you, I have friends in many places. Ruiz and I are playing a game of chess. I now have his queen, and soon he will be in checkmate."

"He's outsmarted you at every turn," she replied, folding her soaking sleeves across her chest in an attempt to cover her erect nipples, which she felt poking through the thin muslin blouse.

Fontaneau whistled toward the woods, and two men appeared from the brush. "Help Miss Woodfield out of here," he ordered. She complied without argument. The men each took an arm and guided her through the brush and trees to Mr. Fontaneau's carriage, which sat on a thin, dusty and rutted road, if it could be called as such. She noticed a faded arrow-shaped sign nailed to a wooden spike. It pointed to toward the dock path and read "Delacroi".

* * *

"I'se glad to see you, Miz Summah," Dancie said, pouring another large kettle of boiling water into the copper tub.

"And I'm glad to see you, too, Dancie," she replied, moving her feet away from the waterfall of steaming water. "This bath is wonderful." Indeed it was. The water was clear when she slipped into its welcomed warmth twenty minutes beforehand. Now, it was murky from the mud and sweat of her adventures of the past few days. The one good thing about being back in civilization was definitely soaking in the copper tub.

"Mistah Fontaneau wants you to be lookin' pretty tonight."

"Why? What's tonight?" She had hoped to be back in a clean nightgown and under the covers of the four-poster for some much needed sleep. She needed to think, to figure out how to get to Ruiz; and she couldn't do that if Mr. Fontaneau planned on taking up her time. Besides, she was exhausted! She had nearly fallen asleep in the carriage on the return to his mansion, despite the constant bumps and dips of the long, broken road from the path that read "Delacroix".

"Oh, this is wonderful" she said, sinking deeper into the tub. When finally she forced herself from its cooling waters, Dancie had laid out a blue satin gown, lace trimmed bloomers and shimmy, the dreaded corset, satin slippers and a four-hooped petticoat.

"What the heck is going on tonight that I need to dress so fancy?"

"Dem soldiers comin' fo' suppah."

"Well, oh crap." *Now what?* Do you mean Captain McAllister?"

"Sho nuf, he comin' too, I 'spect."

Summer groaned again, stepping into the prison of clothing piece by piece. "Not so tight!" she cried, when Dancie pulled on the corset strings. "You know it makes me faint!"

Trussed to the gills, her breasts swelling over the lace trim of the gown's bodice, she sat at the dressing table with Dancie, attempting to shape her hair into something acceptable. Soon, a few rosettes and pearls graced her blond mop

Danice stood back. "Der! You's lookin' nice, now."

Summer stood and admired herself in the full length mirror. The gown was beautiful, its yards of satin expanded and falling gracefully over the four-hooped petticoat. The hem, in several places, was hiked up as if by an invisible string and secured with a bow and rosettes, leaving a triangle of white French lace that peeked from beneath the layer of satin, the lace matching the trim of the bodice. She enjoyed the gentle sway of the hoops as she shifted from side to side, watching the effect in the mirror.

"Dat's all, girl," Dancie said, straightening up the dressing table. "I gots to git to da kitchen now."

"You work so hard, Dancie. Thanks."

"Jes doin' what's I'se always done, slave or free," she said, and left.

* * *

"My name is Summer Woodfield. I come from Magnolia Plantation in Bluebell, Georgia, what's left of it, since the—*your*—soldiers went through." She dabbed her mouth with a napkin. "Now, can we stop the third degree?" McAllister held her hostage at the dinner table.

"How did you get to Fort Jefferson?" he asked, ignoring her request.

"I don't know."

"Oh come now, Miss Woodfield! Of course you know!" said Lieutenant Franks, Captain McAllister's companion.

"I do not—*sir,*" she said, glaring. She did not like Lieutenant Franks at all. He was 30ish and held himself in a pompous self-worshiping way. He was not nearly as polite as Captain McAllister, who at least exhibited a bit of respect in the presence of a lady.

"How do you know Captain Ruiz, then? Why did you help him escape from prison?" McAllister asked.

"Who said I helped him escape?"

"We are not fools, Miss Woodfield. You and Miss de Peau helped Captain Ruiz escape. We have it from witnesses that Miss de Peau kept the guards busy while you, and perhaps some of Ruiz's friends, helped free him."

"If you know all this, then why are you asking?"

"Miss Woodfield," began the lieutenant, "might I remind you that we could very well hold you at the Cabildo until you confess. We have all the time in the world."

McAllister cleared his throat. "However, Mr. Fontaneau has welcomed you into his home, and here you will stay until you share the whereabouts of Captain Ruiz with us." He flashed the lieutenant a look of disapproval.

She eyed Fontaneau, who smiled pleasantly at her. Before the soldiers arrived, he had warned her with bodily harm not to mention anything she knew about the whereabouts of Ruiz. *As if I knew anything!* She was caught between a rock and a hard place. Fontaneau wanted it all; he wanted Ruiz's promised plantation, *and* he wanted Ruiz locked up and executed. *Covering up proof of his double-cross, I'll bet. And what will he do with me—provided I haven't been whisked back to my own time?* Again, thoughts of her death in this time zone crossed her mind.

"And I do thank Mr. Fontaneau for his generous hospitality," she said, smiling snidely at her capture. "If you'll excuse me, gentlemen," she said, rising. "I've had enough persecution for one night. I think I will retire." She curtsied to the three men whose chairs scraped in muffled tones across the Persian rug beneath the dining table as they rose.

"Sit!" Fontaneau ordered, from his place at the head of the table. "I don't believe these men are through with you." Fontaneau's previous smile had vanished.

"Do not talk to me like that! You may be my jailer, Fontaneau but I will *not put up with this friggin' crap* from you!" Her voice had risen sharply, and a gasp from the men filled the room at the use of her language, which certainly should never, ever, come from the dainty mouth of a Southern belle!

She rushed to leave the room, but Fontaneau had raised forcefully from his chair, rushing to grip her by her shoulders. "And don't you ever speak to me like that in public again!" He shook her violently and pushed her backward until she bumped painfully into the sideboard, causing the china dishes atop it to shake and clink. Bouncing from the sideboard, she lost her footing and fell to the floor in a fluffy blue heap.

"Stop it, Fontaneau!" McAllister had come to her rescue. "That is no way to treat a woman." Anger edged the captain's voice as he lifted Summer from the floor.

She glared at Fontaneau as she brushed at her satin skirt, trying desperately to keep her voice from shaking. "Thank you, captain," she said, and realized for the first time, that Fontaneau could be dangerous to her physical self. He had frightened her with this sudden display of violence. He obviously had a streak in him that she was not aware of, and to her, it was a red flag.

Chapter 27

"What can I do to gain back your trust?" Fontaneau asked the next morning.

"Nothing. I've never trusted you, and now I trust you even less, if that is possible."

"We're even, then. I can't trust the trollop of a blackguard criminal."

"And what is trustworthy about you, might I ask? You're a double-crossing turncoat!"

Fontaneau slammed his fork down onto the table, as they had begun the day together in the breakfast room. Anger pierced his eyes, but she could see he was trying hard to control himself.

"Let us bury the hatchet, so to say," he said, leaning back in his chair. "Captain McAllister and I have devised a plan in which to entrap Ruiz, and you are the most integral part of it."

"Oh?"

"I am going to arrange a meeting between Ruiz and myself, with you as bait, of course.

"I will promise to trade you to Ruiz as planned, for the ship and coins in return for the Bella Vista plantation. When the papers are signed and all is legal and proper, you…" he smiled…"will simply disappear, Ruiz will be accidentally killed and delivered to McAllister. I will collect my generous reward from the Federals for capturing a most desperately wanted war criminal, *and,*" he smirked, "the Bella Vista."

Pompous ass.

Fontaneau sat against his high-back chair drumming his fingers on his chest. A wicked grin spread across his face as he stared at Summer, obviously waiting for her reply.

"What about Ruiz's men? Will you kill them, too?"

"Of course! Ruiz and his cohorts will have attacked me, and I will have killed them all in self-defense!"

"And, where is it I'm disappearing to?"

"Well, my dear." He leaned forward. "You don't really exist, do you?"

Her heart skipped a beat. *He knows?*

"Our Captain McAllister cannot find any information on you, so we must assume you are simply a figment of our imaginations." He arched his eyebrows. "Is it not true?"

He plans to kill me! No wonder reoccurring thoughts of death! The trip back in time was getting way out of hand. Sure, she'd been in danger before, but here was Fontaneau telling her outright, in so many words, that his plan was to kill her!

No more fancy dresses, copper tubs, and Dancie to make her look beautiful. Get your act together and get out of here! There was no time to waste; she had to reach Mama Dolly, reach the captain, and leave this place before they were all dead!

Upstairs, she paced the floor, which was certainly not a new habit in Fontaneau's mansion. She had concentrated on Mama Dolly until her head hurt. Surely the woman knew that the escape plan had failed, that Fontaneau had come for her instead of the planned boat! *Is Mama working up more mumbo-jumbo in her shack? Is this why she hasn't come?*

Late afternoon, and before the diner hour, Dancie entered her room. "Time to git dressed. Mistah Fontaneau want you ready at half-past."

"Half-past what?" Summer asked, having no clue of the time.

"Half past 5:00."

"What's the deal tonight?"

"Da carriage gettin' ready and dat's all I knows. I thinks you's goin' somewheres."

Her mind raced, but she could not think of how to change the events to come. Ruiz's whereabouts were a complete mystery to her, but Fontaneau seemed to break through all the cracks; after all, he knew where she was when he picked her up on a dock at the edge of nowhere. *He must know where Ruiz is hiding! Perhaps he's waiting for me at the boat at Black Bay?*

The slow-paced "getting ready" of prior times was gone. Fontaneau was in a hurry to leave, so Dancie was on full speed. No pearls or rosettes in the hair this time; no mirror-twirling, and no fancy ball gown. The dull day dress that Summer had found in the dressing room, was the dress Dancie laid on the bed.

Is this the execution dress? Summer shuddered with the thought. She had no recourse, but to meet Fontaneau at the bottom of the stairs to be led to the carriage where she joined a stout older gentleman who sat with a satchel resting on his lap. She assumed this was the lawyer with the legal papers.

"Where are we going?" she asked Fontaneau, once settled for the ride.

"I told you, to meet Ruiz."

"Just the three of us?" Perhaps Ruiz could get away, if that were the case.

"Do you think me a simpleton? Ha! You shall see."

They rode in silence on a road so bumpy and rutted that she thought perhaps they were returning to the 'Delacroix' path. When they stopped at a fork in the road, several miles from Fontaneau's, she realized that they were not at the 'Delacroix' path, but somewhere she did not recognize. Eight mounted horsemen waited at the fork, and her heart sank at the sight. *We are too outnumbered!*

As a caravan, they traveled down the right fork with two horsemen now leading the carriage and the others riding behind. Her nerves hissed through her body like shorted electrical wires. They would reach the end of the road eventually, and then what?

* * *

With shaking hands she stepped out of the carriage. The mast of a ship spired from behind the trees and brush. *The water!* Ruiz was there, somewhere in that brush, about to be ambushed. Throwing caution to the wind, she broke free of her captors who were busy whispering orders to the horsemen.

"Ruiz!" she screamed, running into the brush. "It's a trap! Fontaneau has…" she fell to the ground, branches scrapping her face and arms. He was heavy, the man who lay upon her, and she strained to breathe.

"Damn!" she heard Fontaneau say. "She's ruined it!"

The man who had jumped her, pulled her up to a standing position, his hand roughly covering her mouth. "Shut up," he said, and by the look in his eyes, he meant it. "Yell again and I'll break your neck."

Please have heard me, Ruiz, she prayed as the man dragged her back through the brush to where Fontaneau stood, his arms crossed, his face red with anger.

"I look forward to your disappearance, Miss Woodfield," Fontaneau said through gritted teeth. "Put her in the carriage until I call for her," he ordered.

In the carriage, with one of the horsemen glaring at her from the opposite seat, she peered out the window. The men were huddled together, and she supposed they were going from plan A to plan B, since she had (hopefully) ruined the surprise.

Shortly, Fontaneau, the lawyer, who was much shorter and plumper than he looked sitting in the carriage beforehand, and one horseman, disappeared through the brush and trees toward the mast of the ship. Dismally, she watched as the other horsemen, who had tied their horses to branches, dispatched into the forest in various directions.

"I've come with the papers and a lawyer. All legal and proper." Fontaneau yelled. "Miss Woodfield is a bit of an actress. There is no trap, so don't shoot!"

Oh, she wanted to scream bloody murder out the window, but casting a sideward glance at her jailer, she realized it would be death sentence before she had a chance to escape. *You're on your own now, Ruiz; be careful, my love!* She closed her eyes, waiting for guns to fire, for yelling, for anything but it was silence that encompassed the carriage.

Soon, the horsemen who had left with Fontaneau and the lawyer, returned to retrieve her. A handkerchief was slipped through her mouth and tied in the back of her head. He then led her through the short span of cypress toward the mast of the ship, her body trembling in fear of the unknown. When they reached the edge of the clearing, he pulled her right arm behind her back and yanked upward until she thought her shoulder would break. She whimpered with pain.

"Shut up now. I'm taking the gag off, and if you say a word, you're dead right here and now. Got it?"

Yes, she nodded and the gag was removed.

Ruiz appeared pathetically bedraggled, tired and unkempt. Otto and Alvarez looked the same as they stood against a backdrop of sloop and the bay. Somewhere a bird cawed.

"Captain Ruiz has signed the papers, Miss Woodfield. Now, I am keeping my end of the bargain."

"Which bargain is that, Fontaneau? The bargain to set us free, or the bargain with yourself to kill us all!" She yelled the last part. "It's a trap, Ruiz!"

Suddenly, Ruiz didn't appear so bedraggled, nor did Otto and Alvarez. It all happened so quickly! Summer was tossed to the side, as the seven other horsemen literally sprang from the forest and onto the bank of the bay. Guns were drawn, as well as a knife or two. The chubby lawyer stumbled backward, heading toward the path to the carriage and safety, but Summer had the presence of mind to trip him as he passed. He fell to the ground, and she sat on him, *hard.*

"No you don't, you stuffed potato!" The chubby lawyer began to bounce beneath her, trying to shake her off. For a moment, she was reminded of her childhood and riding her father's back in such a manner once or twice. "Stop it!" she said, bopping him on the head.

All the while she watched, terrified that Ruiz and cronies would lose this battle. After all, they were outnumbered! But she soon realized that the bedraggled tired appearance was as ploy to relax Fontaneau, to make it appear that Ruiz and his men were too tired to fight.

When a bullet whizzed by her head, it all became too real. She knew she had to let the lawyer go and help Ruiz and the men; with bullets flying, it was a whole new ballgame. For a few moments, the scene played out in slow motion. She felt as if she were in another place, far away, a voyeur watching a story she was not a part of. Then, she was there, amidst the chaos, the sound of men grunting, hitting and being hit. Shots fired, piercing her ears. Three of the horsemen were down, and not moving. Dead, she assumed. She saw two others race off into the trees, along with the chubby lawyer. Spotting the lawyer's cane on the ground, she lifted it, only to have a sword slip from its holder! *What a sneaky thing!* But it was providence, and she had a weapon. Though she couldn't picture herself harming anyone with it, it did give her a boost of power.

Alvarez and Otto were now in the sloop fighting off the remaining horsemen, whose adrenaline had risen to a frightening level; powerful men, all, in a battle for their lives.

Ruiz had fallen to the ground. She watched in horror as his pistol slipped off the bank into the water.

"I have you now, bastard!" Fontaneau yelled, his face glistening red with sweat while his pistol dug into Ruiz's chest. "Ha! It's all mine, you bloody blackguard!"

"Stop!" Summer screamed, running toward her fallen lover, the sword held outward with both hands. "Stop, Fontaneau! Don't shoot!"

Fontaneau turned, looking very much confused. For a split second, he glanced at his fallen soldiers, and then at Summer, who raced at him at full speed, the sword leading her on a path to his demise. He ducked away from her aim, and she, sword in hand, tripped over Ruiz and fell over the bank into the water. It was surprisingly deep, and she sank until she wondered if she would come up again. The dress was heavy, pulling her down. She released the sword and fought like the men above, to bring herself to the surface.

Ruiz had taken the opportunity to clamber into the sloop with his cronies. She was nearer the bank, and he leaned far over the side of the ship, his arm outstretched to her. "Hurry, Verano! Take my hand!"

Out of the corner of her eye she saw Fontaneau, bent to the ground. He was all who was left on the bank. He rose with a pistol in his hand. First, he pointed at Ruiz, but Ruiz had untethered the sloop, and it drifted away from the dock. Alvarez and Otto scrambled to hoist sail.

"Hurry, Vernao!" Ruiz sounded panic stricken that they should drift away without her on board.

"Get back here, Ruiz!" Fontaneau yelled. "I'll shoot your little whore if you don't!"

The pistol was now pointed at her—so close! She looked at the sloop which had drifted even further, and she knew she could not catch it, not in the heavy dress that felt like an anchor. She was desperately treading water as it was, just to keep afloat.

"Go!" she screamed. "Go! I'll…." She swallowed water and coughed, treading harder to keep from sinking.

Fontaneau was now kneeling on the bank, holding out a hand to her, the pistol out of sight. "Oh, take my hand," he said, totally frustrated.

The sails were now up on the sloop. "I will find you, Verano!" Ruiz yelled, his voice fainter than before with distance between them. "I will come for you!"

She now stood on the bank, soaked through and through, water from her hair dripping into her eyes, mixing with the tears that fell like a waterfall.

"He will come for you, and I will get him then." Fontaneau said, putting a hand on her shoulder, turning her, nudging her toward the trees. "Until then, you will be my guest, and you will never, *ever* breathe a word of Bella Vista to the Federals. Do you understand?"

She nodded, her heart broken as she squished her way back through the brush and trees to the carriage.

"What about the dead men?" she asked, trying to wring water from her skirt before entering the carriage where the chubby lawyer sat, his face and double chins red as beets from fear *or* exertion—she couldn't tell which.

"Get rid of the bodies," Fontaneau said to the remaining horsemen. "And bring the horses with you"

Chapter 28

But he didn't come. Summer's spirit sank lower and lower as the days passed, trapped in Fontaneau's home without chance of escape. Mama Dolly did not come to save her. She had not seen Lila since viewing the snake tattooed on her face. *Where are they?* Ruiz, Mama and Lila had vanished as if they had never existed. She wondered if she were losing her mind. Without her mission of saving Ruiz to occupy her time, she questioned the reason for being jailed in Fontaneau's residence. *Why am I still here?* She wanted her life back—*desperately*. She wanted to be with Guy, to plan for the twins, to laugh with Jesse. But, here she sat, day after day in the lavish bedroom in another place and time. Dancie tried to cheer her. Even Fontaneau tried to cheer her with a new gown and a party, but it was to no avail.

"He'll come." he said, as if trying to appease them both for separate reasons.

She lost her appetite and her desire to get out of bed in the mornings. All was lost.

Then, she snapped out of it. As if someone had turned on the light in her head, she woke one morning determined to get free of Fontaneau's grasp. She would walk home to Magnolia if need be! She would leave this place and walk home to Georgia! Dancie and Fontaneau were both pleased to hear her pacing the floor of the bedroom again. She paced, and thought... paced, and thought. She thought hard until she came up with a feasible plan of escape. Her mind was rusty from her depression and seclusion.

"I can't stand being locked in this house day after day" she said at breakfast. "Can't we go for a ride? Perhaps to the dock and walk a while? Have a coffee and beignet?"

Fontaneau eyed her suspiciously. "Do you have a plan?" he asked, eyebrows raised in that pompous way of his. "Have you somehow heard from your lover, or worse, that voodoo witch?"

"I only wish," she replied, keeping her focus steady on his face. "I'm bored…bored out of my mind!"

"Perhaps your lover has decided he doesn't need you? Well, well, what will I do with you then?"

"Honestly? I don't want to think of what you'll do with me. I think I have a pretty good idea. For now, though, while I still live and breathe,"she said, haughtily, "I would like to go for a ride…to walk on the dock for air…to have a little coffee and beignet. Is it too much to ask?"

Fontaneau rang a small silver bell that always sat at his side at the dining table. Dancie appeared almost immediately, as if she had been listening at the kitchen door. "Yes sah?" she said, causing both Fontaneau and Summer to jump slightly at her unexpected quick arrival.

"Please ask for the carriage to be brought around. Miss Woodfield and I will be going out."

Dancie looked questioningly at Summer, as if recalling the last time Summer went out with Mr. Fontaneau and returned a wet and dripping mess.

"Why you's so quiet all da time?" Dancie asked later, as she prepared Summer for her "outing".

"I'm sorry. I'm just thinking, and I'm better now too, honestly!"

"I'se glad to hear dat. You's had us worried to da death!"

"You can relax now."

"Amen."

When Dancie left the room, Summer stepped onto the balcony and closed her eyes. *Please Mama Dolly! Please hear me. I need you desperately! Please hear me and come!* Perhaps it would work, perhaps it wouldn't. Maybe her powers, her own form of black magic, had left on the sloop with Ruiz. Perhaps she had used it all up; perhaps that was all there was, and she was stuck forever in 1864 New Orleans, trapped in the clutches of Mr. Fontaneau.

Not if I can help it! I have a life and I'm going back! Even if she returned to Magnolia and it was tattered and broken from the war, she would still be *home,* and it sounded mighty good.

* * *

"Happy now?" Fontaneau asked, helping her from the carriage at the square.

"Yes, thank you." She wore the red satin dress, yards and yards of fabric billowing over the four hoops, along with a matching bonnet and parasol. *Yes, I'm happy! I'm leaving this place forever!*

They strolled along the dock amidst the crowds of vendors, sailors, stevedores, prostitutes and the ever-present Union army that patrolled the port for danger. Masts of ships jutting into the air foretold of the clogged port with barely a whisper of space between the rocking ships. Thick ropes secured the ships to pilings which squeaked and stretched against the rolling swells caused by the endless activity of the Port of New Orleans.

"It's a lovely day," Fontaneau said, Summer's arm hooked into his. Anyone witnessing their walk would think they were lovers, or man and wife out on a stroll.

"It is," she answered, her eyes beneath the parasol constantly in search of Mama Dolly. She stopped in her tracks when she thought she saw… Lila! Yes, it was Lila up ahead, talking to a sailor! She fought the urge to run up and hug the little traitor.

"The whore is back at it, I see," Fontaneau said. When they reached Lila, she stuck her nose in the air, turned her back to them and continued her deal with the sailor. The snake tattoo was gone. After they passed, Summer glanced over her shoulder and sighed; bittersweet, it was; she had somehow grown a fondness for the little witch.

Ahead, a paddleboat spewed a rocket of black smoke into the sky; it was about to sail. They stopped, as the sailing ships were moored further away from the paddleboat dock giving them a clear view of its departure. Passengers lined the railing of the boat, waving to those onshore. Summer wished she were on it. She waved in return, stepping closer to the dock's edge as the boat, untethered, was now beginning its journey down the Mississippi. The bright red paddle on the stern churned the water in steady fashion as it grew smaller to the eye. She thought of Ruiz, somewhere out there. Did he make it to Buck Key? Did he reconnect with his mother and daughter? All this time saving him, and here she was, ignorant of the answers to her questions. Would she always have to wonder?

She turned to look at Mr. Fontaneau and there, behind him in the shadow of a saloon, stood Mama Dolly! Mama beckoned, in that silent way she had of speaking, and which Summer understood.

"Come and look at this!" she said to Fontaneau. He strolled to the dock's edge and looked downward into the water. "What? I don't see anything."

"There, just below the surface. What is it?"

Fontaneau leaned further over the water, which gave Mama Dolly the perfect advantage of *mistakenly* bumping him.

Splash! The women did not wait for someone to help Fontaneau out of the river. As a crowd gathered of laughing sailors and alarmed soldiers, the women slipped away, between the saloons, down the cobblestone streets, *running...running... running*...until they reached Congo Square and then, the safety of Mama Dolly's shanty.

"Oh my God!" Summer exclaimed, gasping for air, leaning against the inside closed door of the shanty. "Where have you been, Mama? I was so alone!"

"You shut me out, gal. I try and try to find you, but you shut me out. Today, I hear you and I says "well der's my girl!" and here I is."

Summer ran to the woman who had answered her prayers. She wrapped her arms (as far as they would stretch) around the bull of woman who had saved her countless times in this adventure. "I want to go home, now, Mama. I don't know how to get back. I don't know where the captain is, and I can't help him anymore. I just want to go home."

"And you will, chile," Mama said, hugging Summer tightly to her bosom. "You's goin' home. Wait an' see."

"What do I do now?"

"You know da answer."

"I can't wear this," Summer said grabbing a handful of the red satin.

Again, Mama dug around in the old trunk in the corner of her little house. "I'se runnin' out o' clothes!" She held up a dismal dark colored skirt and a red, billowy blouse.

"I would love to repay you Mama, but I have no money."

"I don' want no money. Jes' havin' you heah, da white lady wid da magic from another place, been good; it been a gran' ting, girl."

"I'll never forget you, or your kindness."

Mama Dolly wiped a tear from her eye. "Hesh up," she said and turned away.

* * *

She headed north, and like a hobo carried a bundle full of food, water and 'useful objects', which included a scary looking doll, and gris-gris to keep her safe. Mama insisted she take these things, and assured her she would get home. "Jes follow da railroad tracks n' keep on goin' girl! You's gonna git der, I knows it!" Mama pointed her north. "Go roun' da lake, and keep on goin.'"

When night fell, dark and thick, she tucked herself away amidst the trees and brush that lined the tracks, and slept. A passing train woke her in the night, but she was exhausted and fell back to sleep easily. In the morning, her spirits lifted, despite feeling dirty, sweaty, covered with bites and tired. She was going home to Magnolia! No matter how long it took, she would get there; Mama Dolly said so!

What Mama Dolly didn't tell her, was that Mr. Fontaneau was not going to give her up so easily.

* * *

She heard the horses before she noticed the two riders coming up behind her on the dusty sides of the tracks. By the time she realized it was she they were after, it was too late to dash into the woods. Her spirits fell dramatically as the riders approached. *It's hopeless—I'll never get home!* She wondered how Fontaneau knew where to look? Surely Mama Dolly would not have told, but who knew what evil Fontaneau was capable of? Had he tortured the poor woman?

"Hold it there, Miss Wooodfield." The riders, sweaty and fairly breathless, had halted their horses on either side of her. One man held out a hand for her to mount the horse and ride behind him.

"I don't ride horses," she said.

"Well, you're riding this one, lady."

The second rider took her satchel, and she could do nothing but relent, holding out a hand to be lifted upon the fidgeting beast before her.

A few embarrassing and fumbled attempts to mount passed before she plopped onto the horse's hot behind.

"Hold on!" the rider said, turning the animal.

The rider gave his mount a kick and off they went at a trot, she, flopping haphazardly on the horse's behind. "Don't go so fast!" she pleaded, but the rider trotted on. Along with feeling hopelessly trapped and depressed, she was terribly nervous about this scenario. "Slow down!" she yelled. "I can't stay on!"

She couldn't hear his reply, but he grasped her knuckled hands, which couldn't quite encircle the man's waist, and pushed them into his belly, indicating that she should perhaps hold on tighter.

She did grasp tighter, but still flopped precariously, each contact between her rear end and the horse's making her wince with pain. "Slow down, damn...," she began but then all hell broke loose. The rider had whipped the horse (and her leg along with it), and took off at a gallop. The rider ahead was also galloping.

Stop!" she screamed, holding desperately to her captor as she flopped from one side of the horse's rump to the other. When she felt a sudden distance between her and the rider, and the lump of the horse's tail pounding in her crotch, she panicked even further. *I'm falling!*

Then, she heard it—Ruiz's voice! "Hold on, Vernano!"

In her bouncing and frantic state, and from the corner of her eye, she saw that another horse gained on them. She dare not turn to look, but *it has to be Ruiz!*

"I've come for you!" he shouted, and then drew beside her, his face red with adrenaline. Another horse came up beside him, and she realized with great relief that her rescue party had arrived. Ruiz's horse lunged ahead, putting him fully side by side with her captor. "Stop!" he yelled to the man. "Stop or you are dead!"

A shot rang out; and now, frantic with fear of falling and being trampled, she tried to duck, having no idea who was shooting at whom. It wasn't Ruiz, because with one hand, he was punching at her rider and trying to grab his reins, while holding onto his own galloping beast. The rider fought back, but Ruiz gave him no opportunity to pull a weapon. It was a harrowing race for survival, taken none too lightly by Summer. Ruiz's horse continuously bumped against her leg, pushing her back further from the saddle. In the chaos she heard hooves pounding behind her and prayed that this was not her end—trampled by a horse in another century! She screamed, as the last bounce sent her crashing to the ground, where she rolled and tossed like a rag doll thrown from a moving train. Again and again she thumped across the ground, covering her face, trying to protect her eyes. Then, she was in the air and crashed onto something very hard….

* * *

She groaned and opened her eyes to see Guy kneeling beside her.

"What happened? Are you alright?" he asked, the worry written across his face.

"Guy?"

"Who else were you expecting? What happened? Are you okay?"

Remembering the twins, her hand ran over a large lump of a belly. "Oh," she said. "I'm here—uh—on the floor."

"Yes, you're here and….oh, no. Tell me you weren't time traveling again." Guy looked very unhappy.

"No…no… it was a dream—a scary one. I guess I fell out of bed. Help me up." She hoped he believed her. No sense rocking the boat. Upon standing, her belly settled heavily downward.

"Do you have pain?"

She thought a moment. "No, I think all is well. "I just want to rest a moment. I'm okay. Go ahead, do whatever you were doing."

After he left the room, she sat at Elizabeth's dressing table. "I'm back," she said to her reflection. She was both happy and sad. *What's happened to Ruiz?* Shaking her memory into place, she remembered that Ruiz and his buddies had come to save her, the crazy horse chase, falling off the horse and rolling across the dirt. How did Fontaneau know where to find her, and how did Ruiz find out? Where did Ruiz get the horses? It was all such a mystery, and she was too tired to even think about all that had happened.

"I'm putting you out of my mind, Ruiz. I have babies to be born, I'm marrying a man I love; I have a beautiful home. Please, *please* stay away!" How could she live her life always wondering when she would find herself back in another century? And, if she did return to another century, would Ruiz be there? Would it even be 1864 or another century and another group of people she would grow to love? It was all exasperatedly unknown.

"Ruiz," she whispered wiping away a tear. A pain stabbed her heart, and she wished she could rip him from her memory.

Chapter 29

"Remember that old man in the nursing home?" she asked one evening at dinner.

"You mean the nasty old goat who doesn't want to be Jesse's cousin? Yes. Why?"

"I got a note from him today." She handed Guy a letter handwritten on yellow, lined paper.

"Dear Miss Woodfield'—guess he doesn't know you're married now—*"It would be much appreciated if you could visit me again in the very near future. My health is failing, and there are a few things I've remembered and would like to share with you."*

Guy peered over the yellow paper at her. "And?" he asked.

"And I'm going, of course. Tomorrow. I just wanted you to know."

He sighed. "…and the saga continues."

"It does, Guy. It's important for Jesse, *and* for me."

"I know. I just hope no ghosts of the past come to retrieve you because of this."

She shrugged. "Whatever happens, I have no control. You do realize that."

"I realize that we are now a married couple, soon to be parents; that's what I realize. Hopefully you won't be traipsing off with some ancient Egyptian ancestor or Scottish king."

"Let's hope it never comes to that." She couldn't promise anything when it came to time travel.

* * *

Driving to the nursing home she reflected on what had transpired in the past weeks. Her wedding ring had not yet sat on her finger for more than a month, and in that time she had pledged herself to Guy Mason in an official ceremony; pledged herself to their soon-to-be-born children; pledged herself to their future together. But nothing was certain in her topsy-turvy world, and especially where Captain Ruiz was concerned.

Mental visions of him floated past her mind's eye and painfully crossed her heart on occasion, but she tried desperately to shoo them away as quickly as they appeared. Her focus was on the birth of her babies and making a life with the husband she had here on earth, the husband she loved, and not the dashing Spanish captain she had fallen madly in love with in a different time and place.

Waddling (or so she felt) down the hallway to the library where her meeting with Taylor Woodfield was to be held, she felt butterflies in her stomach; anticipation and excitement prevailed. She peeked around the library door first, to see if he was there. He was, sitting in the wheelchair with his back to her, his bald spot reflecting the overhead lights.

"Hello Mr. Woodfield," she said, stepping in front of him.

"Well, look at you," he said, as her belly was in direct line with his vision.

"I'm married now," she said hurriedly, lest he think otherwise.

"Good for you. I never married, myself. Was too busy keeping up the empire that was left me by my ancestors."

It dawned on her that she had no knowledge of his life prior to the nursing home. "What empire is that?" She was honestly curious.

"Why, the cattle ranch, of course! I guess you don't know anything about that part of the Woodfield clan."

"Well…no, I don't, but I would certainly like to hear about it."

"That's why I've called for you," he said, indicating for her to sit in a chair across from him. He coughed into a handkerchief. "We need to clean up this mess between us. My lungs aren't so good anymore. I'm afraid my time is running out—another reason I wanted you here. I had to hide it all my life, you know."

"Hide what?"

"That black grandma of mine."

"Do you mean Cherry?"

"That's the one, Cherry was her name. My granddaddy told me that his mama was a black slave-woman and that he was born on a key, out there in the Florida islands. Buck Key, that's what it was called, and still is, I think. Buck was the man who raised my granddaddy. He was a black fellow but my great-granddaddy was a white man—the son of a damned Yankee soldier, and a deserter at that." The old man shook his head in disgust.

"Go on," Summer said, barely audible as this outpouring of facts from Taylor Woodfield, facts she knew to be true, had left her nearly breathless.

"The way I heard tell, it was a Spanish pirate, a hooligan of sorts, who was responsible for everything involved way back then. Can't exactly remember his real name, even though he is one of my mixed-up ancestors. It started with an "R" I think.

"Ancestor?" Summer was shocked. *Ancestor?* "Ruiz?" she asked, without realizing she had even spoken his name.

"Taylor looked surprised. "Yes, that's it, *Ruiz.*" How the devil did you know?"

"I…I can't explain it, sir."

"You give me the willies, young lady. You already know a lot about my—I guess it's *our*— family."

The butterflies swarmed in her gut. This was an incredulous turn of events! She leaned toward Taylor Woodfield. "Tell me about Ruiz."

"Well, let me get this straight in my head…. Ruiz, or Granddaddy Alvarez, as I knew of him, had a daughter hiding out on Buck Key. I think he was in some kind of trouble with the Union army. He was hiding out with his young daughter, that fellow, Buck, my granddaddy Yank, and some other folks during the War-Between-the-States. After the war, my granddaddies and the folks left the key, and moved to southern Florida. They bought some land with that gold you told me about. Then, they bought some cattle, and that was the beginning of the W-A Bella Vista Ranch; Woodfield/Alvarez. Buck used the Woodfield name instead of his own. I guess he wanted to do right by my granddaddy's mama, the black one."

Summer was flabbergasted. "Wait," she said, her head reeling with this new information. "Tell me how are you related to Ruiz?" How could this blue-eyed crusty old man be from the same family as her beloved captain?

"He was my great-granddaddy. His daughter married my granddaddy, Yank. She had a changed name too, because of the troubles they left behind, but I knew her as Granny Marsha. Her and my granddad, well, they grew up together on the Bella Vista.

Marguerite? Summer sat back in her chair, speechless.

"You okay?" Taylor asked.

Silence.

"Miss Woodfield?"

"Oh!" She sat up, realizing she had blanked out for a moment—forgotten where she was—as she absorbed the shocking news of Taylor's heritage. "And…and…." It was difficult to even think or speak coherently! "And…where…where is the Bella Vista? What's happened to it?"

"Why, nothing has happened to it. I have a foreman, lawyers, and a business manager. The Bella Vista lives on, thanks to Alvarez, a Negro, a pot of gold, and, naturally, my good business sense. Are you alright, young lady? You look like you've seen a ghost."

I have seen a ghost, lived with a ghost, loved a ghost. Loved two, ghosts as a matter of fact; Robert[72] *and Ruiz.* She became conscious of the twins stirring in her belly; they had chased the butterflies away.

"Can I see it?" she asked. "The ranch. Can I see it?"

"You'll have to go to Florida to see it and I don't think you look in any condition to traipse around a cattle ranch."

---

[72] Robert Mason, a character from Book I

She laid a hand across her belly. "Maybe after…." *Surely after! I have to see where Ruiz lived, where Buck and Yank lived…Marguerite…the Señora…Dilly.* She wanted to ask Tayor about the others, but how could she? He hadn't mentioned the Señora or Dilly, and he was already obviously curious about her knowledge of the past.

"There you have it, he said."

"What happened to Alvarez, and Buck?"

"Why they died, eventually of course. They're both buried right there on the property with the others. I'll join them, one day.

"*Dead?* It was difficult to believe they were gone, even though she knew it had to be so after 150 years. "Who else is buried there?"

"Granny Marsha and a few of her babies that didn't make it. My parents…."

"Your parents, what were their names?"

"My pop was Yank Buck Woodfield, and my mama, Jane. I have no brothers or sisters, so it's just me. I have no heirs and that leads me to another reason why I called on you."

"Oh?"

"Since you seem to be so knowledgeable of the Woodfield family, I thought you could help with establishing a connection with that…that black woman you brought here the first time."

"You mean Jesse? The one you so rudely insulted?"

"Yes…*that* one."

"To tell you the truth, she and I have been working on that; not the connection with you directly, but her connection to Cherry, your great-grandmother."

"Hurry, then. I don't think I have much time left." He coughed into the handkerchief to stress the point.

Chapter 30

"You have got to be joking, girl!" Jesse's eyes were big as saucers. She sat forward in the rocker on the porch at Magnolia. "That old buzzard wants to know how he's connected to *me?* Why, he didn't want a thing to do with me last time! He called me the 'N' word, which I didn't much appreciate."

"I'm just as surprised as you are." Summer was still flying high from her meeting with Taylor Woodfield. "What a turnaround, huh? Now we need to get down to brass tacks and find the connection."

"You think he's going to leave me that cow ranch? I don't know anything about cows except they make good ice cream."

Summer laughed. "He didn't exactly say he was going to leave you a cattle ranch, but this request certainly lights a fire under me; and I think it would you, too."

"I hate to admit it, but it does. Guess we need to look into little Percy."

"I don't know what happened to him after Evaline died, but we're going to find out."

Back to the library and the town clerk they went, determined to find the link. They searched cemetery records, white and black, but Percy's name did not appear anywhere in the cemetery records, nor in the county census records.

"Well," Summer said, exasperated after days of empty research. "Your family has to know *something.* Ask again, Jesse. Ask your siblings, your parents, your grandparents. Somebody somewhere has a clue, and we're just missing it."

"Where could a poor black boy go in the Reconstruction period? He was practically a baby." Jesse sighed.

"Wait a minute!" Summer exclaimed. Maybe we're barking up the wrong tree? Suppose Percy left Bluebell—left Magnolia. Suppose he grew up and moved on? What was keeping him here, anyway? His mother was gone, perhaps his grandmother died, and his rotten father, Arthur Ascot, wouldn't claim him. Arthur wanted my g-g-g-grandfather James, instead, because James looked white."

"I guess the closest place he could go to would be…Savannah? Unless he went up north.

Due to Taylor Woodfield's failing health, Summer prayed he would hold on until she and Jesse found the link between his worlds, white *and* black.

Later, after Jesse left and the sun hung lower in the sky, she remained on the porch, rocking in the chair, gazing out at the land she had fallen in love with over time. It was hard to believe that there was a time in the beginning when she was terrified of it and wanted to leave. Her belly was now huge, and she assumed the births were near and she would have to let Jesse do the footwork. Yes…she would, most definitely. The rocker stilled as she relaxed and her head fell gently to her chest.

* * *

She moaned, her body throbbing in pain. It was difficult to open her eyes. With a weak hand, she attempted to brush dirt from her face. Oh, how she ached!

"Verano, my love!" Ruiz held her in his arms at the edge of the woods where she had rolled from the galloping horse. "Speak to me, Verano! Do not die!"

"Huh?" Eyes caked in dust, she opened them to a blurred vision of Ruiz, his face plastered against a cloudless sky. "Where am I?" She could swear she had fallen asleep on the porch at Magnolia.

"You are safe with me, Verano. I have come to take you away."

"The men…the horses…what happened?" It was all coming back to her now; she had fallen from a horse!

"Do not worry about them; they are gone."

"You didn't kill them, did you?" With no reply, her heart sank. "You can't keep killing people, Ruiz. You're in so much trouble already!" She struggled to a sitting position and looked him square in the eye. "Seriously, you are becoming a dangerous outlaw."

"This is war, Verano. You do not understand. And, I have come to save you, not for a lecture."

She realized he couldn't understand the implications of his actions. Yes, it was war, but he truly was an outlaw; she could see that now. How could she love such a man?

"Come. Can you stand? Can you walk? We must return to the boat. Soon Fontaneau will realize his men are not returning."

"He didn't hurt Mama Dolly, did he?"

"Whatever for?"

"She helped me escape, told me to follow the tracks. I thought you were lost to me forever, so I left." Stabs of pain shot through her body as Ruiz helped her to standing. "I hurt all over, she said, closing her eyes against the unmerciful sharpness and dull aches."

"You had a bad fall, but now we get you to the ship. We have been hiding for many days waiting for the right time."

"I don't understand how Fontaneau knew where to find me," she said, letting Ruiz lead her to where his horse stood tied to the brush. She warily looked for bodies, but saw none.

"It was Lila."

"How did Lila know?" This was very curious. She had seen Lila at the dock that day with Fontaneau, but the woman had turned her back to them as they passed; it was an obvious snub. "And how do you know that it was Lila?"

"I asked her."

"And just how did you ask her?"

He had lifted her to mount the horse. It was an awkward moment or two before her foot connected with the stirrup and her leg swung over the saddle. "I'm not good at this horse business, you know."

"I will have my arms around you, my love. You will not fall again."

"Why did you ask Lila anything? She's in cahoots with Fontaneau. She'll tell him she saw you!"

"No, do not fret. She will not tell him because Mama Dolly is keeping her company until we are safely away. Then, it will be too late."

Ruiz's foot took place of hers in the stirrup and swung himself onto the horse's behind. The horse shuffled from the weight of two upon its back, but when Ruiz tapped him lightly they took off at a slow walk through a forest thick with brush and brambles. Soon, they came across two unsaddled horses that had stopped to eat greenery along the shoddy path.

"Otto and Alvarez have gone ahead. Those are their horses. We will bring them."

Alvarez? That's where Ruiz got the name he used after he left New Orleans! It was much too inconvenient a ride for conversation, with the constant bumping from the less trodden path, not to mention pulling the two horses along. Summer leaned her head back against Ruiz's chest and wondered what was happening at Magnolia. Just a while ago she had been at home on the porch in the rocking chair, and suddenly she was back in New Orleans! What of the babies? Running a hand across her flat stomach, she couldn't fathom how she could be pregnant one moment, and not at all pregnant in the next. "Are you sure Lila can't get to Fontaneau?" she asked, coming back to the *now* of things.

"Mama Dolly put a mark her. She will not want to be seen with this mark."

"Is it a snake down the side of her face?"

"Yes. How did you know?

"Mama likes to see snakes on Lila."

Ruiz chuckled, his breath warm on her neck.

With their enemies behind them, they rode on in peaceful silence. Perhaps they would make it safely out of this place after all. The bushes and occasional tree branch brushed against their arms and faces as they passed, but it was a small inconvenience compared to the events beforehand.

The sloop was tucked neatly away into a small cut of a river, the water apparently deep enough for the keel, but too far out for them to reach without transport.

At the riverbank, Ruiz slipped off the horse's rump and jumped to the ground before helping Summer dismount.

"Oh," she moaned, her hands rubbing the small of her back, as the sharp landing was a reminder of how banged up she was already, not only from the tumble, but from the wild ride with Fontaneau's horseman as well.

Ruiz unsaddled the horses, tossing the saddles to the side. The animals, obviously joyful for the blessings of freedom, shook their manes and ran off into the trees and down the overgrown path from which they had just emerged.

A short ride in the ship's dory brought them swiftly to the sloop. Once onboard, Otto and Alvarez eyed her distrustfully. She straightened, mustering up the courage to eye them back boldly. Perhaps they held her responsible for the delay in their escape from certain execution? *Well, I can't argue that; I am holding them up*, she thought, but was helpless to change the situation, as she was hopelessly stuck in the events that had transpired.

She took a tally of the amenities onboard, which were practically nil aside from an open hatch and ladder indicating there was a cabin below. She did not relish traveling with Otto and Alvarez, and wondered how many days it would take to sail from this place to their destination, Buck Key. With minimal privacy, and men who apparently did not hold her in the same regard as did Captain Ruiz, she was not looking forward to the journey. Of course, having made the journey to Buck Key before, she knew full well that the weather would determine their progress, and she hoped for sunny, breezy days ahead to get them there quickly.

"Hoist the mainsail!" Ruiz yelled, shaking her from her thoughts. "Ahora! Now! We leave this place!"

She stood aside as a flurry of activity from the men scooted her further and further from midship to the transom, praying fervently that the wind would billow the sails and take them off into the Gulf and to safety. The journey ahead was not appealing in the least.

"Go below," Ruiz ordered, nodding toward the open hatch.

"Why?" she asked, knowing full well she would be near to suffocating in an airless, hot cabin.

"Perhaps there will be trouble; we do not know this yet. Go and rest! There is nothing you can do here."

She complied, crawling down the ladder into the stuffy cabin which resembled a dumping ground once she had both feet planted and could view her surroundings. Boots, raingear, blankets, dirty pillows, dishes, bottles; it all littered the cabin in a most unappealing way. She wondered if she had the energy to tidy up, make it livable, knowing instinctively well that it would be solely up to her to do so, whether she had the energy or not.

For a brief moment she lost her footing, putting a hand out onto a small counter for support. When steady, she poked her head up through the hatch to see the sails had caught the wind. *On our way!* A surge of excitement energized the desire to organize the small living space, while above the men shouted orders to one another as they set the course for freedom.

* * *

"Un barco hacia el sur. ¡ Rápido, rápido![73]"

Summer dropped the pair of boots she was holding and ran to the ladder. Top deck she found Ruiz red-faced at the wheel.

"What is it?" Her heart pounded in her chest. She had been tidying the cabin below, even humming to herself from sheer happiness at being out of danger, when the alarm came.

"Look!" Ruiz pointed southward to another sloop.

"Maybe it's just a fisherman?"

"No, it is Fontaneau's boat, the bastard. We must gain speed." He shouted again to the men, who were adjusting the sails, muscles bulging, sweat pouring, and faces as red as the captain's.

"We have no canons," Ruiz said. "We do not have enough weapons to war them off. This is not good, Verano, but we will outrun them; I will not let them take us!" He forced a smile, his white teeth gleaming against his rugged, dark face, but his eyes told another tale; he was not quite as convinced as he tried to sound.

She put a hand on his, which gripped the wheel like a vise. "You will get away, Ruiz. Believe me."

"You are so sure...."

"I *know* you will get away."

"Where I go, you go, my love."

"Yes," she said. *But where I go, you cannot go.*

---

[73]"*Un barco hacia el sur.¡ Rápido, rápido*!" A boat to the south! Quick! Quick!"

She looked again at the sloop in the distance. It did appear to be gaining on them, which caused her stomach to flip-flop. "How are they getting closer?"

"His boat is newer and faster. You must go below, now!"

"Let me help!" she pleaded, not having a clue as to how she could.

"My brave Verano. Kiss me and go!"

She complied, first touching his lips gently, then folding herself into his arms, holding him near. She stood sandwiched between him and the wheel, lodged between his strong arms.

"We are in this together," she said, gripping the wheel between his two hands of steel. "We will stay together." She leaned against him, feeling the taut, hard muscles of his chest against her back.

"Remember that I love you always, Verano."

He could not see the tears that flew with the wind from her eyes. *Where does this end?* Fighting hard against welling fear, she straightened, gained control of her emotions, and concentrated on the job ahead: escaping Fontaneau and helping Ruiz gain his freedom.

When the first shots fired, they struck and splintered the wooden roof of the cabin. Ruiz pushed her aside. "Below!" he ordered. When she refused, he pushed her away from the wheel. "I do not want you killed!" he yelled.

"I will not leave you!"

Her face was now as red as his, their eyes locked in a battle of wills. Shots rang again, close enough to feel a spray of wooden splinters of wood exploding like fireworks, stinging face and arms. The natural reaction was to duck, and she did. Another bullet fired, whizzing over her head, striking the mainsail mast, and yet she refused to leave.

"You are stubborn, Verano!" Ruiz yelled, neck veins bulging. "Lie on the deck!" he ordered and just in time, as more shots fired, one barely missing the captain.

Otto and Alverez were now kneeling at the transom next to her, firing back at Fontaneau's ship, which was close behind, and the distance closing quickly.

"Give me a gun!" Summer yelled. But, there was no time to search for or hand out guns. She remained crouched and soon heard shouts from Fontaneau's side.

"Give it up, Ruiz. You've lost!"

"Never!" Ruiz answered.

They're so close! How will we escape?

"I don't care if I take you dead or alive, Ruiz!"

"You will not take me at all!"

Summer raised her head over the transom to see Fontaneau's sloop perhaps 300 yards away. They were so close she could see Fontaneau's jacket flapping in the wind as he raised his pistol aiming toward them.

"Get down," Otto snarled. "Can't let anything happen to the captain's precious cargo." Summer ducked, wanting to punch the man where it hurt. He obviously held her in great distain.

Alvarez fired, which only brought return fire from Fontaneau's side. As Alvarez reloaded his pistol beside her, she glanced at Ruiz who held tight the wheel keeping the sails into the wind, but she knew in her heart that his determination could not help the situation.

The next fire from Fontaneau's sloop hit Otto's shoulder. He flew backward and fell, cursing. Blood gushed from the wound, from between his fingers and onto the deck. He rocked, moaning in pain. She crawled to him, thinking she could rip her skirt to make a bandage.

"Get away from me!" he yelled. "You ain't been nothin' but trouble!"

She recoiled, shocked that his anger overshadowed the desire for help.

"There's only one thing to do with you," he said. She watched in amazement as the injured man staggered to his feet. Then, with superhuman strength, his arm bleeding profusely, he reached down and pulled her up…and up…and up until she was off the ground and precariously tossed over his shoulder. In a split second, she felt herself sailing away from the safety of the boat. She screamed as she flew over the wake of the ship and then down into the ominous sea. Water filled her mouth, the skirt weighed her down, but she struggled to the top, choking on sea water, bobbing and rolling in the wake.

In the distance Ruiz struggled with Otto, who fell from sight. "I'm coming for you, Verano!" Ruiz's voice was barely audible as it carried off with the wind.

At that moment, another shot rang out from Fontaneau's ship, which was now closing in on her.

"Go! Go! I will be alright!" It was futile; the wind and waves made it impossible for her voice to carry.

"You're dead, Ruiz!" Fontaneau yelled, and then another shot fired, sending Ruiz backward, grasping his arm.

In horror, she fought the cold, gray, rolling sea as it tried to claim her, sucking her into its watery underworld then shooting her out again as she choked on its salty brine. *I'm dead for sure,* she thought, furiously pumping her legs to stay afloat in the unforgiving gulf waters. Ruiz's sloop was turning back as Fontaneau's approached.

"Take me. Let him go!" she yelled, though if anyone heard she hadn't a clue. She bobbed and dipped in minor swells that appeared to be giants when struggling at the same level as the water's surface.

She tried to wave Ruiz off, but she was invisibly nestled between the swells. *Don't come for me!*

"Hold on, Miss Woodfield!" Fontaneau's sloop had slowed; he was apparently going to save her from the choppy water. Knowing full well that his objective was to capture Ruiz—preferably dead— she was surprised that he would give up the chase, but ever so grateful!

She beat the water with her hands to stay afloat, as her legs were now twisted hopelessly into the fabric of the long skirt. "Help!" Her voice held a notch above a whisper as exhaustion overtook her struggling body and she began to feel numb from the cold water. "Help! Please, help!"

"Come on!" Fontaneau waved her forward.

"I can't! I'm sinking!" Her head dipped below the surface. She kicked her legs frantically, mermaid style, in their prison of fabric, but the swells pushed her back, pulling her under in a deadly tug of war with the sea.

Her first thought was of sharks when she felt a thud against her body. But then, *saints be praised!* Fontaneau had sent one of his crew to save her! By the time she secured an arm through the rough bottom rung of the ladder, she was gasping for air and holding on for dear life, too tired to move. She just wanted to stay a while, to dangle from the ladder as the sloop sailed on, but the crew member was behind her, encouraging her to begin her climb.

It was a body heavy with soaked yards of fabric that grunted and banged against the bulwarks, as she slowly brought herself up the ladder. Her rescuer held tightly to the bottom rung in order to keep the ladder as secure as it could be held in a rolling sea.

"So nice to see you again." Fontaneau grinned. "Climb aboard."

Chapter 31

"Well, here you is agin', Miz Summah."

"Yep, here I is again," Summer echoed. She was dry now, but her body felt sticky with sea salt. "Do you think you could draw me one of those nice hot baths of yours?"

"I sho'ly will. Now you jes' lay down on dis bed and relax."

"I won't argue, Dancie."

She sank into the soft, down-filled mattress, disregarding the whiteness of the coverlet and the stains her filthy clothes would leave behind. She was exhausted—totally! At least Ruiz was safely on his way to Buck Key, and she knew he wouldn't die from the bullet wound. In fact, he would go on to become a cattle baron! "He's safe," she whispered. She had thought as she bobbed in the water, that he had turned the sloop toward her, but she was mistaken. When Fontaneau helped her over the gunwale of his sloop, all that could be seen of Ruiz were the two sails in the distance.

Out of the corner of her eye she watched Dancie hustle about. She was ashamed to lay on the bed doing nothing, and a few times attempted to rise and at least help haul the water for her bath, but it was useless; she was paralyzed with fatigue.

Later, when she descended the grand stairway to dine with Mr. Fontaneau, squeezed into the bodice of yet another elaborate gown of his choice, she wondered if Captain McAllister would be present. Her question was answered quickly.

"Miss Woodfield." The captain stood, bowing slightly as she entered. "So nice to see you again."

She nodded and took her seat, which was directly across from him. "Need I guess what brings you here?" she asked.

"Probably not. As you know, we are very anxious to capture Captain Ruiz. He is a war criminal, and we will not rest until we have him in custody."

"Good luck," she said smiling while unfolding her napkin. A glass of wine sat invitingly in front of her place setting; and feeling that she needed something to quiet her nerves, she took a sip. In fact, she took several sips before setting the glass down.

"You must be thirsty after swallowing so much salt water," Fontaneau said, snidely.

"You should know," she replied.

"A nice payback for all the Mississippi River I swallowed."

Summer smiled, remembering Fontaneau flying past her at the dock and into the river.

"So, Miss Woodfield, we are under the impression that you know the whereabouts of Captain Ruiz," interjected McAllister.

"Why should I?" *Haven't we been through this before?*

"Because you were with him!" Fontaneau blurted, his chin jutting forward in ugly fashion. It wouldn't have surprised her if flares of fire shot from his nostrils. His desire to capture Ruiz devoured him.

"No, I do not know. Yes, I was with him, but he did not share his destination with me. My guess is that he would have headed far away from this place and this war".

"She's lying!" Fontaneau pounded a fist on the table, which brought Dancie flying in from the kitchen.

"Yes sah!" she said, eyes big. "You's ready?"

"Bring the soup," Fontaneau ordered, glaring at Summer.

"Yes sah!" she said, and vanished back into the kitchen.

With Dancie's procession of many fine dishes reflecting her expert magic in the kitchen, the trio sat in silence enjoying a fine gumbo, followed by an étouffée of shellfish and rice. Summer was starving from her exertion of treading the waters of the gulf, but recalled the time she had fainted from exertion and too much of Dancie's good cooking. She nibbled, and convinced herself she was satisfied with the tiny portions. Dinner was followed by chicory coffee, beignets and a plate of pralines. These lavish meals always reminded of the starving days at Magnolia, which further increased her hatred of Fontaneau—not that she would have dreamed of passing up even the few nibbles she allowed herself—because after all, he ate like a king because he was a traitor!

Feeling Fontaneau's eyes burn into her flesh, she tried hard not to look at him. Instead, she concentrated on smiling at Captain McAllister when she caught him staring across the table from her. Finally, feeling quite on display, she dabbed the beignets' sugar off her mouth and set her napkin on the table, and leaned back in the chair. "You can imagine how difficult it is to enjoy Dancie's cooking with two men staring at me. Is there nothing else in this room to look at?"

Captain McAllister cleared his throat and looked away, while Fontaneau's eyes only burned more deeply into her own. "You could change this situation very easily and quickly," he said.

"I have nothing more to say except 'goodnight'. The two of you may now stare at each other." She rose to leave the room, but Fontaneau stood abruptly.

"You may *not* leave, Miss Woodfield. I'm tired of your bull-headed ways."

"And I'm tired of being your prisoner!" She turned to the captain. "Take me to your jail! If I'm to be a prisoner, I do not wish to be in this house with *that* man." She glared at Fontaneau.

The captain had also risen at this point. "I think you would be much more comfortable here where you have amenities, Miss Woodfield. As you know, there is little comfort at the Cabildo."

"Surely, you can find a place for me, captain. You saw him push me once. Perhaps he will beat me the next time. He hates me, and the feeling is mutual, I might add."

The captain appeared to consider her request for a moment. "Um, perhaps it is a better idea, Fontaneau."

"This is absurd. I am not going to beat the woman. Why would I spoil the bait? What better place to capture Ruiz than here, where she is?"

"He simply doesn't want to lose the reward you've offered him, captain." She knew it to be the truth; he wanted it all! He wanted Ruiz's Bella Vista, *and* she was convinced that he wanted Ruiz dead. Fontaneau glared at her in a most alarming way, certainly a warning to keep her mouth shut. He did not want the Federals to know that he had double crossed them.

The dead tell no tales. Summer winced at her own thoughts. She was certain that if Fontaneau could have reached across the table to punch her, he would have. She could not stay in this place; the man was seething. She could feel the heat emanate from his body as he tried to control his temper. *Pompous bastard.* She supposed the captain picked up on it as well, because he straightened himself before speaking.

"I will take Miss Woodfield to the Cabildo for the evening, and find a place for her in the morning."

* * *

She woke to a *tap-tap-tap* at the barred window of her room in her new quarters, a townhouse. McAllister had placed her here, not far from the Cabildo. It was the same townhouse where he lived at present, as well as several other officers. The original owners had lost their fortune during the war and relocated elsewhere, surely to lesser means, leaving the Federals free to claim the vacated house as officer's quarters for the duration of the occupation. There was, of course, no one to argue the matter.

Her barred window was on the ground floor. The captain had explained that the bars had been placed upon construction of the building not to keep prisoners in, but to keep thieves out.

"Very convenient in this case, I'd say." She ran her hand across the row of vertical bars.

"I would have to agree with you, Miss Woodfield. Now, is everything satisfactory?

"Yes, everything is as satisfactory as it could be, and I do appreciate my removal from that horrid man's house."

"Good. I shall leave you to unpack."

"It should not take long," she replied, looking at the small trunk next to her bed. Dancie had packed the trunk with two extra day dresses for her use, a nightgown, along with an extra pair of satin slippers and the required undergarments. Fontaneau objected to the removal of the clothing he reserved for the women he brought in to entertain his guests, not to mention the fact that he would lose his bait and a better chance at killing Ruiz. With Summer gone from his home, his mission to deliver Ruiz would only become more difficult, if not impossible. However,

Captain McAllister was adamant that she have decent clothing, and after a brief argument, Fontaneau complied.

At McAllister's departure, the door locked behind him and she set about unpacking the trunk. *Locked in, but little do they know that nothing can hold me when the time is right!*

* * *

Tap-tap-tap. She tossed the covers to the side. Remarkably, she had slept fairly well now that she was out of the grasp of Mr. Fontaneau. The night before, she dined alone in her room having been served by a plump, cheerful woman with graying hair and a soiled apron. Her name was Mary O'Brien from the Emerald Isle, and she had the lilt in her voice to prove it. The woman had sailed into Summer's room carrying a tray laden with spicy jambalaya, rolls and chicory coffee, and babbling up a storm, which had worked to put Summer at ease. Perhaps Mary O'Brien's parting words had inspired her peaceful night: *"A good laugh and a long sleep are the two best cures."*

Summer smiled, remembering the cheerful woman; but suddenly it struck her that the tapping at the window could be none other than Mama Dolly!

"Der you is." Mama sent her thoughts telepathically through the glass and iron bars.

Two things about Mama Dolly amazed Summer. One was her size. Through the window her shoulders stood above the bottom sill and well above the top of Summer's head. The other, was the way in which she and Mama communicated without speaking; it certainly came in handy in this instance.

"I been thinkin' hard, but you lock me out again, gal."

"It's been a difficult time. You said I'd get home to Magnolia, but here I am, a prisoner again! Fontaneau sent his men after me."

"I knows. I got dat nasty Lila at my house." She then let out a hearty laugh. *"Lawdy, she fussin' wid dat snake on her face!"*

"I'd love to laugh with you, Mama, but here I am, stuck behind bars and it's not very funny. I've been either imprisoned or chased since this whole episode began. What now? Did you bring any magic to get me out of here? Have you heard from the captain?"

"No, I ain't heard from da cap'n, but I'se talkin' to da queen 'bout some magic. She workin' on sometin' special. I come back in da night. Be ready."

You don't need to ask twice. Summer had a sneaky suspicion that she was stuck in a warp, a situation that replayed itself time after time; every attempt to get out of New Orleans had failed. Perhaps the exalted voodoo queen could be of service.

Hours of the day passed like a snail's race. Summer paced her quarters, stared through the bars of the window, enjoyed a few minutes chatting with Mary O'Brien, and, by supper time, was ready to pull her hair out. When darkness fell, she was more than grateful to see the day end and anticipated Mama Dolly's return.

"Come on! Come on!" she whispered through the window, her breath steaming the glass. "Where are you, Mama?" She glanced at the clock on the fireplace mantle; 10:15. At 10:33 she heard the key in the lock, and was speechless when Mama Dolly appeared in the doorway looking even larger by lantern light.

"How the heck did you get in here? How'd you get the key?"

"It ain't magic dis time," Mama said, beckoning her to hurry. "We gots to go now b'fo da soldiers come on back."

"Where are they?" Summer asked as they slipped out the back door.

"Da queen makin' a big rukus at da square. All dem soldiers race like da devil to get der."

"Where's Mary O'Brien?"

"She sleepin' up in her room."

It was déjà vu, as they raced toward Mama's little shack in Backtown, down the grilled balcony streets, through Congo Square and finally, Mama's place. *I've done this before....* It was a fleeting observation, and once inside she leaned against the inside of shack door catching her breath.

"Zummer!" Lila flew off of Mama's bed to stand before her, pointing to the snake tattoo that blackened half of her face.

"Look what she done to me, Zummer!"

"Wait!" Summer said, chills creeping up her spine. *Something is wrong. We've been through this already.* She backed away from the wooden door watching Lila all the while—Lila, who stood blankly staring after her—until she felt the gris-gris table stool against the back of her knees. She sat, but stood abruptly remembering that this was her exact movement before—*before I left for Magnolia. Something isn't kosher, here.*

"Look," Mama said, picking up a bundle wrapped in cloth. I put together some tings for you to take wid you. You's gonna git home gal, I knows it for sho'!"

"What about me, Zummer? I cannot make zee money with theez on my face!"

Neck hairs stood on end as the scene replayed itself. "Stand back!" she said holding out her hands like a traffic cop. "Don't come near me. I'm thinking...."

"If you follow da tracks north, you's gonna git home, gal!"

"What weel I do, Zummer?" Lila pleaded.

Something was definitely very wrong. This was more than déjà vu, it really *had* happened before. She tried to fight the creepy feeling that had started small, but now crept like a million spiders over her flesh. She fought the urge to run screaming from the cabin. *What's going on here?*

Lila and Mama Dolly approached her as she stood plastered against the wall next to the gris-gris table. Their voices were hollow, echoing eerily throughout the small confines of the shack. Catching a movement out of the corner of her eye, she turned to see that the gris-gris with which Mama had decorated her walls, was *moving.* She watched in horror as the button eyes of the strange dolls rotated simultaneously to stare in her direction. The crosses spun rapidly, pinned by the nails that had been hammered to hold them. Everything wriggled, or spun! Mama and Lila now stood only inches from her face, the candlelight casting their shadows ominously on the wall behind them.

"What weel I do? Zummer?"

"Take dis and you's gonna git home, gal...."

"Look what she done to me, Zummer!"

"Jes stay by da tracks and you's gonna get home...."

Over and over they repeated their lines, their eyes growing larger, and their voices ringing in her ears.

"Don't touch me!" Summer screamed, running past the women to the door, which she opened with such strength, that it crash against the wall. She ran from the shack, away from Backtown, away from the city. She ran and ran until she came to the cypress swamp. There, at the edge of the Spanish mossed-draped trees she stopped to catch her breath, looking back to make sure that Lila and Mama Dolly had not followed; she was nothing short of terrified. *Where will I go?* Ruiz was gone, and with him, safety.

"Take me home!" she yelled moving further into the trees. "I want to go home! I want to go home…." She fell to her knees, and sank a few inches into the damp, muddy soil.

Get up. Make yourself get up…. Something was definitely wrong, and she felt dizzy with confusion. A bullfrog bellowed, and then the swamp became quiet, dead quiet. She held her breath, listening for any small sound, but there was none…nothing until she heard it, someone—or some*thing*—coming near. *Hide!* She braced herself on a cypress knee and raised up, frantically searching for a hiding place. At first, she couldn't tell in which direction the rustling and splashing came from; but as it grew closer, she peered through the surrounding trees until she spotted what looked like a figure coming near, weaving through the cypress forest, sometimes visible, sometimes not. When it finally came into view, she gasped.

"Verano! I have been looking for you. Come." Ruiz signaled for her to follow, but she stood fast, with dropped jaw and eyes wide. *It can't be….*

He did not approach, but stood in the shade of the tall trees, his white shirt cut to a 'v', exposing the hairs of his chest. His sleeves billowed in a slight breeze, reminding her so much of the way she had first seen him: black hair combed away from his face, the white, billowing shirt, black pants tucked into tall black boots. He was a handsome and enticing picture, but she would not be fooled!

"It's not you," she said, more to herself than to him.

"Of course it is I! Who do you expect? Come now, Otto and Alvarez await us."

"But Ruiz, I saw you sail away."

"I have not sailed, Verano. How could I sail without my love? Come now." He motioned her forward, but she hesitated.

It's impossible; it's a trick. "But… Otto was shot—and you, too, you were hurt."

"You are dreaming, Verano." He signaled again for her to follow and she took a step forward. "Look at me, I am here, and strong as a bull."

What am I to do? There's no place else to run! She continued to step toward him, sloshing through the swamp waters, her slippers slimy with mud. As soon as she was near, he held out his hand. "Good," he said. "We go now."

His behavior was not typical; it worried her. Instead of projecting himself as the Ruiz she knew and loved, he was strangely odd and, in a sense, *creepy;* but, despite the intense premonition that something was very, very wrong, she took his hand. It fit oddly into her own. Where her hand was solid, his felt soft and mushy, like the mud that embedded her feet into the swampy earth.

"We go, Verano. We will be together forever, safe and far away from this place." He led her once more through the swamp forest to the small inlet tucked away beside the river that led to the Gulf of Mexico. The dory that had taken them previously to the sloop, was tied at the same spot. The sloop also appeared to be moored in the same area as before. She spotted Otto and Alvarez aboard, with Otto shirtless and working as if he had never suffered a bullet wound.

"Ruiz…." She started to ask if something was wrong, but couldn't finish. When he turned to her, his eyes appeared gray and glassy. Her hackles rose.

"What is it, my love?"

"Where are we going?"

"Home!"

"Home? Where is home?"

"Why, Buck Key, of course. I must get to mi madre and Margeurite."

"Of course."

"Come."

She glanced at the sloop over his shoulder. It was not so far that she couldn't see that Otto and Alvarez had halted work to stare at her and Ruiz—*just as they had before.* She wondered if Fontaneau waited and watched in his own faster sloop, and if today would be a repeat of the open sea battle between the two ships?

Ruiz stepped into the dory and held his hand to her. Again, it felt mushy in her own when she squeezed to steady herself as she entered the small craft. As Ruiz rowed to the waiting sloop, he stared; but she could not tell if he was staring at her, over her, or *through* her. It was almost as if she wasn't there at all, as his eyes were even odder than before; the black pupils had faded somewhat into cloudy gray orbs.

"Set sail!" Ruiz ordered, once onboard the sloop, but his voice normally strong and full, now sounded distant and hollow. Ruiz stood at the wheel, his back to her; and when he turned and grinned, her flesh crawled. His eyes were now solid gray-white orbs! "We will be together forever," he said in the strange, new voice. Come stand with me, my love."

She looked behind at the diminishing river bank as the sails had caught wind. *I can still make it to shore.* It was no mistake that something major was occurring, or about to occur. She trembled as she walked toward him. *This is all wrong.* He was different. She reluctantly reached to take his outstretched hand, but her hand slipped right through his! Again she reached, and again her hand slipped through his.

"What's happening, Ruiz?"

He continued to hold his hand out, smiling, as if he couldn't hear her speak.

A movement caught her eye, and with extreme and alarming shock, she realized that she could see Otto watching her directly *through* Ruiz's head! She screamed at this new horror, but it did not phase Ruiz in the least; he continued to hold out his hand, smiling and staring through the gray orbs.

She stepped backward as far as she could before the feel of the transom stopped her. Alvarez and Otto, both, now approached, each passing on either side of Ruiz.

"You're nothing but trouble," Otto said, his voice as hollow and distant as Ruiz's. A terror as she'd never known sent her adrenaline sky high as the men advanced. As was Ruiz, they, too, were now transparent, their eyes the same glassy grayish white, the pupils, gone.

"Stop!" She yelled, holding out her palms as if it would halt the horror. "Stop there!" But, they did not stop. The two came forward while Ruiz stood at the wheel, smiling, his hand outstretched.

"Come Verano, we are going home…."

"You'd better come in off the porch, Summer."

"What?" Her head whipped around; *Was that Guy? Where is he? This is crazy!* She could see that Otto and Alvarez were nearly upon her, and she was frantic

"Guy! Where are you? Help! Hurry!"

"Time to come in, Summer."

"I'm trying!" she screamed.

"Try a little harder," Guy said.

She heard him as if he were standing next to her, here, on this horror vessel, but she could not see him.

"Where are you?" she screamed. "They're going to get me!"

"There's only one thing to do with you," Otto said, reaching for her. Though his hands passed *through* her body, she felt the impact, bending forward as if someone had punched her in the gut. Again, Otto tried, but she ducked and stepped aside.

"Guy!"

"I don't know how you can sleep in that position," he said. She heard him plainly, and yet she was here and he was….*somewhere else.*

With Otto trying to capture her, and Alvarez staring with the blank frightening eyes, she looked once more at her love, her dashing, blockade running angel who had saved her, Cherry and Buck from a watery grave. Her dashing Capitán whom she had saved from the gallows, and for whom she had felt such passion. Her heart cracked; a pain as sharp and real as if someone was trying to chisel it apart; yet, Ruiz stood smiling, plastered against a blue sky that shone through his quickly fading self. His outstretched hand, the toothy grin, his devilish eyes, the billowing shirt…he was all but invisible, now.

Then, one last grin. "Come, Verano…come…co…." He was gone; they were *all* gone.

She sat on the transom staring at the ship's wheel as it stood alone without its captain; there was no one to guide it home.

"Goodbye, my love," she said to nothing, feeling strongly that she would never see him again. Tears filled her eyes as she forced herself to search out the riverbank. *Perhaps there is still time;* she could not sail alone. Shifting her legs over the transom, she held her breath and jumped into the river. When she reached the bank, she looked again for the sloop, but it was gone. The swamp birds sang, as the chisel broke her heart in two.

Chapter 32

"We're on a roll, girl!" Jesse was very excited. "While you were off visiting the ancients…." She looked to make sure she hadn't offended Summer. "Just joking, my friend. Anyway, while you were…*not here,* I found something very important."

Summer's ears perked. She had been in a bittersweet limbo since returning to the real and present world. It was a tough reality to swallow, that the adventure with Ruiz had come to an end. Even though she loved Guy, even though she was excited about the twins, and even though she was happy to be back in her own safe world where she understood how things worked, it was still bittersweet. "Well? Don't keep me waiting," she replied.

"I found Percy in Savannah!"

"Where? How?"

"In Savannah, I went over and over the census, the births, all that we've done before; but on a whim I searched under a different surname—Ascot—and I found him! I found a Percy Ascot living in

Savannah in 1890! *Ascot*, not Woodfield. He took his father's name and not Cherry's!"

"It has to be him." Summer's adrenaline had kicked in. "You're brilliant, Jesse. I never thought of looking for him with the surname of Ascot. Wait…what year was he born?"

"He's 32 at the time of the census, just the right age to be born in 1858 making him 6 years old during the war, and that was his age in the time period you knew him."

"This is fabulous, Jesse!"

"That's not all."

"Oh?"

"He was married to a woman named Della, and had two children; A girl—and get this—named Cherry, and a boy named James!"

Summer's jaw dropped. "A girl named Cherry…this can't be a coincidence, Jesse, not a Cherry *and* James. No way."

"This is our guy, all the pieces fit."

"How about that?" A warm feeling filled the empty space. "He didn't forget his mother, *or* James, his half-brother and my great-great-great grandfather! We have to find out what happened to the children, so we can place you on that family tree. So exciting!" *Something else to look forward to….*

"But wait, that's not all!"

Summer eyed Jesse who was obviously brimming with extreme joy. "The best for last?"

"You bet! I managed to trace Percy's descendants all the way to my dad!"

Elation overflowed as the news took root. "Do you have the documents to prove this?"

"I sure do."

"But your surname isn't Ascot, it's Williams."

"Easily enough explained. Percy's daughter Cherry married a Williams, and the Williams name is still going, after all these generations. Percy Ascot was my great-great-grandfather."

"I wonder why he chose the surname Ascot, instead of Woodfield?"

"Probably from spite, I'd say. Maybe he knew that Arthur Ascot was his birth father. The father wouldn't claim him, so out of spite, he took his name. I don't know this for sure, but it kind of makes sense, doesn't it? We don't know that part of the story and never will, unless you have more magic time travel up your sleeve."

"Perish the thought! Look at me, I'm ready to explode!" And explode she did, for at that moment, her water broke sending a puddle to the wooden flooring of the porch.

"Oh, my God!" Jesse's eyes nearly popped out of their sockets.

"Get Guy!"

"Hold on, don't move!" Jesse ran down the porch stairs, following the sound of the tractor. The last they'd seen of Guy, he was mowing the lawn.

"Just hold on," Summer said, trying to still her racing heart. All these months of waiting, fixing up the nursery... *time traveling.* All these months, and the time had finally arrived. She and Guy would be parents soon—maybe today! She was both excited and afraid. Life was changing and she was scared, scared of what was ahead, considering the fact that one moment she could be here in the present, and the next, gone on some crazy adventure in a different century.

* * *

Guy held the babies up one at a time for her to see.

"Look at this chubby fellow!" The baby was fair-haired with round cheeks and three chins. "He's a bruiser, alright."

"Just like his dad, huh?" Summer smiled. She was deliriously happy that the twins were finally with them, and healthy, as was obvious by the pink skinned chunky bundle in Guy's arms.

"Let me see him."

Guy placed the fellow on her lap as she sat up in the hospital bed resting on freshly plumped pillows. She gently unwrapped the blanket, exposing his soft flesh, the clip on his belly button, and the newborn diaper that he filled out. "Pretty hearty for a twin, I think. What would you like to name him?" They had decided that he should name the boy, and her, the girl.

"Now that I see him, I think we should call him Alex. Alex Mason. Sounds good, doesn't it? Sounds like a good, strong name."

"Alex." She let the name roll over her tongue. "How about Alex Guy Mason?"

"Done deal," he said. "Come on, Alex." He wrapped the baby into his blanket and lay him back in the basinet. "Now for the little princess. Wait until you get a look at her now that she's all cleaned up. Gorgeous creature…really."

Summer had only seen her briefly after the birth, and now Guy came toward her with a small bundle wrapped in pink. A shock of black hair sprouted upward out of the pink flannel. “May I present this little dark-haired beauty to her highness? She’s a princess, so you must be a queen!”

Summer gently unwrapped the baby from the tight folds of her pink cocoon. She was darker skinned than Alex, the black hair thick and straight, standing on end.

“Gee, Guy, I wonder if she’s a throwback to Evaline?” Eyes as black as night peered from squinted lids. Her arms suddenly flayed in the way a newborn’s arms will; and when Summer placed her finger into the baby’s tiny palm, she grabbed hold.

“Whatever she is, she’s a beauty.” Guy said, leaning over the bed. “Look at that face. Perfect. Look at those…wait…look at this—this proves she’s going to be a knockout!”

“What?”

Guy held a tiny arm up. “*That.*”

Summer’s eyes grew large. Her heart pounded in her ears, stars flashed before her eyes.

“Are you alright, Summer? You like you’ve seen one of your ghosts.”

She couldn’t answer. She was speechless as she stared at the heart-shaped mole just below the baby’s armpit.

Chapter 33

"Stop fidgeting!" Summer said. She and Jesse had arrived at the nursing home after an hour's drive. Guy was home taking care of Alex and Marguerite—Maggie, for short—while she and Jesse visited with the ailing Taylor Woodfield.

"I'm nervous. I can't help it."

"If you recall, *he* wants this meeting. I doubt he'll be calling you names this time. Now straighten up, stop fidgeting and be brave. You have the papers, right?"

"I do." She lifted her briefcase. "In here."

"Good."

The meeting was held in Taylor's private room, as he was now in extreme failing health and sitting in the library would have been out of the question. Summer gasped silently when she caught sight of him in his bed. He was very frail and thin, much more so than he had been the last time she visited, before the twins were born.

"There you are," he said, turning his head to watch the women approach. "Please pull up a couple of chairs." He weakly raised a hand, pointing a bony finger to the corner where two folding chairs leaned against the wall.

The women complied, setting their chairs bedside. Several moments of silence passed in which time Taylor's eyes seemed to be glued to Jesse until she shuffled in her seat.

"Don't get nervous, girl, I'm not in any shape to bite. I owe you an apology for the first time we met. You see, I've hidden the fact that I had a nig…black woman in my family line. Now that I'm on my way out of this world, it's come to me that I was a fool, an idiot, in doing so. Without that black woman, I wouldn't be here; and from what Miss Woodfield tells me, she suffered terribly." His voice stilled a moment, perhaps waiting for enough energy to continue. His watery eyes had lost any bit of vivaciousness they may have held, having been at one time the same brilliant blue that had belonged to his forefather, Thomas C. Quinn, the *only* thing of value that Summer could perceive as worth passing down.

"Anyway, I'm sorry for what I called you the last time. Please accept my apology."

"Yes, sir," Jesse replied.

"Miss Woodfield says you have proof of our connection, is that so?"

"It is, sir."

"I want you to give it to my lawyer. These old eyes are too tired to read anymore. Confounded pain in the ass to have to lie in bed all day without a damn thing to do but wait to die."

"I'll do that, sir."

"And stop calling me 'sir'."

Jesse swallowed hard. "What should I call you?"

"Well, we're cousins, aren't we? Call me Taylor."

"Yes, sir…uh…Taylor."

"You're a responsible young woman, aren't you?"

"I am. I work in a law office. I'm an assistant to Blaine Ascot."

"I don't know Blaine Ascot, but I'm glad to hear you have a responsible job. I have no descendants, you know. I was always too wrapped up in the ranch business, too wrapped up making a fortune to marry and have a family. And for what?"

Two weeks later, Taylor Woodfield passed away, leaving his entire fortune to Jesse Williams.

* * *

When Summer felt the twins were old enough to leave for a few days, she left them in the care of Guy and Jesse's mother, who had graciously volunteered her services. She, Jesse and Blaine were off to Florida to visit the W – A Bella Vista Ranch in southern Florida, which now belonged one-hundred percent to Jesse Williams.

"Look at this property, it's endless!" Jesse had her nose pressed to the glass window of the rental car. It seemed ages since they had passed beneath the overhead wrought-iron sign displaying the ranch's name. So far, they had not seen any sign of Taylor's home, but plenty of Black Angus cattle out on the range.

"You sure hit the jackpot," Blaine said. "I suppose you're going to throw away your career with me now and become a ranch woman?"

"I don't know that yet…there it is!." Blaine pulled up to an immense two-story structure. "What a house!"

"That's no house—that's a mansion!" Summer said opening the car door.

The trio stood and stared a while at the brick mansion that seemed so out of place in a setting of Spanish moss and range cattle.

A Hispanic woman appeared on the massive front porch. "*Hola!* Come!" She waved them forward and as they approached, she wiped her hands on a red-ruffled apron tied around her ample waist. "Welcome to your home! My name is Rosa."

After greetings, they were led into a large foyer, complete with a wide, winding staircase leading to the second floor, and then into a rustic parlor. "I get refreshments," she said, and disappeared back into the foyer leaving the trio to freely peruse the room.

"Hm. Seems like there was more to Taylor Woodfield than met the eye," Summer said, walking the length of an immense bookcase. She ran a finger along the leather spines of westerns, historical biographies, and classics. As she walked, she stopped occasionally to view one of the many framed photographs. Most were black and white, and some were obviously very old and faded.

"I wonder…"she started to say, and then stopped; a framed photo caught her eye. "Jesse…come here."

In a flash, Jesse was beside her. "You gave me goose bumps, the way you said that. What's wrong?"

Summer pointed to an old photo, a grouping of men and women. Six men stood in back, long-sleeved arms resting on the shoulders of the women sitting in front. The men wore cowboy hats which partially covered their foreheads and shaded their faces. A young man stood on the left end of the row and two young black men on the opposite end next to the tall, elderly black man. In the front row sat an elderly woman with a mess of frizzed hair piled high on her head; a graying middle-aged woman who appeared to be of Hispanic descent; a teenaged girl and an old white-haired black woman.

"I think…." Summer leaned in closer, squinting. Her heart beat rapidly. She raised a shaking hand to point at a stocky man standing behind the graying haired woman. "I think…" she whispered. "I think it's Ruiz! And that man," she pointed to the tall black man. "It's Buck! I'm sure of it! Oh, my God—it's *them!* She wavered and grabbed the bookcase shelf.

"What's wrong? What's going on over here?" Blaine asked.

"Not a thing, nosey. Go check out that gator hide on the wall," Jesse said, waving Blaine back.

"You okay, Summer?" he asked, giving Jesse a dirty look.

"Yes…yes. Just a moment of dizziness. It's okay."

Both women now leaned into the photo. "I wish I had a magnifying glass." Summer carried the framed photo to a large window that overlooked the side yard of the mansion. In the distance, a black fence circled a stand of moss-draped trees.

"I can name these people," she said, staring wildly at Jesse. "This is Captain Ruiz. He's old here, but it's him." She paused, feeling her heart sink into the pit of her stomach. "And this, this is Buck. Why of course it's him; he's big and tall—though he's much paunchier in this photo, but of course he must be what, 70? 75? Maybe these boys next to him are his sons? Maybe this is his wife sitting in front." She put a finger on the face of the gray-haired black woman and then pulled the photo closer. "Could this be Dilly?" My God, I'll bet Buck married Dilly, and these are their boys standing here in back!"

She then drew her attention to the other women sitting in the front row. "I don't know who this old lady is, but looking at the frizzy hair, she sure reminds me of Lila. No…can't be. But this woman," she pointed to the graying middle-aged woman. "I'll bet this is Marguerite. She looks Spanish to me."

At that moment Rosa entered carrying a tray of finger sandwiches, cookies and iced tea. "Come and eat! Señor Bill will be here shortly to take you for a tour. He is the foreman."

"Rosa, do you know who these people are in this photo?" Summer asked.

Rosa set the tray down on a live-edged, free-formed slab of redwood that served as a coffee table. "Let me see," she said, crossing to the window where the women stood.

"Oh yes, Señora. This is a picture of the old ones, the ancestors to Mr. Taylor, bless-his-heart-may-he-go-with-God." Rosa crossed herself.

"You weren't here when this photo was taken, were you?"

"Oh no, Señora, I was not even born!"

"I didn't think so; I know you're not *that* old…I mean *old*."

"Stop while you're ahead," Jesse whispered.

"Oh, but my mama was here then. She was a small girl, and her mama was here as well. They lived on the ranchero. We have always lived on the ranchero. My grandfather was a *vaquero*[74] and he work for Señor Alvarez here," she pointed to Ruiz. "And this man," she said, pointing to Buck. "*And* Señor Woodfield…the first Señor Woodfield, but he is not in this picture because he die. This is his son, Señor Yank, the father of my boss, Señor Taylor. This is Señor Woodfield's wife, Señora Margeurite. She was a Spanish lady. Señor Alvarez was her father." She pointed again at Ruiz, and Summer's heart flip-flopped just to see his face, shadowed as it was.

"They are all buried here," Rosa said with a sigh, as if she had known them all personally.

Summer came to attention. "Oh, yes, where is the cemetery?"

Rosa looked out the tall window. "There, under the trees. It is the family cemetery."

Summer rested her hands on the bottom sill and peered through the window at the black wrought iron fencing that enclosed her beloved Ruiz and the others, the others she had known in another century.

"And who's this?" Jesse asked, breaking the spell. She pointed to the thin, frizzy-haired old woman on the left end of the sitting row.

"Oh, *that* woman…my mama tell me that a long, long time ago that woman come begging for Alvarez to take her in. He know her from

---

[74] *Vaquero: a ranch hand*

somewhere, New Orleans, I think. Mama say they fight with words, the woman cry, and Alvarez tell her to stay. She stay until she die."

"What was her name?" Summer felt a tremble deep inside. *Could it possibly be? Could it possibly be Lila?*

"She was a French lady. Lila De…De…something. You will see it on the headstone if you go there." She nodded at the window and the cemetery beyond.

Summer felt overwhelmed with this new and astounding information. She thanked Rosa and sat in an overstuffed leather chair staring at the cold fireplace. *Ruiz…Buck…Lila. They're all here!* She stood abruptly and raced to the front door, alarming Jesse who was just stepping through it to greet the foreman who had rumbled up in his Jeep.

"I'm going out there, Jesse. I want to go alone." She raced past Jesse, down the steps and broke through the tight circle of Blaine and the foreman, who were standing in her way on the landing. "So sorry" she said. "I'm Summer, how'd you do." She kept walking, focused on one thing—the cemetery.

The gate creaked a bit as it swung open. She forced herself to read the other headstones that lined near the cemetery fence, when all she wanted was to rush to Ruiz's grave, to throw herself on the ground and proclaim her undying love, to tell him that he had never left her heart, to tell him about her baby, Maggie, who carried the Ruiz family birthmark beneath her armpit.

They were all here, resting beneath a canopy of the moss-draped trees; Lila, Buck, Dilly, Marguerite, Yank, and his son, Taylor's father, Yank. Even the stern-faced Señora, Ruiz's mother, was laid to rest in this place. The fresher grave belonged to Taylor; he had come home. A few very small headstones lined up beside Dilly and Marguerite, and she assumed that they were infants who had died young. Then she spotted the last headstone. It stood against a setting of savannah, speckled by the Black Angus who were unconcerned that Ruiz had ever lived.

She took a deep breath and lowered herself to the ground, fighting hard the tears that that threatened to fall. "Hello, my love," she said softly, patting the grass that grew over him. "I remember you so well." She laid her head upon the ground and listened to the emptiness below. There was no heartbeat; there was no laughter, no sound of Ruiz rustling about, ordering to "hoist the sails". There was nothing but the silence of what was left—*nothing.* She raised up and ran her fingers over the name carved into the headstone;

Capitain Alejandro Verón Gutierrez Ruiz. ***1835 – 1901*** ***Sail on into heaven our beloved friend***

"At least you could be yourself in death, Ruiz, and not the alias of "Alvarez". She sighed. "I'm speaking to nothing, to nobody." This she said aloud, then looked to see if anyone was within hearing distance, but the others had gone off to check the barn or perhaps the other outer buildings that made up the ranch. "I guess I'm just crazy, Ruiz, sitting here next to your old grave remembering our time together. But I *do* remember. Do you remember me?" It suddenly occurred to her that perhaps he didn't remember her as he grew older on this vast ranch. Perhaps she had never existed for him. It was so confusing—time travel.

A slight breeze ruffled her hair. She closed her eyes letting it caress her face, and tickle the back of her neck…*neck!*

"Verano…."

Is it the wind?

"Verano…."

There it was again! She jumped to her feet, turning in all directions trying to find him.

"Where are you?" she asked. "I hear you!"

The breeze grew stronger; and once more, as it had happened so long ago, she felt his breath on the back of her neck as his lips touched her tender skin. She melted into it. Her head turned upward, her eyes closed as his arms wrapped around her body; it was a moment to savor.

"Do you remember me, my love?" she asked.

"Verano…."

And he was gone.

It took a moment for her to regain her composure; and when she did, she brushed the grass and dirt from her clothing and closed the cemetery gate behind her, stepping back into the real world. She couldn't resist turning once more to view the place beneath the moss-draped trees that held the remains of people she had once known and cared for, and a man she had loved desperately, a man she still loved, and always would. He had a special place in her heart. She turned again toward the grand house that now belonged to Jesse. First, slowly, and then with purpose she walked forward, her spirits rising, her step growing lively. *I have been blessed not only to know, but to live my history.* In doing so, she had brought history with her in the form of little Marguerite with the heart-shaped mole beneath her arm. "Ah, you sneaky devil, Ruiz. Just like you said, my love, "*We will always be together*"."

Chapter 34

At times, when the house was quiet, when the twins were napping and not running about her feet, and when Guy was outdoors, she found herself in Evaline's old room standing before the attic door. Sometimes she put her hand on the latch, wanting to look up the stairwell to see if anyone waited there; but she never opened it. She waited to hear the scratching, or tapping that beckoned her to come, to help a soul in need. But the door stood shut and silent, leaving her to stand alone in the dusty room with her memories.

On one of these occasions, as she stood as a statue staring at the closed attic door, her mind lost in memories, she heard it; *scratch... scratch... scratch.* She jumped backward, as she had expected today to be as any other day—silent! Once over the shock, and after hearing yet another set of muffled scratching, she so wanted to run to the door, fling it open, and see who awaited her! Instead, she backed away, fearful that the captain would leap out and disrupt her world, rekindling the passion and longing. Oh, how she'd love to see him—if it *were* him— but, instead, she took another step backward.

"Stay where you are!" she ordered. "I can't help you now. The children are too young, and I can't leave them!"

Scratch...scratch...scratch.

"You've waited this long, whoever you are, so you will have to wait a little longer. I *will* help you, *I promise*! When the time is right, I will help you!"

And, she did.

THE END

Books by Jocelyn Miller

- **Broken Chords**
- **Tanglewood Plantation**
- **Tanglewood Plantation II: Adventure in the Everglades**
- **Tanglewood Plantation III: Adventure in New Orleans**

Available in paperback and Kindle at

www.amazon.com

Made in the USA
Middletown, DE
20 February 2015